I0593174

~ TURN LEFT ~

OUTBACK QUEENSLAND ROMANCE
BOOK THREE

RHONDA FORREST

Valeena Press

For my long-time friend - Denise

~ all the best as you set off on your
'turn left' adventure ~

ALSO BY RHONDA FORREST

OUTBACK QUEENSLAND ROMANCE SERIES

With a cast of eclectic characters and set amidst the rugged outback of Australia, the *Outback Queensland Romance Series* will introduce you to stories of friendship, resilience, and loving relationships that come together to triumph over obstacles defined by the past.

Two Heartbeats (Book 1) is followed by the sequel, *Time Will Tell* (Book 2)

Turn Left (Book 3), *A New Start* (Book 4), *Outback Magic* (Book 5) and *Echoes of the Outback* (Book 6) are stand-alone books with some links to the other books in this series.

~ TURN LEFT ~

CHAPTER 1

Amy jumped up and down, her arms flailing frantically in the air with the hope that the old red truck chugging towards her would stop. There was no way she would be able to change the flat tyre on her little white car by herself and being stuck on the side of an outback road on a sweltering summer day was nearly more than she could take.

Biting her top lip, she took deep breaths and crossed her arms, jumping when the truck backfired loudly before slowing. The flat tyre was just another calamity to add to the list, a list so long there was no end to it. A list that covered mistakes and disasters that had taken place during the last four weeks. A month that should have been exciting and invigorating; her first position as the new music teacher in the remote town of Matfield. Who would have ever guessed that the new start she had been so eager for would so far be one of the most difficult experiences of her life?

The truck skidded to a halt, a cloud of dust concealing

it as it pulled in behind where she stood. As the dust settled, the driver's door opened and a well-dressed young man jumped down, his boots disappearing into the soft red powder that filled the ditches on the edge of the road.

He shielded his eyes and looked towards her and she tensed, aware that she was by herself and in the middle of nowhere. Thankfully, when she looked closer through the windscreen of the truck, she spotted an elderly lady waving at her.

As the man strode towards her he pushed an Akubra hat down on his black curly hair. She guessed that he was about thirty and a local, the tell-tale slow gait and friendly greeting he gave her, leaving her thankful that today, perhaps some luck had come her way.

He tipped his hat when he spoke, a broad smile across his face. 'G'day. That tyre looks flat.'

She pushed her brown hair back from her face and smiled in response, a sense of relief washing over her that his arrival had saved her from trying to work out how she was going to get help in such an isolated spot. Being from the suburbs of the east coast, she was accustomed to decent mobile coverage. Her usually handy, roadside assistance membership didn't quite cut it out here.

Wiping her hand across her forehead she looked up, noticing his dark eyes and handsome face. 'Yes, the tyre's flat and I don't think I can change it.'

Her father's words rang in her ears. 'You just need to learn one thing about cars. How to check the oil and water, and how to change a busted tyre.' He'd tried several times to show her but she'd taken scant notice. That was what he was for. After all, when she wasn't travelling overseas, she lived at home and if she ever got a flat tyre she could just call RACQ. Wasn't that why she paid the yearly membership?

She looked up at the young man. 'I'm on my way to a funeral at Billa Station. My phone doesn't get reception here so maybe you could ring a breakdown service for me? I really can't be late.'

He held his arm out, a worker's hand, tanned and rough on her skin as he firmly gripped her hand. She noticed his strong arms and physique. Most likely he was a worker on one of the properties out this way. After all, there weren't too many different options for work in these small towns. He looked like a stockman or a station hand.

His eyes met hers. 'Name's Angus,' he said. 'We're going to the funeral also. Lucky for you because this is not the usual way to get to Billa Station and certainly not the way you should be going. That's my Nana in the truck and she wanted to come this way. Hammer Road isn't used much anymore, but it holds some good memories for her. It's the only reason we're out here.'

She shook his hand and then waved to the lady in the truck. Turning back to him, Amy spoke quickly, her words tumbling out. 'Thank you for stopping. I was so stressed when I had to stop. My dad tried to teach me how to change a tyre, many times, but I didn't listen. Now I don't know what to do and I really, really, need to get to this funeral.'

'It's okay. Calm down.' His slow drawl sounded the opposite of her jumbled monologue and she tried to take his advice and settle down. These people would help her. She wouldn't die out here.

She held the car manual booklet over her head like a hat. 'I'm not sure what I should do. There are instructions here on how to change the tyre. My name is Amy and I'm the new music teacher. I'm at the high school mostly, but I also teach music at the primary school when needed. Elliot Gantarro, the principal, rang me last night and said I had to be at this funeral by ten o'clock to conduct the school choir. I don't know the person who the funeral is for but their usual teacher, Mrs Sanderson, has unfortunately left. Elliot is there with the band. He said not to be late.' She didn't add that Elliot had not given her a choice and after she'd declined his offer to go with him in his car he had been quite rude and abrupt. 'Find your own way then. Make sure to go out the Hammer Road, way. You're a city girl, so don't go thinking you know everything. Listen to what I say.'

Angus shook his head. 'That'd be right. That fella's only been here a couple of years and thinks he knows the roads and how to get about, but he doesn't.' He walked to the back of her car and opened the boot. She watched as he located the spare tyre, his hands running around the rim of it. She followed him as he walked back to the busted tyre. 'That spare won't fit your car. The rim size is different.'

'Whoops. One of my friends swapped theirs for mine, just before I left for out here. I presumed the tyre would be the same.'

He stood up straight and turned to her. 'I tell you what, how about you jump in the truck with Nana and me. At least that way you'll get there.'

Waves of heat pressed against her skin and she wished she'd brought a water bottle with her. The gauge that showed the temperature outside her flat this morning had nudged forty degrees, the wide sky above the small town of Matfield, cloudless and stretching endlessly across the plains that surrounded her new home. A blast of hot air rippled across where they stood and her hair—which she had blow-dried and sprayed to stay in place—flew in every direction. It wasn't usual for her to spend so much time on her hair or make-up, but today she needed to make a good impression.

Struggling to gather the loose strands with one hand she went to answer but a sneaky breeze picked up more dust and pushed it around her legs, lifting her dress at the back. Her spare hand quickly gripped the fabric, her attempts at holding everything in place having very little success. She gripped tight with both hands her hair flying in every direction so that she could no longer see. So much for all her time spent preparing how she looked and wearing her best outfit and matching white sandals.

She turned around, making sure that her dress was where it should be. Using one hand to smooth her hair down and the other hand to hold her dress in place, she smiled at Angus. 'Thank you. That's so good of you. Going in the truck would save the day for me. Elliot is never happy with me, and being late will really stir him up, so I need to get there as soon as I can if it's possible. That's lucky that you're also going to the funeral.'

Angus chuckled, a deep dimple forming on the left side of his face. 'Elliot. Good old Elliot. Wouldn't want to upset him.'

She looked back at the truck, the old lady with white hair staring at them both, beckoning them to hurry up. Angus followed her gaze. 'We better get moving. Nana's giving me the signal to get a move on. It'll be easy to pick your car up on the way back. There's a trailer out at the property where we're going. I'll hitch it up when we're ready to leave and we can put your car on it and bring it back to town when we return. There'll be a tyre to fit in the workshop and,' he raised his eyebrows, 'another one to have as your spare. One that fits.'

Pushing her hair back from her face, she drew her shoulders back. What a day, taking the wrong road, a flat tyre, and now relying on someone she had just met to bring her and her car back to town. 'That would be great and really kind of you to go out of your way for me.'

'No worries and it's no bother. I'm still curious why Elliot sent you this way though.'

'I followed his directions to the dot. I even wrote them down. I was very careful and checked several times and when it seemed to get more and more remote, I tried the maps on my phone. That worked until everything dropped out. I had to go through a few gates and I wasn't even sure if this was a road.' She looked around. 'I hope no one steals my car?'

He laughed, his entire face lighting up. 'Are you kidding? Who's going to take it out here.'

There wasn't any other option and as she grabbed her bag out of the car she thought about how everything was so different out here in Western Queensland. She looked at her phone. There was still no reception. Visions of outback Australia that she had seen on the television rattled in her mind. Dead animals lying in the dust, their white bones picked dry by crows; bodies of people found years later, miles from their abandoned vehicle. Whatever had she been thinking to keep going when it was obviously remote and no other vehicles in sight. Then again, Elliot had insisted she come this way.

With everything going on at school, and trying to settle in, she had not thought rationally or safely. Her only concern had been to get there on time and not get in trouble again from Elliot. This was a good reminder that distances were large in these places and without water or a way to get back to civilisation, one could end up dying of the heat and dehydration. She followed Angus to the truck. Luckily he had come this way, otherwise she could have been stuck out here forever. Dead or alive.

CHAPTER 2

*a*ngus helped Amy up into the cab of the truck. It was a 1940 Ford and his grandfather and he had spent the last five years restoring it to its former glory. That was before Grandad got sick. After that, the old man had mainly been bed-bound but sometimes he managed to get out to the shed and sit on a chair and watch Angus work on the truck. 'Bloody proud of you, boy,' he'd said, the last time they'd been together. 'You'll never be out of work being a mechanic. This truck is yours once I'm gone.'

He'd hated it when Grandpa talked like that, but they knew it was inevitable. Years of smoking had taken their toll and it wasn't long after that last conversation with Angus, that Grandpa had passed away.

He cast his thoughts back to the present as he helped Amy into the truck. The cab was high off the ground and he held onto her arm as she pulled herself up. 'Amy, meet Nana Mavis. It might be better if you climb over the top of Nana and sit in the middle. She likes to be next to the window and hang onto that special handle and use the footrest we put in there for her.'

He tried not to laugh as their new passenger clambered over into the space, wriggling into her place as Nana guided her and helped her settle in the narrow area between them. Even though she was covered in dust and her long hair was messy from blowing all over the place, she was a very attractive girl and he noticed a dimple in her left cheek. Her shapely legs were pushed up beside Nana and she moved over a little as he explained that he had to get to the gear stick which she had thankfully noticed and made sure to keep one side of.

'Right,' he announced. 'Off we go. How are we going for time, Nana?'

'Plenty of time, Angus. No rush, they'll have to wait for us anyway.' The elderly lady turned to Amy who sat quietly, no doubt thankful to be rescued from the dust and heat.

'You're lucky we came along. No one usually uses Hammer Road. You're not from around here are you, love?'

'No, I'm from Maroochy, on the Sunshine Coast.'

'Oh yes, I've been there but it's many years ago. Just a row of beachside cottages.' Nana tut-tutted. 'Well, this should be a lesson for you. People perish out in these parts when they're not equipped for breakdowns or the unexpected.' The old lady's voice softened as Amy looked ahead, nodding her head up and down to show she was taking in the lecture. 'Now, my dear, how old are you and what has brought you to Matfield? What is your story?'

Amy took the neatly folded handkerchief that Nana offered her, wiping her face and grimacing at the dirt that came off on the fabric. 'Oh, my goodness. I must look terrible. I'll have to clean up before joining with the students.'

Angus kept his eyes on the road. It hadn't been used much lately and he gripped the steering wheel tightly as he navigated the corrugations and potholes. 'There's a bathroom there you can use,' he said, 'and we'll make sure it doesn't start until you're ready. Don't panic, like Nana said, they'll have to wait for us.'

Amy turned to Nana, her body bouncing up and down from the bumpy road. 'Sorry, you asked me what my story is. I'm twenty-four and I moved here four weeks ago, at the start of the term. I'm the new music teacher and by new, I mean really new. This is my first teaching position ever. I've worked in other jobs before this and I travelled overseas for quite a while, but a few years ago I decided to study and become a music teacher. The high school is my central position and I have music students there as well as some other classes. I also have some students at the primary school.'

'Wow. Fresh out of uni,' Angus said, intrigued why she would want to move somewhere like Matfield. 'Was it hard to leave the coast? Bit different out here.'

'There wasn't anything to keep me there apart from family, and my friends who all have their own busy lives. It was time for a change.'

Amy shuffled in her seat and he moved over a bit to give her some more room, aware that his arm and hip were pressed right up next to hers. Her body was small next to his and he glanced down, trying to avert his eyes from her legs. Women didn't usually arouse his interest, in fact, he ran a mile if anyone even suggested they were keen on him. But Amy was cute and in need of rescuing; if not from being stranded in the middle of nowhere, then definitely saved from the bullying nature of the school principal, Elliot.

Angus worked at the local mechanic's and he'd had a bit to do with Elliot when he brought his car in to get fixed. He was an arrogant man and had been quick to let Angus know that he was the principal at the high school and that it was important that his car be fixed promptly and before the others that were lined up ready for services and mechanical repairs. Angus hadn't been impressed with Elliot's demands and informed him firmly that his vehicle would get fixed when they could slot it in.

The principal's complaints that day had been loud and annoying. He was full of himself and the entire time he'd been in the workshop he'd complained about young teachers at the school not knowing what they were doing, or that they had come from the cities and didn't realise they had to work hard and put the hours in. It had been easy to take an instant dislike to him and from what Elliot had said, Angus got the impression that not only was he a bully, but he also seemed like a regular pain in the arse. There had been stories from others in town about the principal and some of his antics, the loud self-important middle-aged man who always seemed to be in a dispute with someone, perfect fodder for town gossip. It was interesting that the stories he had heard had come from those who didn't usually exaggerate but rather told it as it was. Although he'd only just met Amy, he could tell she'd be a perfect target for Elliot's nasty ways.

She really did look like she was from the city. Her legs were slender and tanned and he stifled his laughter as he caught a glimpse of brightly painted toe-nails peeping through the dusty red of the dirt that covered her once white sandals and slender feet. Long elegant fingers gripped the dashboard as she tried to hang on, balancing herself as they bumped across a corrugated section of the road. What a well-poised attractive young woman, he thought. It wouldn't take long for word to get around that there was a new teacher in town and he was surprised he hadn't heard about her before now.

Matfield had a population of just under three thousand, and usually if someone new arrived the entire town would be talking about what, who, where, and why the newcomer was here. Drawing his eyes back to the road he focussed on traversing the large potholes that were filled with fine dust. Better to concentrate on the road rather than scrutinise how beautiful the new teacher was.

Anyway, he'd sworn off women years ago. He'd never had a long-term relationship, in fact, he hadn't had a girl-friend since he'd come back to Matfield. Most of his time he spent at work and then helping out on Nana's property. There really wasn't much downtime and when spare days did come around he preferred to be by himself, fishing at the dam or camping further out. It suited him to be alone.

'How's the school going for you? I've heard different things about that principal. Not all good,' Nana asked.

Angus listened, watching Nana who would be enjoying the company of someone young and new to the town. Amy's shoulders slumped. 'I must admit the school hasn't been what I thought it would be. They seemed so desperate for teachers and I thought I'd give it a go. I guess I was looking for something different. I like the idea of a small town but I don't think I was prepared for how remote it is. Don't get me wrong, most of the teachers are lovely and some have been supportive, it's just completely the opposite of where I come from.'

Angus piped in. 'It's always hard when you're not from a rural area. Life is very different. I've lived on the coast for a while and you would have got a shock coming here, especially in summer and when it's so dry. It'll take you a while to settle in.'

She turned to him when she answered and he couldn't help but look sideways at her, her dark green eyes looking straight back at him. 'The work situation has been a bit tough. But I guess I'll get used to it. My contract is for six months so I'll see after that.'

He could tell she didn't want to say too much. Smart girl, you never knew who was connected to who in these small towns. There was unhappiness in her tone though and he wondered if the egotistical Elliot had given her a hard time. Nana made a hmph sound and turned to Amy. 'We need good teachers for our kids. Have you made many friends yet? There're quite a few young teachers at the school.'

'Yes, there are some other teachers around my age and a lot of the staff have been friendly. It's just everyone is so busy with school and then some of them have families so there hasn't been time to get to know anyone that well.' A frown creased her forehead. 'I do miss my friends from home. Just someone to have a drink and a laugh with.'

Nana patted her on the leg. 'Well, you can be friends with Angus here. He's a loner and needs someone to talk to. Wonderful young man. Sometimes a bit grumpy in the morning but you won't find a better friend.'

'Nana!' Angus frowned as he turned towards the old lady. 'I'm fine.'

Nana wriggled in her seat, her hand stretched out to hold the dashboard as the truck bounced over a particularly bumpy part of the road. Hanging on tightly, she continued. 'No, Angus, you need a friend. You spend too much time alone. I think the two of you will get on fine. Just friends.' She looked out of the corner of her eye at Amy. 'Nothing more.' Nana stared across Amy, trying to draw Angus's attention but he concentrated on the road. 'You know he's the youngest of our grandchildren. The baby. All the other cousins are older with families of their own. Maybe the best was saved until last.'

Angus shook his head as he gripped the wheel, slowing a little as the track narrowed and they crossed a dry creek bed.

Nana smiled at Amy and then turned and looked through the side window, her next words causing Angus to slow the truck and eventually grind to a halt. 'Friends. The two of you. Angus and Amy. Perfect. Now just stop the truck here for a moment. Right here is good.'

Nana waited until the cloud of dust that had kicked up when they stopped, dispersed. She wound her window down. 'I just want a couple of minutes to let him have a last look.'

Angus whispered in Amy's ear. 'Grandpa's in the casket in the back of the truck. It's his funeral. This was one of his and Nana's favourite views.'

Amy's eyes widened with disbelief as she looked through the back window of the cab. In the back of the truck, a dust covered mahogany casket was strapped in, bales of hay positioned around it. 'Oh, my goodness. I didn't realise.'

Nana patted her leg. 'It's okay, Amy. This is exactly what he wanted, dust and all. He would probably find it interesting that we picked you up on the way. He always liked meeting and talking to young people.'

Amy drew her eyes away from the casket and turned back as they all looked out the window together. The only sound was a clanging noise of a loose part under the truck that eventually also fell silent. They'd stopped next to a lone gum tree, its twisted trunk, white and ancient, rising from the dust like a sentry guarding the plains beyond. Their gazes turned to the branches, three galahs staring straight back at them. The birds' claws gripped the grey brittle branches, the faint green of a few dry leaves also clinging on. One tilted its head, perhaps inquisitive about why the truck had stopped in the middle of nowhere.

'Your grandpa hated them, Angus. But I can't help but love their colours, that pink and grey splash of colour. So pretty and a sign of good things to come.'

Nana pointed towards the dusty plains that stretched out behind the tree. Tufts of grey spinifex grass poked through the flat terrain and a flock of emus lifted their heads to look back at them. The huge birds stood like statues, staring with wide eyes, their bodies and beaks all pointed in the same direction, towards the truck. Eventually, the huge birds turned and raced off, dust flying out from their feet as they sprinted behind a rocky outcrop and out of view. Amy followed their path, her eyes drawn to the distant line of mountains that framed the horizon. A hazy mirage flickered across the plain and Nana wiped a tear from her eye. Her voice was steady when she spoke.

'There you go, Grandpa Ken, one last look. I know you'll be somewhere watching us.' She stopped and turned to Angus and Amy, a serious look on her face. 'And … you'll be happy to know, Angus has a new friend.'

Amy suppressed her laughter as Angus shook his head and closed his eyes, his words hardly audible. 'Nana, you couldn't resist could you.'

The old lady turned back, her gaze once again focussed on the horizon. 'Rest in peace and one day I will be there with you.'

She looked across the plains for a bit longer, the three of them silent before she took a deep breath and wound the window up. She turned to Angus, looked at her watch and nodded. 'Right on time. Let's get this over with.'

*A*ngus pulled the truck up outside a large shed that had been prepared for the funeral service. He gave Amy the rundown on the family. 'This property belongs to my cousin now, but it was where Grandpa Ken was born and lived before he and Nana married. After that they moved to their own property where he spent the rest of his life. The original family home was where he wanted his funeral to be.'

Nana turned to Amy and took her hand. 'It's been lovely to meet you. I probably won't get time to chat today, everyone will be fussing over me. I'm staying the night here, but Angus will make sure you get home and look after your car. Don't be a stranger, will you? Come and visit me in the coming weeks. I'd love to talk to you. Give yourself time with your job. You might settle in and small towns are lovely places to live. And remember, Angus and you will be great friends.'

Amy gazed Angus's way as he shook his head and looked at the ground. She gently squeezed Mavis's hand.

The old lady's weathered soft skin and gentle fingers reminded Amy of her own grandmother who had passed away the year before. 'I'd love that. Thank you for the invite and for picking me up today.'

As Angus helped Mavis down from the truck, a group of people standing nearby walked towards them. Looking through the back windscreen Amy took one last look at the casket, still amazed at the unusual way to transport someone to their funeral. She liked it. And she liked Nana.

Now a throng of people milled around and she was grateful for Angus who helped her get out of the truck. He gave her a quick smile. 'If you head towards the smaller shed on the left there, you'll find a bathroom if you want to freshen up.' He paused and smiled. 'Good luck with the choir.'

'Thank you once again. I really appreciate you stopping and I hope everything goes well for the funeral.'

'We're a big mob when we're all together. I'll make sure to find you afterwards and get you home. I'll have the trailer and we'll stop and pick up your car. Nana will stay here the night and I'll stick around for a bit, but not too late. I'm not one for hanging around and there are plenty of others here who will carry on into the night. You'll probably be hungry after the service, so make sure to help yourself to the food and drinks.'

She blushed when he winked at her, his voice deep and husky when he added, 'I apologise for Nana's directness. She's always trying to get me to socialise more so pay no attention to her. Now, watch out for Elliot. I could tell you a few stories about him.'

'Thanks, Angus, and I'll find you later.' With that, she turned and walked towards the shed. Her feet and face needed cleaning, her hair also, and then she'd have to find the choir.

* * *

She didn't need to look too far. Three students she knew from the primary school were all standing on a chair, jostling each other as they looked at themselves in the bathroom mirror. They squealed when she walked in, all of them jumping down and standing in a straight row in front of her. Their school uniforms were pressed, their hair back in neat plaits, with shiny black shoes and white socks completing their outfits. Pleased to see familiar faces, she smiled at them and gave them a look of approval.

'Girls, you must be in the choir? Miss Sanderson isn't here, but she's left instructions for me to direct you. I'm your conductor today. You all look fabulous.'

The children jumped up and down with excitement when she spoke and one of them passed her a small towel. 'We were told you would be the teacher today. My name's Lisa. Remember me? You have dirt on your face. Here you go Miss Coops. Yes, we're part of the choir and the others are inside waiting. Mr Gantarro has his cranky face on.' Lisa put on an angry face. 'He said he'd sack you if you didn't turn up.'

'Did he now!' Amy replied, raising her eyebrows as she spoke. 'Thank you, girls. Wait for me and I'll clean up.'

She did a speedy wipe with the wet cloth, ensuring that everything was as it should be. Turning around she asked the girls to check that she was looking okay.

'You look beautiful, Miss Coops,' they chorused, 'but what about your feet and sandals?'

Grabbing some paper towels, she slipped her sandals off and put one foot up in the basin. Scrubbing with the paper towel she managed to remove the dirt from her feet. The girls laughed as she did the same to her other foot. Next she wiped over her sandals making sure there wasn't a trace of dust on them. The girls supported her as she put them back on, their excited chatter about dust and dirt, music, and cousins, making them forget for a moment that they were at a funeral.

She laughed with them. It was why she had become a teacher. She found kids and teenagers more interesting sometimes than adults. If only she had got off to a better start at the high school.

Standing in front of the mirror she took another quick look, patted her hair and nodded to herself.

Lisa grabbed her arm and squeezed it tight. 'I think I'll hang onto you, Miss Coops. 'There're so many people here and funerals are a bit scary. Everyone will be looking at us. I'm only doing this for Nana and Grandpa. They're really our great grandparents but we just call them, Nana and Grandpa. It's a pity you didn't meet our Grandpa Ken, he was the best.'

She put her arm around Lisa.

'Thank you, girls. You all look amazing. I think I might have just met your Nana. Her name is Mavis.'

One of the girls called Cindy, jumped up and down. 'She is our Nana and eight of us in the choir are her grandkids. Even Ethan and Peter are going to sing today.'

Lily, who was in Amy's year three music class, grabbed

her hand. 'I hope I don't cry. Funerals are sad and I cried so much when Grandpa died.'

'Funerals are often sad, Lily, but you have to remember, your grandpa wouldn't want you to be unhappy. In fact, after meeting your Nana I would say that your grandpa would be really happy if you smile when you sing. That's exactly what I'm going to tell the rest of the choir. Do you think you can do that?'

The three girls smiled at her, practising how they would achieve that. 'Yes, we can do really big smiles as we sing.'

'I also might have met your Uncle Angus. Or is he someone's dad?'

Lily giggled. 'Uncle Angus, are you kidding, he doesn't even have a wife or a girlfriend.'

Cindy chimed in, 'He's our favourite and the best uncle in the world and the most fun. He takes us to the pool and teaches us how to swim and sometimes when there's a family party he spends the whole time playing soccer with us.'

'The other adults don't do that,' Lisa said. 'They all sit and talk. Boring!'

Interesting, Amy thought, no wife or girlfriend. Her curiosity was pushed aside when she looked at her watch. 'Right, let's do this,' she said. 'I'm assuming Mr Gantarro has a run sheet for me.'

'There are five songs,' Lily piped up. 'They're all Grandpa's favourites. We've practised a million times with Mrs Sanderson. She was sad to leave. She cried when she said goodbye. Everyone knows the songs by heart. We're a really really good choir.'

Amy crossed her fingers, inspired by the girls' confidence and enthusiasm.

* * *

It was easy to spot Elliot once they got inside. The band and the choir were set up next to each other. She gulped, her body tense as she took in the setting and the number of people milling around, many of them now taking their seats. The music students were right at the front of the shed, in full view for everyone to watch them. Checking her dress and shoes were sitting right, she tucked her hair behind her ears. Act confidently, she chided herself, noticing Elliot giving her a death stare and waving his arms wildly at her, leaving no doubt that he wanted her to quickly make her way to the front. Walking slowly, she reminded herself to remain poised and not let him get under her skin. Something he was very good at.

Elliot had been unfriendly and domineering from her very first day at Matfield High School. Although she spent some time at the primary school, most of her lessons were at the high school where he was principal. He spoke to her like she was a child and had already lectured her several times already over minor incidents. As a new teacher she thought she would have been given some support from the principal but it had been the opposite and now she tried as hard as she could not to cross paths with him. But he always seemed to find an excuse to email her or call her up to the office.

It wasn't her fault that no one had bothered to tell her that chairs had to go up on the desks each afternoon or that the meeting on Tuesday started at 3.15 not 3.30 like the emails stated. The fact that one of her students had stumbled over a rug in her classroom on the first day and broken their arm wasn't her fault. The rug had been in the room in exactly the same spot when she had started and, no, she had not noticed that the corner sometimes curled up and caused a tripping hazard. In the second week when she'd accidentally locked herself out of her class-room, he had threatened her with a code of conduct. Who knew that one of her students would faint in the heat and hit his head on the concrete while waiting for her to get a spare key from another teacher.

With a class of thirty kids, all with different needs and behaviour, she was just trying to do her best and keep her head above water. A bit of support from him would have made the world of difference but she'd found out right from the start that it wasn't going to be like that. The fancy marketing ads that the education department had probably spent a fortune on—to lure staff to fill the dire shortages of teachers in regional areas—showed caring admin staff and welcoming teachers. That wasn't her reality on the ground. Photos of smiling, angelic students looking up at the teacher like they were idolised educa-tors were in fact the opposite of what she'd experienced in her first few weeks.

She jumped as Elliot came up beside her and growled in her ear, his usual bad breath wafting across her face. Why didn't someone tell him that his breath was bad? 'You're late. I said nine thirty and it's now ten. The service will start soon and you aren't ready. This will be another black mark against your name.'

Behind Elliot were the first rows of seats and she could see Angus watching and giving her the thumbs up. Anger filled her as she turned to Elliot and smiled as sweetly as she could, ignoring his icy stare as he looked her up and down. She pulled her shoulders back, grateful she'd had time to clean up and look professional. Music was her business and when it came to choirs and bands she knew what she was doing. The main thing was to keep calm and not let anyone rattle you, particularly when you were about to perform. She looked past him at the students who were all staring at her waiting for some direction. Turning back to him she gave him her most nonchalant look. 'I'm here now. Thank you for your patience. Do you have the run list?'

He snarled a response and she could feel her face burning as she tried to keep a pleasant look on her face. 'Thank you,' she said as he passed her a list, his eyes narrowing, a sneer on his face.

His voice was low so no one else could hear. 'You new teachers think this job is easy. Well, girlie, you have a long way to go. Look smart now.'

It would have been so good to tell him to jam his list and walk out the door. But her car wasn't waiting outside for her to escape and besides … she turned around, breathing deeply as twenty little expectant faces looked at her for confirmation that everything was going to be alright. Picking up the conductor's stick that was resting on the music stand in front of her, she placed the list on the stand and turned the first page in the music book. Everything was in order. Mrs Sanderson would have made sure it was. From the corner of her eye, she saw

Angus and Nana Mavis watching her, their smiles making her calmer. She turned slightly to give them a quick smile back before returning her focus to the children in front of her. 'Right. Gather around now. I just want to quickly talk to you before we begin.'

CHAPTER 4

$\mathcal{I}$t had taken all of Angus's strength not to break down during the service. Grandpa Ken, who had been one of seven, had been the central figure of their extended family for as long as he could remember.

The Carmody family had been in the area for generations and today they gathered at Billa Station to pay their respects. It was where Grandpa had come into the world just over eighty-five years ago. Although the property had changed slightly over the years, with plenty of modern facilities and buildings added, it remained the central spot for the family.

Billa's thousands of sprawling acres had years ago provided enough room for Ken's siblings to split separate blocks off and build their own homes. Angus's aunts, uncles and cousins were spread out across the land that produced cattle whose meat was distributed throughout the country. Over the years many had stayed and still worked on the properties. Angus, along with a multitude of cousins, were the next generation who would continue the family tradition.

Not everyone had remained though and over the years family members had come and gone, some like Angus's parents, Susan and Bill, seeking another life away from the dusty cattle properties and remoteness. They had wanted a change several years ago and had moved further north to Cairns. A beautiful house on a hill that overlooked the ocean had become their new home, the salty sea breeze and thick rainforest they backed onto, a far cry from where they had previously lived. Angus had also moved away from the area around the same time. At one stage he considered never returning, there were many reasons to stay away. But eventually, the pull of the outback was stronger than his urge to keep his distance. When he was ready to return, Nana offered for him to live with her and Grandpa. He had the use of a spare cottage and a shed not far from their own house. It was rundown but he had quickly turned it into a liveable home, the shed a perfect spot for him to work on vehicles and farm machinery.

He had not been sure about returning to where he had grown up, there were years and events that he'd rather forget. However, the bush and familiar places he'd loved as a kid had nagged at him and the teenager who at nineteen had left was a vastly different person from the man who had returned.

It hadn't been easy coming back. His life experiences should have given him strength, there had been plenty to overcome. But there were ghosts of the past to contend with and just as he expected, they were there to greet him. He had left but they hadn't. Every day was a struggle but

Nana and Grandpa had helped him, getting him through the tough times and allowing him space when he needed it the most. Even though Grandpa had needed help on the property and there had been plenty of work around the homestead to keep him busy it hadn't taken Angus long to work out that coming back was a mistake. His heart wasn't in it and working with cattle wasn't what he wanted to do full-time. When he was offered a job at the local mechanics he'd been tentative, but it had proven to be a step in the right direction and kept him in the town for a bit longer.

Now he was grateful he had come back. At least he had been around for his grandfather's last couple of years. If it wasn't for his grandparents he wouldn't have stayed. The old man's deep voice echoed in his mind and he closed his eyes, the past wrapping around him. 'Don't waste time mulling over the past. You can't change it. Just get on with it.'

As the sweet tones of the children's choir echoed around the old shed, Angus opened his eyes and couldn't help but smile as he watched Amy wave her hands gently through the air, keeping the beat and encouraging the children to raise their voices. Grandpa would have loved the music and the way they sang with a happy lilt in their tone and smiles on their faces. He focussed on his nieces and nephews who kept looking towards him and Nana. Poor little Cindy, she'd had to take a tissue off Amy during the main song, *Wind Beneath My Wings*, wiping her eyes and taking deep breaths before continuing.

Considering, as Amy had said, it was the first time she'd worked with the choir, she'd done an awesome job and the singing and music of the band made for an uplifting service.

When Nana gripped Angus's arm and nodded solemnly to remind him to stand up, his chest ached and he took a deep breath as he rose from his seat. The crowd stood together and he walked with some of the others from his family, towards the casket. The haunting sounds of the choir singing, *Amazing Grace*, echoed throughout the shed and what seemed like a hundred youthful voices crescendoed into the chorus.

His tears fell and his body filled with grief as he concentrated on putting one foot in front of the other.

His mind blurred with other memories. Another death. Billy. His mate. A boy who never got to grow into a man. Angus tensed his body, glad of the weight of the casket against his arms. The sweet tones of the choir pulled him back to the moment and he held tight as the pallbearers walked slowly through the middle of those gathered and out into the sunlight. He tried not to think of the finality of death and the overriding grief of losing someone and never being able to see them again.

His grandfather had lived a long and full life and had no regrets. He'd talked at length to Angus about life and how to get the most out of it. He was going to miss the old man but amidst the sadness, there was a warm feeling that Grandpa had been given the time to say goodbye and had even give instructions to Nana about how his body should arrive at the funeral. He had been adamant that only Angus was to drive the truck with Nana in the front and Grandpa in the back.

Angus had been with Grandpa not long before he passed. He'd held the old man's hand as he struggled to tell him his last wishes. 'Drive me there in the truck with your nana. She knows where to stop and I want you to give her some time there. It was our spot.' He'd also overheard what Grandpa had said to Nana, just before Angus had left the room, leaving Nana to be alone with her husband. His voice had been low but Angus had heard him. 'When he wants to go, Mavis, let him go. He needs to get away. He'll come back one day.'

Angus had gone back to the bed and gripped Grandpa's outstretched hand, the old man's voice barely audible. 'Let it go, boy, let it go,' Grandpa said. 'Don't waste time.'

Thank goodness he had driven to the funeral with Nana. Just the two of them and Grandpa. And then Amy.

Standing tall, he wiped his eyes before pulling his sunglasses down as everyone emptied out of the barn and stood together. Two of his nieces, Lisa and Cindy, joined Nana next to the hearse, ensuring everything was in order. Nana wrapped her arms around the children's shoulders and they in turn hung onto her. Grandpa had wished to be cremated and the hearse would return his body to town. Billa Station had its own family graveyard and Grandpa's gravesite and tombstone, where his ashes would be scattered later in the week, would be there, right next to four generations of his family who had worked the land before him.

Nana stood tall, wiping her eyes as Lisa and Cindy waved at the hearse as it started up and made its way towards the road that would lead it back to town. Angus smiled a little when Lisa called out after the vehicle. 'Bye Grandpa, we'll look after Nana for you.'

*a*my breathed a sigh of relief when the service ended and the pallbearers, with the coffin held between them, made their way out through the barn doors. The choir had performed better than she could have hoped and she hugged and thanked the children who had stayed with her, waiting until the rest of the mourners left. As she watched the last one leave through the shed door she turned and started to pack up the music stands, gathering the sheet music and making sure she had everything. Thankfully Elliot had already exited with the band. She wasn't in the mood for his criticism.

A man approached her, his hand outstretched for her to shake. He looked a lot like Angus and she smiled back as he spoke. 'G'day, pleased to meet you,' he said. 'You must be the new teacher, Miss Coops. I'm Edwin Carmody, the eldest of Ken's grandchildren. My two kids were in the choir, Cindy and Peter. They talk about you all the time. You teach them piano, is that right?'

'I'm pleased to meet you. Yes, I'm Amy or Miss Coops. They sang beautifully today and Peter nailed his solo part.'

'They did, and yes, he was spot on. Grandpa would have loved it. You did an amazing job with them. Thanks for being at the school and putting so much effort and time in. Like I said, the kids adore you. You're doing a great job with them.'

She blushed. Were all the men good-looking in the Carmody family? Edwin was older, taller and more solid than Angus but he had the same black curly hair and dark eyes. He looked directly at her when he spoke and touched her on the arm when he said his thanks.

She responded, watching as he wiped his eyes, took a deep breath, and looked away.

'They're talented kids and they love music. The credit isn't mine though, Mrs Sanderson has done all the hard work with them. I only led them today and it was easy because they knew exactly what to do.'

His words were mumbled when he replied, his tone melancholic. 'Well, I just wanted to say thank you. The kids don't have their mother here so it meant a lot that you looked after them today. Are you going to stay for something to eat and drink?'

Edwin stood close to her and she could smell his after-shave, a sweet sexy scent that matched his well-fitting jeans and a dark blue collared shirt. Taking a step back she rearranged the music books in her hands. 'I guess I will. I'm getting a lift back with someone in your family. I broke down on the way here and they picked me up. Angus, and Nana Mavis.'

Just as she spoke, Angus appeared beside Edwin. 'G'day Edwin, I see you've met Amy, the new teacher.'

For a moment she thought a scowl crossed Edwin's face as he took a while to respond to Angus's outstretched hand. He gripped it quickly, with a short handshake and no reciprocating smile. She sensed a tone of sarcasm in his voice. 'Looks like you met her first.' He thumped Angus on the back. 'Time for a beer.'

CHAPTER 6

*T*he attending crowd gathered under a marquee beside the shed. A couple of the mothers from the school recognised Amy and came to talk to her. It was reassuring to have someone familiar to stand with and she appreciated the students who milled around her and made sure she had a cup of tea and something to eat. Many of the guests were relatives and she listened as they explained how they fitted into the family.

The women were all curious to know if she had a partner and she noticed the looks between them when she said she was single. 'That won't last,' one of them said. 'There're a few single men in town who are always looking for a beautiful young woman like yourself.'

She wanted to say that intelligence was usually what she looked for first but she minded her manners and laughed off the suggestions that she'd soon find a farmer who wanted a wife.

'I'm only twenty-four. I have plenty of time for that later.' Thank goodness the conversation had ended as

Edwin made his way towards them. She watched him as he greeted all the women. He was poised and slick, piling compliments on each of them, rewarded with fluttering eyes and wide smiles. Polished and definitely at ease around females, she thought. When he turned to her she was lost in her thoughts. It had been a while since she'd been in a relationship. There had been a number of boyfriends at school and then a couple more at university. But none had lasted and she'd learned that not all could be trusted. She wasn't sure yet what to make of Edwin. Was he genuinely a nice guy or was it all a front?

He passed her a glass of wine. 'I thought you might like a drink to wind down after that performance. I bet Elliot asked you to help with the choir at the last moment. The other music teacher Penny Sanderson only left town a couple of days ago. Left everyone in the lurch, apparently. No commitment.'

'Thank you, and yes, it was rather late notice. As I said before, I was lucky that the kids all knew what they were doing.'

'Their singing was the highlight, such beautiful voices and their little faces trying to smile. Grandpa would have loved it and Nana smiled the entire way through the performances,' one of the ladies said.

Eileen—one of the mums from school—broke into the conversation, her question directed to Edwin. 'Why did Penny leave? I thought she had settled in.'

Edwin looked a bit bashful. 'Must have been the school, or maybe family obligations back in the city. She rang me yesterday morning and said she'd packed her things and was leaving. I'm not sure of anything more than that.' He took a long sip from his beer and Amy noticed some looks between some of the women. 'Anyway, we have Amy now to lead our children to their musical success.' He lifted his glass high. 'Here's to our new teacher.'

It was embarrassing to have all the attention focussed on her and she tried to avert more questions from the ladies and turn the conversation to something else other than getting quizzed about every detail of her life. Edwin stood quietly listening, every so often throwing a smile her way. There was something about him that she liked. He was strong in his opinions, and it seemed like he was well-respected in his role at the council. She wondered what had happened to his wife.

A lady who appeared beside her tapped her on the shoulder. 'Hi, I'm Cheryl. Nana would like to hear the children sing again. She said to come and ask you if it was possible to get them together and have them sing another few songs. She said their singing has made the day exactly what Grandpa would have wanted.'

'Oh, of course. I would love to.'

Cheryl pointed towards the verandah, where Nana sat on a cane chair, surrounded by family. The old lady lifted her hand and waved at Amy, who gave her a wave back before turning to Cheryl. 'Right. Let's round up these kids.'

It hadn't taken long to get the children together and now they stood in formation with Amy at the front to conduct. Nana looked on proudly and everyone gathered around to hear one more performance. They looked a little bedraggled and dusty, but they held their heads high and their little voices filled the air. They'd even done some hand actions in time and the audience had cheered and clapped, their cries of 'more, more,' and 'encore' making Amy laugh along with the children before turning back to them for one last song.

When they had finished she took a moment to look around at the people gathered, many of them wiping their eyes and cheering the children who all bowed together in time when she gestured for them to do so. Nana blew her a kiss and she smiled back as the children gathered around her, giving her hugs and jumping up and down in excitement at the success of their performance.

Edwin appeared beside her, putting his arm around her shoulders and giving her a squeeze. 'That was fantastic. What a choir. They sing with real heart for you. Well done.'

'Oh, I can't take the credit. Their usual choir teacher has done amazing work with them. They did perform beautifully though.' Emotion filled her as she looked at the children who had dispersed and were now running around, some of them going back to a game of cricket being played on the small patch of grass to the side of the house. 'It's lovely to see family together like this.'

Edwin took her arm and led her over to a group of people who congratulated her on the choir's performance. They were mostly family and she enjoyed the talk about the cattle and sales that were coming up. Different conversation in a different place. She had to admit she was starting to enjoy herself and with Edwin beside her, adding in his bit and making sure she was included she started to relax and forget about the last few weeks and the aggravation of Elliot.

* * *

As time went on and the crowd started to thin, she looked around for Angus, hoping that he hadn't forgotten about giving her a lift back. Edwin tried to persuade her to return with him and his children, but she said she'd already told Angus she'd take his offer. She was deep in conversation with Edwin, when Angus appeared, his wide grin causing her to smile back at him. The men today were all dressed similarly. Dark jeans and collared shirts with no ties. Angus had told her when they'd been in the truck. 'It was what Grandpa wanted. He hated formal wear. Nana told all of us not to wear ties.'

This funeral was different from the ones she'd been to before. A tin shed instead of a church and a community gathering including children. A bush funeral where everyone was dressed for the occasion, but also for the heat.

Angus had joined the group she was talking to. He was full of energy compared to his older cousin, Edwin, and he jumped around, hugging some of the women and making jokes when they commented about how well he scrubbed up.

'Angus is the black sheep of the family,' Edwin piped up, nodding towards her to make sure she heard. 'He's covered in tatts under that shirt and he's only got decent clothes on because Nana told him he had to.'

Angus stopped bouncing around and came and wrapped his arm around Edwin. 'Thanks, mate. Tell me, how am I the black sheep and perhaps if I am that's not a bad thing. It might pay you to remember on such a day, one of Grandpa's lessons. If you haven't got something good to say, don't say it.'

Amy sensed the animosity between the two. They looked alike but were very different in personality. She watched them closely, perhaps it was just friendly banter.

Edwin pulled himself away from Angus and gave him a playful punch on the arm. 'Nana's boy. Could never do a thing wrong in her eyes.'

Angus jumped up and down pretending to jab punches at Edwin's body. 'Jealous. You're just jealous.' He went to say more but then looked around and stood still. 'I won't tell any stories, Edwin. Family secrets stay that way.' Turning to Amy he lowered his voice. 'I'll leave in about ten minutes. The trailer's hitched up ready to go and we can pick your car up on the way back.' With that he nodded to the group and turned towards the shed. He was out of earshot when Edwin, who she thought may have had one too many beers, had one final go at him. 'Rough as guts he is. Trouble with a capital T. You're lucky, Amy, that he doesn't have any kids at the school.'

Angus must have heard but he kept walking, a couple of the kids running up to him. He hoisted one on his shoulders and held the other's hand as he walked towards the house, probably to say goodbye to other families who were inside preparing more food.

She didn't reply to Edwin's comments, instead taking long sips of her drink, her eyes cast down. Matfield was going to be full of local characters and gossip. She'd have to make sure she kept her head down and mouth closed. Around here, everyone knew everyone and even at a funeral, gossip and local news were being shared. As she put her empty glass back on a tray she suddenly felt like a stranger in an unfamiliar setting. This was something she had experienced a bit lately and she was learning that it was a mixed bag of emotions due to stepping outside her comfort zone and making a big move by herself. Insecurities were becoming part of her everyday life as she tried to find what it was she was looking for in life. A career? An old wooden cottage with a verandah that she dreamed about, or just a friend, or a group of friends that made her happy. At the moment it was just her, with no one else to rely on or share her concerns, and now amongst strangers, she was overwhelmed with the thought of being so far away from home and everything she was used to. What was she doing here in the middle of the outback and were the pangs of loneliness and the situation at school going to improve?

She watched the crowd dispersing and groups getting into their cars to return home. The day had been long and Elliot unrelenting in his attitude towards her. As Angus waved her over to his truck she felt a sense of relief. For now, she just wanted to get home and get her car fixed.

CHAPTER 7

*A*ngus had stayed a bit longer than he had originally expected. At first he had as usual wanted to leave as soon as possible, to get away from everyone, particularly Edwin who was always a thorn in his side. The two of them were at separate ends of the family line. Edwin, the eldest of Ken and Mavis's grandchildren, and Angus, the youngest. He usually managed to stay out of Edwin's way but in a small town that wasn't always easy and today with his parents away overseas he was the sole representative of his family. When he listened and shared stories about Grandpa and grieved with others in the family he was grateful he had stayed. Nana had asked earlier in the week if he could please hang around and talk to the others. 'I know you and Edwin don't get on but the kids love seeing you and all the others. Don't let his animosity ruin your connection to our family. Stay for a while and talk. I'll need you there for support. We're not supposed to have favourites as grandparents, but...' She'd smiled sweetly at him and he promised he'd hang around and be social. The satisfied look she gave him showed that she had won but really, who could say 'no' to her.

There were plenty of others to mingle with apart from Edwin and although it was a sombre occasion the kids had lifted everyone's spirits with another impromptu choir performance that really turned the funeral into a celebration of life.

When Amy had gathered the kids together at Nana's request and they'd gone through a rendition of songs, he'd watched how they all focussed on Amy, singing their hearts out to please her and Nana. Grandpa would have loved it, a chorus of children's voices filling the yard, the old homestead with its verandahs full of people in the background, and even the cows in the paddocks nearby, lifting their heads and staring.

When it was time to go he'd gestured to Amy who was talking to some of the kids, that he was ready to leave. Nana had already hugged him and thanked him for the day. 'You've done well, Angus. Everyone loves you and Grandpa was always proud of you and your kind nature.' Now as he walked to the truck with Amy, he waved back to Nana who sat on the verandah, a small glass of sherry in her hand.

'She's amazing, your Nana Mavis,' Amy said as he opened the truck door for her.

'She is. She held up well today.'

It had been a relief to get in the truck and away from the crowd who were left on the front lawn. The older members of the family were settled in on the verandah and it was mainly a younger crowd who were left outside, the conversation getting louder and more boisterous as the afternoon grew long and the effects of alcohol settled in.

Angus held her elbow and helped her into her seat. He took a final look back at the others clustered in groups around long tables that were set up on the lawn. A few raised their hands and waved. 'That lot will carry on until the sun comes up,' he said, relieved that he was under no obligation to stay any longer. There were plenty of others there to carry on the festivities and as long as Nana was comfortable he was ready to go home.

Angus wanting to leave had been good timing for Amy. Although everyone had been friendly and the kids had kept her company and brought her plenty of food and a drink, she had still felt somewhat out of place. Everyone knew each other and their conversations were often about places she had never been to and people she didn't know.

Edwin had come back and forth to her. 'Always tricky when you're the new person in town,' he'd said as he passed her a glass of wine. 'I'll take you out and show you around. I know everyone in the district so when you need something you just come and see me.'

She took tiny sips from the wine. 'Thank you. That's really kind of you.' She'd listened as he talked about his job and the cattle, the weather, the dry seasons, and how hard he worked to look after his kids. He didn't say anything about what had happened to his wife, but he made it clear that she wasn't living with them and that he was responsible for the children.'

He'd left when a couple of the other ladies came over to talk to her. There were a variety of different charity clubs in town and they were keen to get her to join. She talked with them for a while, until Angus signalled to go.

'Don't forget, love,' one of them said as she said goodbye to them. 'We always need volunteers at the cake stall on a Saturday morning. Right outside the hardware shop. Every weekend. You just have to bake one or two and then we only need an hour of your time. The money goes to such a good cause.'

It had been on the tip of her tongue to tell them that every weekend was filled with doing schoolwork and other paperwork that Elliot constantly emailed to her. There was not going to be any time for baking cakes or standing behind a stall. Besides the shop in town sold cakes, why on earth would you need to bake them?

A couple of the kids had run up to the truck, waving and calling out to her as Angus started the vehicle up and pulled slowly out of the yard. Out of the corner of her eye she glimpsed Edwin staring at them, his gaze steady, his face unsmiling. Who knew what the trouble was between him and Angus. Whatever it was though it seemed fairly serious. As she settled back in her seat and looked to the road ahead she thought about how Edwin had tried to rattle Angus. Best not to get involved in family arguments. There was obviously bad blood between them. For now, she was happy to be going back with Angus. It had been a long day and she couldn't wait to get home and have a shower. At least tomorrow was Sunday. One more day before school.

The truck rattled along at a good pace, the trailer bouncing along behind. When they reached her car she stared at the colour of it, its thick covering of red dust blending in with the surroundings. 'Just as well we're collecting it now,' she said to Angus, 'otherwise it would just disappear into the earth.'

It hadn't taken Angus long to drive it up onto the tilt trailer and secure it. She stood watching him, her arms folded, her white sandals once again sinking into the dust.

As he tied the car down with ropes he had in the truck, she watched for a while, before turning around in a full circle, looking in every direction. There was no movement as far as she could see, just wide plains, dotted with a few stunted trees and tufts of grass. A warm breeze pushed across her face as the sun sank lower in the west, a deep blue rising above the line of the land. She looked in the other direction above the trees, a white crescent moon rising in the sky, the afternoon light throwing a hazy gold across the land. Thank goodness Angus had driven this way earlier in the day. She shivered at the thought that she might have been still stranded here, sitting and waiting in her car for who knew what.

His voice behind her startled her from her thoughts and she jumped as he called out that he was ready to go. It was as if he had read her mind and she felt a wave of gratitude towards him when he spoke. 'I'm pleased we came this way today. If we'd left a bit earlier you might still be sitting here waiting to be rescued.'

'I can't thank you enough, both for saving me and then

bringing me back and picking up the car. God knows what I would have done if you and Nana hadn't come along.'

He grimaced as he hung onto the steering wheel, the truck bouncing over a corrugated section of the road. 'We only came this way because she wanted to stop at that favourite area of Grandpa's.' He turned to her and shook his head. 'I'll have plenty to say to that idiot Elliot when I see him next. He really put you in danger. You think he'd look after his staff.'

'He hasn't been exactly welcoming. I don't like to say too much, but he doesn't like me. He's made that obvious.'

They talked back and forth, and a weight lifted from her shoulders when she opened up about her experiences of the past month. Angus was not only a good listener but he also seemed to understand her position and how she was feeling.

After a while the subject changed and she started to ask him about where he lived and the history of the area.

He explained how he lived in an old cottage at his grandparent's place, a property called Allub Downs, that had once been part of the original Billa Downs. 'That's how it works for our family. You don't have to worry about big mortgages and finding a place you like some-where. We all have rights to a certain amount of land we can call our own and the freedom to build our own home on that plot.'

She listened intently, pleased that he was chatty and she didn't have to talk too much. The details of how the properties operated and who lived where were inter-esting and she asked him some questions about the cattle and how they kept track of them over such large distances. It was strange, she sensed his connection to where he was living but there was also a certain degree of distance in some of his comments. 'I can't see the properties or houses from where my cottage is, but most of the family still live and work in these parts,' he said. 'Mum and Dad have already handed over their plot to me. Their block was next to mine anyway, so it just doubles the size when I decide to do something with it. Grandpa and Nana use them both for stock but they were always trying to get me to work it myself. They want me to stick around, you know, carry on the family tradition.'

'And are you going to?'

He paused for a long time before replying. 'I'm not sure what I'm going to do yet.'

She sensed his mood shift. There was something about Angus that made her want to take him aside and ask him if he was okay. Like she did with her students. She sensed it in his tone when he talked about his grandparents and now in the conversation about what he was going to do next.

She dropped the topic of what he was going to do next. She was the last person to question someone else about what the future held. Who knew where her life was headed? Matfield was supposed to be her new direction, both in life and her career, but the way the situation was at school she was no longer so sure about any of it.

The subject fortunately changed and she thanked him again for helping her. 'Would it be okay if I just drop you home,' he asked. 'It's getting a bit late and I'll fix your car tomorrow and bring it back then if that's alright with you.'

'Of course, it is,' she replied. 'I'm not going anywhere until school on Monday anyway.'

She didn't need her car tomorrow. It was Sunday and a good day for chilling out at home and getting school-work ready for the week ahead.

Angus had been quieter after that and she realised that he was probably emotionally exhausted after the events of the day. It was a calming silence and she enjoyed not having to think about too much as the old truck rattled along the road back towards the town. Neither of them spoke until she gave him directions to where she was living.

The apartment the Department of Education had allotted her, was tiny. Thankfully she didn't have many belongings and the few pieces of furniture that she had brought with her were small and fitted in easily. A new bed had been delivered the first week she had arrived and with all her boxes now unpacked she finally felt like she had her own space to call home. The oak bedside table and matching dressing table that her grandfather had made her gave her room to display some of her favourite items. Her parents had gifted her a two-seater lounge, perfect for the tiny room that jutted off from the galley kitchen.

Tonight, after such a long day, she felt like she had come home. The drive to Billa Station and back, as well as the funeral service and stress of the choir presentation had left her exhausted. Angus and his truck and trailer had been a godsend and he had dropped her off at the apartment, reminding her he'd be back in the morning with her car.

He'd waited until she unlocked and she gave him a

wave as the truck towing the trailer with her car on, rumbled up the street. A group of dogs fighting in the middle of the road jumped out of the way as he beeped his horn at them. To the west, a red glow shimmering above the roofs of the houses and bats flew overhead. The eerie call of a curlew echoed along her street and a feeling of loneliness descended on her as she shut the door, making sure to pull the safety latches across the heavy timber door. It was a small town but apparently there were still break-ins that occurred so she had been warned to be vigilant.

As she made herself a cup of tea she went over the events of the day. Angus had talked to her at length on the way back about the dangers of driving on the roads without letting someone know where she was going or without backup safety precautions. She'd listened carefully. No one at school had discussed this with her and she appreciated his local knowledge. 'I'm not sure you should go on those dirt roads with that small car of yours,' he said. 'That's why everyone around here has a four-wheel drive vehicle. You don't want to get into a situation and not be able to get out of it. You don't have to go far out of the town before it's remote.'

He must have noticed the look of shock on her face. 'Don't stress about it. Your car is okay for in town and on the bitumen, it's just where you were today you shouldn't have been there in that little vehicle and with those tyres. I'm working at the mechanic's down Main Street so if your car needs servicing or anything else just let me know and I'll help you out.'

'Oh, you're a mechanic,' she'd replied.

'For now. I'm a diesel mechanic but I've done other

jobs, mustering, shearing, anything that needs doing on these properties.'

It was hard to judge how old Angus was. His face was boyish but when he spoke he seemed older than she was; as though he'd been around a bit and lived through different experiences. His personality was intriguing and although he was 'rough around the edges', she liked him. Besides, he and his nana had saved her.

She stirred her tea, jumping when her phone beeped. 'Geez,' she spoke out loud. 'It's Saturday night.'

A message from the school glared out at her, the spelling errors making her inhale sharply. Didn't they read over their messages before sending them? *'ALL STAFF, dont forget FULL STAFF meeting at 8 am prompte Monday mornin. All must attend. Message back to show that you have recieved this message. Elliot.'*

Flicking the silent button on, she turned her phone over so that it was facing down. There was no way she was going to answer any emails or messages until Monday morning. The weekend was her time. A bit of extra preparation or marking was okay, but communication with the school and especially with Elliot, particularly after today's events was strictly off-limits.

CHAPTER 8

*S*leep came easily that night, and in the morning she woke invigorated and motivated for the days ahead. Moving out west had seemed like a simple solution to ease the boredom that had set in when she lived on the coast. Most of her friends had partners and she was tired of feeling like the third wheel. It had been time for a change and regional areas were screaming out for teachers. As soon as she had hinted that she was possibly interested in a job in a remote area the Department had been persistent. Phone calls, emails, and promises of everything she had ever dreamt of. They would give her whatever she wanted and look after her if she agreed to relocate to a regional town.

As she tried to get the hotplate to work on the stove she thought how perhaps an improvement in living quarters might persuade others to make the move to remote towns. The oven barely worked and her shower constantly dripped. She'd reported it and tied a towel around the showerhead to stop the noise keeping her

awake at night. 'I'll pencil it in on the list,' the maintenance man, Riley, had told her.

She'd wanted to tell him to write it in red pen, forget
the pencil part. 'Could you also please add that the
washing machine is broken and the smoke alarms go off
for no reason. It all needs fixing.'

Riley seemed to take a bit more notice once she
mentioned the smoke alarms. 'I'll message you with a time
I can come and fix it,' he replied, muttering something
else about fire hazards and safety.

Turning her music up, she tried to remain positive. An
upbeat song would help the situation and she shook her
body, jigging up and down, stretching her arms high in
the air before dancing to the tune. The kitchen was only a
small space but big enough for her dance moves and she
wiggled and jigged around, letting herself get right into
the rhythm as she got the bread and butter out of the
fridge. Everything had to be kept in the fridge, vegetables,
bread, flour, any edible item. It was too hot to leave food
out and the noisy air conditioner barely worked, making
it sometimes hotter inside than out. Giving up on getting
the stove to work she danced her way over to the kitchen
bench. Toast would have to do this morning, she didn't
have the patience to argue with the stove.

Some dramatic dance moves made her feel even more
energised and she put her plate and cup down on the
bench, letting herself feel the music and forget about
where she was and what the week would bring. Dance
had been one of her passions when she was younger. At
school she'd not only been the band leader and part of the
choir but also involved in every musical and theatre
performance that took place. Once she left school the

clubs and bars of the coast had provided regular dancing places and now as she moved around the kitchen she realised how much she missed the freedom of dancing. Matfield was probably not going to give her many opportunities, apart from in her own kitchen, to let those skills loose. Maybe she could start a dance group at the school.

She twisted and moved, her hair flying wildly, her body feeling alive. A thumping sound on the kitchen wall stopped her in her tracks and she stood with her hands in the air, listening to the noises coming through her wall. A teacher, Eliza Tuls, from the primary school, lived in the apartment next door. She'd been in Matfield a year longer than Amy and loved nothing more than to talk about how much she knew and what she was good at. To put it mildly, she was a major pain in the neck and Amy avoided her like the plague. Resting one hand on her hip, she turned the music down. Eliza acted and looked like she was well in her seventies but she had told Amy she was fifty-two.

Amy had hoped that because Eliza Tuls worked at the primary school she wouldn't need to interact too much with her. But the primary school and high school were situated next to each other and often the teachers attended the same meetings. Of course, as Amy was the music teacher at both, she was expected to attend every meeting. And, she had quickly discovered, that teachers loved meetings, especially Eliza who for some reason was often given the opportunity to speak and air her advice. The allocated time often ran way over, because of Eliza's persistence to give every unnecessary detail for whatever topic she was talking about.

Although Amy had only been working for a month at

the schools, she had already attended more meetings than she could count. There were special meetings because she was a beginning teacher, where she had to sit for two hours and listen to complicated and very impractical theories on a variety of different ways to teach. Weekly meetings discussed the curriculum, assessment and lesson content while other meetings went over and over the paperwork that needed to be completed each week, contact methods for parents and carers, and how to "unpack"—she hated that word—a variety of programs, forms and instructions that must be dealt with every day. Last week there had even been a two-hour meeting to discuss the intricacies of "meetings". When would meetings occur, where would they be held and what would they involve? Words like pedagogy, collaborative, metacognition, and duty of care, swirled in her head, even after she closed her eyes and tried to sleep at night. There were lists and information that came out daily about students in her classes and the different ways she was to cater to each one and their different learning needs. The work was endless.

None of this included her own essential preparation for her music programs and music lessons, not to mention the random year eight maths class that was included on her timetable. After a month her brain was already on overload and she wondered just how much more information or lists of 'to do' would fit in there.

And to add to her inventory of problems, the biggest issue right at the top of the list, was Elliot.

He always seemed to find her and use up even more of her valuable time, chiding her, from the way she dressed, to how she was interacting with the students and why she had so much difficulty turning up to meetings on time. She had asked him for specifics about when she had arrived late. To her knowledge that had only occurred twice and both times she had good reasons that had been unavoidable. Also, both times, her lateness had been less than five minutes and when she arrived most of the others were still taking their seats and chatting before the meeting started.

Often Elliot chaired the meetings and it was despairing to sit for a couple of hours listening to him lauding some amazing program or innovative idea someone had come up with, while all she could think about was her lesson preparation or marking she could have been doing instead of listening to his monotonous lectures. Although she found her body tensed and waves of panic swept through her at the thought of what she should be doing, it appeared that some of the more experienced teachers had learned how to overcome the droning roll of Elliot's voice. An older man, Samson, who was the PE teacher and adored by all the kids at both schools, had fallen asleep in the last meeting, his head resting on Amy's shoulder, his quiet snoring making her giggle and unfortunately draw attention to the situation.

Elliot had not been impressed and Samson had squeezed her shoulders on the way out, whispering in her ear. 'Hope I didn't do the sleep dribble on you, love. Elliot is as boring as bat shit. I wish he'd hurry up and climb the ladder and piss off.'

They were definitely a mixed crew of staff, some who liked Elliot, others who tolerated him, and surely some like her and Samson, who thought he was a bully and a complete idiot.

It hadn't helped her assessment of Elliot that several times she had observed that he was very friendly with Eliza who lived in the apartment next door. If she wasn't mistaken, Eliza openly flirted with him and swooned like a lovestruck teenager in his presence. Yuck, she thought. Another reason to have as little to do with Eliza as possible.

She ran her mind across the rest of the staff, trying to work out who could be trusted and who couldn't. At the moment it was better just to smile and get along with everyone. Keep her mouth shut and try and do her job. A loud knock on her front door woke her from her daydreaming and she slammed her empty cup down on the table. That would be Eliza! It wouldn't be the first time her neighbour had come to complain.

She jiggled her body, pleased that at least she had moved around a little with her dancing, stretched her muscles and released any tension that came instantly whenever she thought about school. Her reflection looked back at her from a mirror that hung on the wall. Her appearance was messy to say the least and she pulled a silly face, building up her nonchalant demeanour for when she opened the door. That would give Eliza something to talk about. The music had served its purpose and some of the stress from the past week and yesterday had disappeared. She looked down at her pyjamas which consisted of tiny cotton shorts and a singlet top that barely covered her body. Her hair was unbrushed and hung wildly around her face. Perhaps her feral appearance might scare her prudish neighbour away. Putting on her 'I don't care' face she strode to the door and flung it open. 'Yes, Eliza,' she said as she pulled the door back, the bottom of it sticking as usual on the uneven floor. Concentrating on pushing the door open, she looked down, making sure she didn't scrape the bottom of the door on her foot.

She hopped out of the way as the door finally swung open, reaching her hand up to push her hair out of her eyes so she could talk to the person standing on her doorstep.

* * *

Angus had risen early the morning after the funeral. For some reason he couldn't stop thinking about the new teacher, Amy. The conversation had flowed in the truck on the drive home and she'd made him laugh with some of her stories about her first few weeks of work. Even though he got the impression that she'd held back and not complained too much, he could tell that it hadn't been easy for her so far and by the sounds of it, Elliot was going out of his way to make her life difficult.

It had been easier to fix the tyre at the workshop rather than his place and he'd left home early and driven into town. As he reversed her car off the trailer and into the shade of the shed where he could work on it, he looked down at his feet. Several pairs of shoes had been left on the floor of her car, so he leaned down and picked them up, placing them in between boxes of books and papers stacked where a passenger would usually put their feet. How did she drive properly with everything under her feet, and so many items near to the accelerator and brake? Lolly wrappers and more papers and books littered the front seat of the car and he smiled to himself when he turned around and observed the array of clothes scattered in the back. It appeared that Amy took off her bra when she got in the car, four of them draped over the back seat where she had tossed them.

* * *

It hadn't taken long to fix her tyre and check the pressure, making sure everything was as it should be. He would drop the car back to her apartment and she could drive him back to the work shed. That way she'd have her car for the day, just in case she needed it.

When he knocked on her front door he noticed her neighbour peering at him through her blinds. She'd quickly snapped them shut when he waved to her. He'd been about to knock again when Amy flung the door open and he'd taken a step back when she greeted him loudly. 'Yes, Eliza.'

He was startled by how she was jumping around and struggling with the door, but he held an appreciative grin in check at the sight of her in barely any clothes. Obviously she was not expecting him, but instead, Eliza.

'Good morning,' he said, trying to keep his eyes on her face and not focus on her scantily clad body.

She stared at him, her mouth open, green eyes wide as she hung onto the door. When she finally spoke, her voice was a squeak. 'I thought you were Eliza from next door, complaining about my music, again!'

'No, I'm Angus and I've brought your car back,' he replied, a deep chuckle he had been trying to hold back finding its way out. She took a step back and blinked several times.

'I wasn't expecting anyone. I'm still in my pyjamas.'

'Obviously,' he said, looking her up and down. 'Nothing wrong with that.' Looking over to the blinds that were opened again next door he tilted his head to the side. 'Eliza must be the person who is peering through the window next door.'

Amy stepped out and looked straight to where he was gesturing, the blinds instantly snapping shut again. 'Yes, that is Eliza Tuls, primary school teacher and a regular thorn in my side. She bangs on the wall and then comes and berates me if my music is what she considers too loud. She gossips about every person in this town.'

'You won the lucky draw getting her as your neighbour.' He held out her keys. 'I've fixed your tyre and adjusted the pressure. You had barely enough in any of them. I've also put in a new spare for you. You need to maintain that car a bit better. I think it might also need new brake pads.' Amy crossed her arms across her chest as he continued talking, obviously aware that her singlet top was loose and also quite see-through. 'I was going to get you to drive me back to the workshop but...'

She interrupted him. 'Of course. Come in.' She held the door open and he followed her inside. 'Have a seat or make yourself a cup of coffee. You have to hold the electric switch down until the jug boils. The basic utensils came with the accommodation. It's broken. Help yourself, I'll just get changed. Give me two seconds.'

By the time she returned, he was sitting at the table, a coffee in hand, and a maths book open in front of him. She'd changed into a loose cotton dress that came to just above her knees. Her hair was brushed and he admired her casual but elegant look. Taking a long sip, he looked over the top of his cup at her as she made herself a cup of tea. When she came to sit beside him they glanced at each other and laughed. She pushed her hair back from her face. 'What a morning. I'm sorry I screeched at you.'

He laughed again. 'I'd yell louder than that if I had to live next door to that woman. I know exactly who she is. I've seen her around town. She's on with your mate, Elliot.'

'On what?'

'You know, they're on with each other.'

Amy nearly spat her tea out, her eyes bulging as she coughed and spluttered. 'Are you kidding me? No way. I've noticed she likes him and she does openly flirt with him. You must have it wrong though, it's just a bit of flirting. They can't be "on" because he's married.'

Angus nodded. 'Yep, he is married. You know he owns this entire apartment block. Leases them back to the department. He regularly pops around to check on hers.' He rolled his eyes. 'I can see a dozen things that need fixing just sitting here for five minutes. You should make a list.'

Her voice shook slightly and she put her cup down. 'I have. My 'fixit' list is as long as my arm. There aren't any other rentals in town so I don't have a choice about where to live. All I can do is keep pestering the maintenance man. I'm not allowed to get my own tradesman in to fix anything. I'll have to watch what I say to her next door though. Thanks for that. I didn't realise they were, like, you said, "on".'

They talked for a bit longer and he noticed Amy staring at his tattoos. She leaned over to look more closely. 'You have a lot of ink on you. It was hidden the other day.'

He ran his hand over his arm. 'I got a lot of them when I was younger. I'm thirty this year. How old are you?'

'Twenty-four, nearly twenty-five, and no tattoos.'

He chuckled. 'Nothing wrong with that. I'm not sure I'd get them again. A different stage in life. When you think something's a good idea at the time but later realise that it wasn't. Nana hates them. She rolls her eyes when she looks at them and then I get a little lecture about how she would be very happy if I did not get any more.'

'It's nice that she suggests what she thinks.'

'Oh, there's no suggestion. I take her words as a demand. It's not often that she tells me what to do, but when it comes to the tattoos, she makes it very clear.'

They talked for a bit more and he was sorry when his coffee was finished and there were no more excuses to sit and chat. Amy was lovely, her voice was soft and calm, although she seemed a bit naïve about how small towns operated and what the safety essentials of living and driving in the outback were. When he brought that subject up however she held up her hand to stop him talking.

'It's okay, you don't need to tell me again about how stupid I was to drive out where I was yesterday.'

'I never said you were stupid.'

'You didn't, but my father did when I rang him last night and told him what happened. Believe me, I have every detail of what I should and should not do. He really was very unhappy with me.'

'Well, I can see why.'

'He was extra annoyed because he said he'd told me all

this before I came out here and when I first started driving.' She took another sip of her tea. 'I sort of listened but I don't think I took in everything he said. You know, you sort of blank out when you're an adult and your parents start telling you what to do.'

'In this case you should have listened.' She glared at him and he softened his voice a little. 'Okay, I won't go on about it. It sounds like your father has it covered.'

'He definitely does. There's nothing he didn't cover in the hour-long rant. I love him and Mum dearly and, yes, I should have listened better. Lesson learned.'

Angus could listen to Amy talk for ages. She was full of energy and he loved that she had definite thoughts on different topics and spoke her mind. On the drive back yesterday, she'd asked questions about his grandparents and their property, drawing stories out of him about his childhood and what it had been like growing up in such a small town.

She hadn't been nosy though. It wasn't often that someone made him relaxed enough to talk about himself. He was usually more of a listener. As their conversation continued, he knew he wanted to see her again. Since returning to Matfield he had kept to himself. Only occasionally when his mates pushed him enough had he gone to the pub to socialise and a few other times he had attended family functions when Nana expected him to go. They were the only outings he bothered with. It was easier to stick to himself. But there was something about Amy he was drawn to. It would be nice to have someone to talk to sometimes, someone who could make him laugh and was interesting. Even better a friend who wasn't a long-time local. Just someone he could hang out with.

* * *

They walked to her car and he opened the door for her, the sun's heat already permeating through his shirt, even though it was only mid-morning. 'You can just drop me at the shed and I'll pick up my ute. It isn't far, but it's too hot to walk,' he said as he opened the car door for her. 'Hang in there at work. Surely it will get better.'

A forlorn look crossed her face. 'Let's hope so, because it can't get any worse.'

When they reached the work sheds he directed her where to park. 'This is it. This is where I work.'

'Do you love it?' she asked.

'Does anyone love their job?'

'Certainly not me.'

'I wouldn't say I love it, but I enjoy it and the boss is great. If I'm going to work in Matfield I couldn't ask for better than this. I do like it once I'm here and working on the machinery or vehicles. Takes my mind off anything else anyway.'

When they both got out of the car and stood next to each other, he had been a bit lost for words. Amy had also seemed reluctant to part ways and she'd stood awkwardly as they said goodbye, her arms crossed, her feet clad in white sandals, drawing circles in the dirt.

'Okay,' Angus finally said. 'I'll see you sometime, Amy.' He resisted the urge to give her a hug. 'Maybe we'll run into each other again. Matfield is a small place.' Her face lit up when he said that and her gaze met his. He found himself drawn in, mesmerised by the dark green of her eyes. 'If you ever need anything or want some company, just give me a call.' He passed her a card. 'That's the contact details for the mechanic business. My name's on there and you can get me on that number. Also, when I fixed your car, I threw all your shoes over the other side. They're on the floor on the passengers' side. Dangerous to have them all there under your feet. They'll get stuck under the brake or accelerator and then you'll have more problems than just a flat tyre.'

'Oh, my goodness. I forgot what sort of mess the car is in. I'm so hot when I leave school that I sort of take … well, no doubt you saw what I take off and throw on the back seat. I'm not known for my tidiness and,' she twisted her mouth in a cute little smile, 'Dad always has a fit when he cleans my car and finds not only all the rubbish but also those shoes under my feet. Thanks, I miss those little reminders about picking up my act.'

He made a tutting sound. 'Mess is okay, but the shoes aren't.'

'Okay, I won't leave them there.'

He narrowed his eyes. 'Really?'

'Yes, I promise.' She'd continued to smile at him and he noticed the dimple in her cheek again. 'Thanks, Angus, I really appreciate everything you've done for me. It's the nicest anyone has been to me since I've been here. I'd better go. I need to get ready for work tomorrow.' He could tell she wanted to say more and he sensed the trepidation in her voice when she mentioned work.

He watched as she got into her car, gave him a wave and drove out onto the road. Hopefully he would see her again. Matfield was a small town and sooner or later their paths would cross again.

CHAPTER 9

*F*amous last words, Amy thought, telling Angus that school couldn't get any worse. On Monday the maintenance man arrived at her apartment just as she was about to leave for work. His round ruddy face grinned at her when she opened her front door ready to leave. Juggling her bag and a large box full of books and papers that she needed for the day she beckoned him to come in. There was no way she was going to send him away. 'It would have been good if you gave me some warning,' she said to him, wishing she hadn't been so abrupt the moment her words left her mouth.

His face fell and he scowled. 'I put you top of the list. Prioritised your maintenance because you're new. Monday morning first up.'

She held her hand out. 'Apologies, I'm so sorry if I sounded rude, it's just there's a meeting at work this morning and I'll be late if I don't leave now.'

He muttered as he shook her hand and put his toolbox

down. 'Meetings, meetings, meetings. Is that all you teachers ever do?'

She smiled at him. 'We do have a lot.' She wanted to add that most of them were a waste of time but instead thought she'd keep the conversation positive. He was probably a friend of Elliot's.

'The name's, Fred Ferally. Fred Ferally, your fixit friend.'

'Pleased to meet you, Fred Ferally. I have a list here. Can I just show you the upstairs shower before I go? Then I'll have to leave it to you and you can put the key under the mat when you're finished. I'm sure no one will break in. There's nothing here for anyone to steal anyway.'

'Sounds good.' He put his tools down and followed her into the bathroom, making all sorts of tut-tutting noises when she told him the dripping shower had been like that for the last few weeks and the noise often kept her awake at night, not to mention the amount of water that was being wasted.

By the time she answered some of his questions and explained what was on her list she knew she was not going to make the school meeting on time. With a hurried goodbye she raced out to her car, threw a box of work and her bag on the back seat and started the engine. The temperature was already soaring into the thirties and she wiped the sweat from her brow. Her little car's air conditioning had long ago decided to stop working and she wound the windows down, the smell of the cattle yards down the other end of the town, wafting through the car and filling her nostrils.

She held her breath against the smell. Heat or stink? Everything she did here was unfamiliar. The street where she had lived with her parents at the Sunshine Coast was quiet and shady, large paperbark trees hanging low over well-manicured lawns that boasted surroundings of gardens filled with colourful native trees. Occasionally a car came up their street, rolling slowly, the occupants usually others who lived nearby. The air was fresh and filled with the smell of the flowering plants that grew along the pristine river that their house backed onto. The scents of melaleuca flowers, gardenias, and roses had often drifted through her open window in the morning and the only sounds were usually the chirping of dainty little birds that flitted through the bushes next to the house.

She wrinkled her nose, the smell overbearing as a cattle truck lumbered up the street towards her. The odours that greeted her each morning reminded her without a doubt where she was. There was no clean air with the hint of a coastal freshness, instead, a fine dust covered everything in its path, throwing its sheet over all her possessions, inside and outside her apartment. She put her hands over her ears as the cattle truck, its four long trailers filled with cattle, blasted its horn. The noise blared across the town, the early morning quietness shattered. She scowled as a group of kids from her high school all held up their middle finger to the driver of the truck who responded with another loud blast of his horn. Further down the street, the dust settled as the truck passed through and rounded the corner.

As she pulled out onto the street she wound her window up, the smell now intensified by the lingering trail of muck that had spilled from the truck. She veered sharply, avoiding running over a dead kangaroo that had obviously wandered into town last night and now lay, flat as a pancake in the middle of the road. A group of crows picked over any meat left on it, jumping and fighting with each other as they battled for the best pieces. A scroungy dog bounded out from behind a fence and she slammed on her brakes as it ran across in front of her before running back the other way to chase the crows away. No doubt the dog was also after any meaty bits that might be left.

Another group of older students forced her to slow right down and she shook her head as they gathered in a group in front of her car. They stood like soldiers in a row, the boys' long hair straggly, their shirts untucked and completing their scruffy look. The girls' skirts were so short they looked like shirts and she ignored the ciga-rettes that two of them hid behind their backs. They laughed and waved at her and she shook her head, refraining from beeping her horn at them and drawing attention to a road blockade of students. Another three students ran over from the other side of the road to join in. The tallest boy in the middle waved at her before saying something to the other students. One by one they saluted her until all of them stood with their hand to their forehead. Now she beeped her horn. The minutes ticking by as they laughed and slowly sauntered off onto the foot-path. They waved like crazy when she drove past, her eyes focussed on the road ahead.

It was just too early in the morning to be greeted by those sights, smells, and sounds. Putting her foot down as she thought about how late she was going to be, she spoke silently to herself. You can do this. Her father's favourite motto came to her. 'Seize the day.' She took deep breaths.

At this rate there would be no day left to seize. It would be over before she even got there. Breathing in through her nose and out through her mouth, she practised the relaxation breathing she had learned years ago at yoga. It was only a school meeting she was late for and the smoke alarms in the apartment were a priority. Hadn't that been what all those workplace health and safety meetings, as well as the courses she'd had to endure, said? Surely Elliot would understand that, particularly when he owned the apartments.

* * *

The door to the room where the meeting was being held was locked and Amy tried to twist the handle several times before resigning herself to the fact that she was not going to be able to open it. The blinds inside were drawn and she knew from previous weeks that anyone who was late would not be let in. There was still ten minutes of the meeting left but if she couldn't open the door there wasn't much she could do.

She was going to be in trouble no matter what she did so she headed back to her empty staffroom. At least the room would be empty and there wouldn't be anyone there to distract her from getting ready for her first class. Monday, she thought, and only her first term at Matfield High. Nothing was ever simple.

As she placed the box of work she'd brought from home down on her desk she could hear her laptop dinging with incoming emails and notifications. The smell from the boys' toilets—that were adjacent to the staffroom—wafted in through the open door and a cockroach swimming in her half-filled cup of coffee she'd left on her desk on Friday sent a shiver through her body. Picking up the cup she walked out through the door to empty the murky contents and the half-dead, largest cockroach she'd ever seen in her life, onto the dust outside. Her eyes closed as a group of Year 12 students blocked her way and she picked up on the conversation detailing what they'd done on the weekend. Their sentences were littered with more 'f' words than anyone could imagine and the explicit details she overheard, forced her to turn on her heels and quickly retreat inside.

She slammed the door behind her and closed her eyes, thinking of her last job, working at a boutique skincare shop on the main street of Noosa. Days filled with sweet-scented oils burning, luxurious skin care products that she spent hours rearranging and tubs of natural moisturising creams that she sampled on her skin. Customers who were always happy and usually wealthy, who loved to talk about nothing in particular, amidst a relaxed atmosphere without the slightest hint of drama, rushing, teenagers or …. stupid meetings.

Back then she'd had time to be a member of the choir and the local string ensemble. When her study at the Conservatorium of Music had ended there had been numerous job offers. Some were from the most elite private schools in Brisbane while other smaller country schools had also been looking for a music teacher. She could have gone anywhere she wanted. Usually, she took the safe path. When she finished high school she attended the Conservatorium and studied music. There had been plenty of time to party and travel but she always returned to her parents on the Sunshine Coast where she had lived since she was born. However an opportunity had presented and she decided it was time to do something adventurous that would tie in with her new career of teaching.

Her parents had encouraged her. They'd spent years travelling around Australia and worked in a variety of different towns. 'Get out there, get amongst it and gain some experience,' they'd told her. 'Where else better to do it than Western Queensland? You can't do all that study and stay in the same shop selling skin care products for the rest of your life.'

Now she felt sick every time she thought of the decision she'd made. Out here she was the odd one out, and everything was unfamiliar and difficult. Some of the other staff were lovely, but everyone was so busy with their own workload and even though they reminded her to let them know if she needed help, there hadn't been a spare second in the day to catch up with them.

Had it been the right decision to leave her easy, comfortable job, or had she looked at the world of education and the dreams of children yearning to learn, through rose-coloured glasses? As another bell rang and the sounds of the other teachers making their way back to the staffroom sounded outside, she took a deep breath and tried to hold back her tears. This morning was not a good start to the week.

CHAPTER 10

Halfway through period three a boy knocked at her classroom door. She had the year eight maths class on track and a moment of quiet and focus from them had given her a chance to get her breath. When she had first started at the school, Elliot had taken delight when she questioned the maths class on her timetable. 'But I'm a music teacher. Maths is not one of my strong points. In fact, it's my weakest point.'

'You young teachers have to learn to teach whatever you're given. This is reality. A real job. A busy school. You're not at uni now. Besides you have a spare at that time. I suppose you think you can just swan around and do nothing when you see that gap in your timetable. Well, girlie, it doesn't work like that in the real world.'

She wanted to remind him that she was a new beginning teacher and entitled to non-contact time. If he wasn't going to allow her to have that, when was she supposed to get her preparation for classes done? Other more experienced teachers might be able to have those resources ready and know everything that needed to be done, but she was new to this and there had been very little left from the last music teacher. Everything she went to do was new, and as the workload snowed her under more and more each week, she thought that perhaps today she might email him and question why she wasn't getting any spares. Other teachers did. She was entitled to three a week and if her memory served her right, as a beginning teacher she was supposed to have more.

The knock at the door broke her thoughts and she stood up from where she had been sitting, helping one of the boys. It was a shame that most of the students didn't know their times tables. When she'd brought that up at a maths meeting, the teacher in charge, who just happened to be Elliot's nephew, had frowned and looked down his nose at her. 'Those days are long gone. Rote learning isn't around anymore. There are inventions called calculators.'

Beckoning the boy at the door to come in she mulled over the issue not for the first time, that she considered it important to know how to multiply. Her maths was basic but she'd managed to get through life because she knew the basics.

The boy passed her a note. 'From the office,' he said. 'They said to tell you that it's urgent.'

The note was written in block letters and her stomach lurched when she read it. 'REPORT TO MR GANTAR-RO'S OFFICE AT 3PM SHARP. THIS IS NOT OPTIONAL.'

Turning to tell some of the students to be quiet, she read it again, her eyes wide.

The boy who had delivered the note turned and walked out the door, not before raising his middle finger to a boy, Jimmy, who was one of her behaviour problems and had once again been sneaky and sat at the back of the classroom, not at the front, where she had moved him yesterday. Jimmy called out loudly, disrupting the entire class. 'Oye, Miss. Did you see what he just did? That's bullying.'

'Calm down Jimmy, and no, I didn't see anything,' she lied. Jimmy was a troublesome student and was an expert at distracting other students and disrupting her classes. If she got into a conversation with him about what had just happened, she might as well forget about the rest of the lesson. To report on such a small behaviour problem, and an action that she often observed Jimmy making to other students, was not worth the trouble or the paperwork. She sent a withering look Jimmy's way. 'Back on track please, you were all working so well.'

At the moment she didn't have the energy to chase up the messenger boy, who strutted off, smirking at the class through the side window. She had bigger issues to be concerned about.

At a quarter to three she tried to make sure she had everything organised to get out the door at the same time as the students. She'd even let them finish their work five minutes early and the chairs were all up on the desks, the rubbish on the floor cleaned up, and the windows closed by the time the bell went. Not every-thing went to plan though, and Jimone, who was one of her high-needs students, had not kept up with her instructions. While everyone else was rushing out the door, screaming loudly and shoving each other as they made their way up the path, Jimone was under his desk trying to gather his pens which had fallen out of his pencil case. One of the girls, Sarah, put her bag down and helped him.

'Thank you, Sarah,' Amy said. 'That's very kind of you.'

Jimone managed to nod and take the pencils from Sarah. The blonde-haired boy had a serious face and big eyes, his range of disabilities requiring a lot of one-on-one time with Amy during lessons. Several times she had requested teacher-aide time so he could have some help with his maths. Her requests had been ignored though and she usually spent most of the lesson moving between Jimone and several others who all worked at a level well below the rest of the class. Sarah must have noticed that Jimone needed help and that the longer it took him to pick everything he had dropped, the more flustered he became. 'I saw one of your drawings, Jimone,' Sarah said. 'You're really good.'

Jimone was unused to praise and his face flushed red as he stopped what he was doing and looked up at Sarah. 'Really, you think I'm good?'

'Yes. I would pay money for one of your paintings.'

His face split into a wide grin. 'I ain't good at nothing.'

Amy interjected. 'Don't say that. You write lovely poetry and I think your drawings are good too. We might have to make sure you do some artwork for the exhibition in town later this year.'

Jimone pulled a sketch book from his bag. It was unlike the other scrunched up books that were twisted and pushed into the dark depths of his school bag. No doubt, Amy thought, shoved in beside sandwiches and other pieces of food that every year eight boy seemed to fill their bag with.

He placed the book, like a precious item, down on the desk. 'You can have a look at these if you like. I've never showed anyone else.'

Amy tapped her foot. Time was ticking and she was now ten minutes late for her meeting with Elliot. However, there was no way she was going to lose the opportunity for Jimone to show off his skills. This was the first time he had voluntarily interacted with her or anyone else in the class since the start of the year.

By the time she locked the door behind Jimone and Sarah, they had looked at all his sketches. He was positively beaming and he stuttered a bashful thank you to Sarah. 'Thank you too, Miss Coops. No one ever looks at my art. I'm going to go straight home and do some more now. Wait until I tell my mum and dad that you think my art is good. Today's the best day ever.'

When Amy approached the closed door to Elliot's office she thought of the smile on Jimone's face as he'd left her classroom. Straightening her clothes and pushing her hair back from her face, she inhaled deeply and knocked on the door. A terse, 'come in,' sounded from inside and she pulled her shoulders back and smiled as she entered. Elliot sat behind his large rosewood desk, leaning over and surveying her over the top of his glasses. She felt like she was a child back at school and about to get in trouble.

'You're late again,' he stated.

She closed the door behind her, nodding at the middle-aged office lady, Gwen, who sat opposite him. Trying not to stare at how short Gwen's dress was, she approached the desk. 'I was held up by a student. Do you want me to come back another time?' she asked.

'No. Now is good and Gwen can listen to what you have to say.'

Gwen gave her a pious look and sat down. Amy could have sworn that Elliot bent over the desk further when Gwen crossed her legs.

She shook her head, not wanting to even consider that he had directly looked at Gwen's legs. Amy was still standing and she wondered if Elliot was going to offer for her to sit down.

He must have read her mind. 'No need for you to sit. This won't take long.'

Gwen swivelled in her chair and pretended to check her nails, almost as if this was all a bit, ho-hum, for her. Her voice was sickly sweet when she spoke. 'Do you want me to take minutes, Mr Garranto?'

'No need. Thanks, Gwen.'

'Now, Miss Coops.' Elliot passed her several sheets of paper. 'If you had checked your emails today you would have noticed these have been sent to you.' He waited as she perused the documents, no doubt the shocked look on her face letting him know that this was the first time she had seen them.

'I thought as much. It's irresponsible not to keep up with the communication sent by email. I've had no response from you to the messages so I can only add that to my list of complaints on this code of conduct that I'm submitting to head office about how you don't respond to communication. That is of course what you are holding. Had you read your emails you would have already known about this.' He held up his hand as she went to speak. 'Silence, girlie. You need to respond to all of this by three o'clock tomorrow. Now did you have a question?'

Anger filled her and she grasped her hands together to stop them from shaking. 'I would like to know how I'm supposed to answer emails when I'm teaching. I had playground duty at first break, I helped a student with an assignment at second break and the rest of the time I have been teaching. I don't see how I'm supposed to check or respond to emails when I'm helping students or out the front giving explicit instructions for learning.'

'Well Miss Coops, once you're a bit more experienced you'll learn to juggle the day better. I'm also going to recommend that you are mentored by one of our more experienced teachers from the primary school, Eliza Tuls. She can give you some pointers and instructions on how to cope better than you are. It's obvious you're not putting in the hours you're supposed to, and you've shown yourself to be lazy and never on time. Arriving late to the funeral on Saturday, setting a bad example to the choir students not to mention what the people gathered, including the family must have thought of your tardiness and furthermore, not even making the meeting this morning are perfect examples.'

Gwen chipped in, looking at her watch as she spoke. 'You were twenty minutes late for this meeting also.'

Amy glared at them. There was no use saying

anymore. Elliot had given her the papers. A code of conduct was serious. She needed to calm down before she said something she regretted.

Elliot shuffled some papers on his desk. 'Anything else, if not, off you go?' He waved his hand to dismiss her. She stared hard at him, taking in the broken veins that ran across his cheeks and his mean little eyes that flitted back and forth. His hair was thin and combed back with some sort of oil and he ran his hand through it, before crossing his arms and leaning back at his desk.

'Good afternoon, Miss Coops.'

As she turned and went out the door she gritted her teeth. Should she just march back in there and tell him to stick his job where it fitted? Hesitating at the doorway she thought how that was probably what he wanted. He'd told her right from the start that he didn't like beginning teachers. He preferred older teachers and he mentioned constantly that he had told the department that was what he needed. It was his belief that the younger teachers lacked resilience and loyalty and left the job without giving it a proper go. There had been quite a few of them who had left before their contracts had finished. Amy pulled her shoulders back and stared straight ahead, her heart thumping hard as anger filled her. There was no way she was giving in that easily. This was what she'd studied for, and to add to it, there was also all the trouble she'd gone to moving away from where life was easy and putting herself out of her comfort zone. Her inner voice told her not to let Elliot win when she hadn't done anything wrong and had tried hard to do what she was supposed to. Chin up and just get out of his office, she reassured herself.

* * *

The office foyer was full of parents lining up to pay for an upcoming excursion. She kept her eyes down and picked up her box of work that she'd left there. Her car was parked in the area straight out the front of the admin office and she'd planned on making a quick exit once she'd talked to Elliot. Grasping onto the box and gritting her teeth she made her way out through the front door, only stopping when someone called out her name.

It was Edwin, standing with his two children. He smiled warmly at her and she clenched her teeth harder, determined not to burst into tears. 'G'day, Miss Coops. 'Good to see you so soon again.'

He leaned in and looked more closely at her, concern in his eyes. She wasn't good at hiding her emotions and obviously the anguish from the meeting was written on her face. 'Hey, are you okay?' he asked. 'You look upset.' He touched her on the arm and she looked up at him. When she went to speak the words wouldn't come out. 'You two go and get in the car,' Edwin said to the kids. He waited until they were out of hearing range, before asking, 'What's up? You look like you're about to cry?'

Taking a deep breath, she pulled her shoulders back and stood up straight. 'I'm okay. I just got in trouble, again, from Elliot.'

'Elliot is an idiot. Here let me take that box from you. Where's your car?'

She pointed and he led the way, her car not parked far from where his was. Edwin looked different today. At the funeral he had been dressed up, but now he was in his work clothes, old jeans and a khaki work shirt, his tanned muscly arms making light of the heavy box crammed full of books and marking that she usually struggled with. Once he'd placed the box on the front seat of the car he turned to her. 'I was going to take the kids for a milkshake at the cafe in town. You're coming with us. They'd love it, and so would I.'

She hesitated. Elliot had been very clear with his rules about not fraternising with parents or children, but Edwin was insistent and the last thing she wanted to do was to go home to an empty apartment and start doing her schoolwork for tomorrow. 'C'mon, we'll cheer you up.'

There was nothing to lose. Elliot was already trying to get rid of her and if going for a milkshake pushed him over the edge, then so be it. 'I will,' she answered. 'I'd love to.'

Edwin's wide grin was charming and some of the angst that had filled her, lifted, as she managed to smile back. 'See you there,' he replied before turning around and walking back to his car.

CHAPTER 11

Thankfully by the time she arrived, Edwin was already seated at a table tucked away at the back of the eating area. Many of the students came into the cafe after school and she waved to a few as she made her way to where Cindy and Peter were waiting for her. They jumped around in their seats, excited that she had joined them.

Edwin stood up and pulled her chair out, waiting until she was seated before sitting back down. 'I ordered for you. On Monday afternoons our regular is vanilla milkshakes and pancakes with the lot.'

Her mouth watered and her stomach rolled. She hadn't eaten anything except an apple while she was on playground duty. 'Thank you,' she managed to reply. 'That's perfect.'

They talked for a while and she asked the children questions about school and how they were going at sport. They were both so cute and sat up straight, using their best behaviour, well-drilled in the manners required when eating out. When the food was served they waited until everyone was ready to start, watching their dad for notice that it was okay to begin.

'I have hardly eaten all day,' Amy said. 'This is the first food, apart from an apple, I've had since six o'clock this morning.'

Edwin wiped his mouth with a serviette, 'What? That's crazy.'

He watched the kids as they finished their food, Amy unsure if it had even hit the sides of their mouths with the speed that they devoured the delicious pancakes. 'These two eat as much as eight kids,' Edwin said. 'I spend my life trying to fill them.' He waved his hand. 'Off you go. Now you're finished you can go across the road to the park.' He turned to Amy. 'That's where all the kids meet on a Monday afternoon.'

She looked across to the park. The one piece of green grass in the otherwise brown dusty streets. Two massive trees threw some shade and a variety of swings and climbing equipment scattered over the grounds was already full of local kids letting off steam after school.

It was quiet after the kids left and Amy sipped her coffee, relishing the taste after the sweet pancakes. Edwin had finished his and leaned back in his seat, his legs stretched out revealing a weathered pair of riding boots. She had already decided that he was very good-looking, with a rugged cowboy look, like he could be on the front cover of a romance book. She dragged her eyes away from his boots, giggling when he gave her a quizzical look. 'Sorry, I didn't mean to stare but the attire out here is so different than where I'm from. Board shorts, singlets, and thongs are what everyone wears when they go for coffee back on the coast.'

He sat up and rolled his sleeves up. 'I know it seems crazy. It's hotter out here and we wear more clothes than you coasties do. You wouldn't last long in that beach getup out in the paddocks though. The sun is so hot you can fry an egg on a tin roof.'

Her shoulders slumped and she looked out the window, a whirlwind of dust flinging twigs and leaves in a twirling spiral across the park. Some of the kids chased it, throwing paper into it and running every which way to avoid it.

'I like the freedom that kids have out here,' she said. 'It's a different world, but...'

'But, you're having trouble adjusting? Would I be right?'

'Yes. Elliot is out to get me. He hasn't let up since I arrived and everything I do is wrong. I know I'm twenty-four, older than some of the new teachers, but I'm still new to the job. Everything is difficult and this morning I had to wait for the maintenance man. There are a lot of things that are broken in the apartment. That made me late for the morning meeting.'

'That'd be right. I tell you what, why don't I have a word to Elliot, you know, a few scare tactics so that he leaves you alone.'

'Oh no, please don't. I need to work it out for myself.'

'Did you know that Elliot owns the apartments that you live in?'

'Yes, your cousin Angus dropped my car back and he told me the same thing.'

Edwin visibly stiffened, his cup clattering as he placed it down on the saucer. 'You're only new to town so you won't know what's happened in the past, but you want to steer clear of my cousin, Angus.' His tone had changed and she sensed anger in his voice, his eyes flashing when he spoke. There was the same antagonism towards Angus that she had noticed at the funeral.

'He has been really helpful. I don't know what I would have done when my car got that flat tyre if he hadn't come along.' She'd thought a lot about Angus after he'd left on Saturday and his cheery face and energetic manner kept flashing through her mind. Edwin on the other hand was also charming, but much older with a swagger of confidence that made her feel a little uneasy. Being young and single in a remote country town she'd need to have her wits about her. She tried to appear unmoved or shocked by his next words.

'Angus's been in jail you know? Bet he didn't tell you that.'

'I've hardly spoken to him. Really?'

'That's why he has all the tattoos. Loves attention and yeah he was in jail for quite a few years.'

'What for?'

'Murder'

Amy tried to maintain her composure but it was hard when faced with such a statement. 'Murder, and he only got three years. That seems strange.'

'Murder, or manslaughter. Something like that. It's all the same, he killed someone.' Edwin reached over and stroked her arm. 'I'm only telling you so you know what he's really like. You're single and very beautiful. He loves that. Just beware.'

Edwin's touch sent pleasant tingles up her arm. It had been a long time since a man had touched her arm, or for that matter, the rest of her body. He gave her a gentle squeeze. 'If you're looking for a real friend and some company, well,' he raised his eyebrows looking directly into her eyes. 'I'm your man. Really I'm not that much older than you. I'm only thirty-four. I've had it tough over the last few years so maybe I have a few more wrinkles than I should have.'

His hand rested on her arm as he continued. 'The kid's mother left a couple of years ago. Just up and went with no warning. I was of course devastated and if it wasn't for the kids well … I don't know … I would have had nothing to live for.' He pulled a sad face and took a long sip from his tea. She got the impression he had stopped talking to add drama to his story and she waited for him to continue.

'I tell you, Amy. It's been rough but I do the best I can, given the situation.'

'That's so sad, for you and the kids. Do they ever get to see their mum?'

'They go to her in the holidays. She lives in Townsville so it's been difficult, but I've soldiered on. I do the cooking, cleaning, and everything for the kids. I read to them every night and sit with them to help with the homework. I'm mother and father all rolled into one. Look at them, they're happy.'

'Oh, my goodness,' She jumped a little as his fingers caressed her arm. 'Yes, um, yes you are definitely doing a good job. They're great kids.'

Silence surrounded them and he eventually pulled his hand away. 'You know, you've really affected me. From the first moment I saw you at the funeral, well, there's just something about you. I don't usually bother with dating or chasing women, my entire focus has been on the kids, but...'

She tensed, her arm still warm from where his fingers had been. 'I'm going to see you again. We'll go on a date. I'm not real good at this but we'll go to the movies at Hillview next weekend.'

Her first instinct was to say no. Edwin was very charming and had a way with flattering words. His touch and words had been comforting after such a difficult day, but he was much older and had two children.

'I hope the fact that I have the kids doesn't put you off. Plenty of women don't like kids, they think they're baggage, but it's just a date I'm asking for. It would do you good after your rough start and take your mind off school. A beautiful woman like you deserves to be spoilt.'

Out of the corner of her eye she spotted the kids running back across the road. Her mind whirled and she answered quickly, surprised at her own words once they were spoken. Everything today seemed jumbled and rushed. 'I will. Yes. Thank you.'

He stood up. 'Great. I'll pick you up at four o'clock Saturday afternoon. We can go for a drive and I'll show you around the area a bit before we go to the movies.'

As they walked out the front door, Cindy and Peter bounded up to them. 'We just saw Uncle Angus and Nana,' they both spoke together. 'They were getting groceries,' Peter said.

'That's good. In the car please.' Edwin's voice was gruff and the two kids stopped in their tracks, their faces falling as they walked back towards the carpark.

Edwin reached over and squeezed her hand. 'See you Saturday.'

'Yes. I'll see you then,' she murmured, waving back to the children who were hanging out the car window. 'Four o'clock.'

$\mathcal{T}$he week flew past and every night she spent preparing work for the following day at school. Elliot had been busy with a string of fights between year nine boys and vaping incidents with the girls in year ten, so he'd had no time to harass her. At least the shower was fixed in her apartment and the smoke alarms now worked. Something to be positive about.

When the bell sounded at three o'clock on Friday afternoon she congratulated herself on getting through another week. Sure, there had been a couple of incidents in the classroom; someone had drawn a large penis on her whiteboard, a girl had painted devil horns, a moustache and blackened teeth on her favourite Gandhi poster and one of the senior boys had asked her out. Just a regular week though and nothing too drastic. At least she hadn't been the teacher on playground duty when a huge fight broke out or missed the fact that over twenty students were vaping in the sports shed at lunch time. She pressed her hand to her forehead and massaged the skin, trying to relieve some of the tension that had built up during the day. Something surely had to go her way.

Mary-Anne, a third-year teacher who was in the room next to her, caught up with her as she walked back to the staff room. 'Come to the pub. We tried to catch you this morning at assembly to ask you but you were with the sick kid.'

She pulled a face. 'Ugh, I'm really bad with vomit. Thank goodness it missed my shoes.'

'You did well. At least Keith came and helped you. I noticed Elliot didn't move a muscle and he was the closest.' Mary-Anne linked her arm through Amy's. 'None of us have come up for breath this first month. It's time for a drink. Leave your car at home if you like and I'll pick you up.'

Friday afternoon. She loved the end of the week. Two entire days to herself. A wave of panic rushed through her at the thought of her date with Edwin on Saturday. A drink and some company this afternoon would be good to stop her thinking about it. 'I'd love that. Thanks. I need to wind down.'

CHAPTER 13

*I*t was a relief to be able to drop her car at home and get a lift. Mary-Anne had been right behind her when she pulled into the carpark and she felt a sense of celebration for the end of a long week as the others in the car called out to her to hurry up. Although she was the only new teacher this year there were quite a few other young teachers. They all had a few years of experience under their belts before coming to Matfield and she was envious of their knowledge. 'Yeah, Elliot told us all he detests—yes, he used the word, detest—first-year teachers, but don't worry, he can't get rid of you. There's no one to replace you.'

Barney, who was about thirty-five sat next to her in the back. 'He's a pain in the arse and it would be heaven if he left. Don't hold your breath waiting for it though. He knows people in high places and this is where he wants to be. He's buying up real estate from one end of town to the other. I don't think he's going anywhere for a while.'

Jason sat on the other side of her. 'We all feel sorry for

you. Everyone can see he's got it in for you. Don't worry, we have your back when we can. It's just been flat out and we're all drowning in work. The trouble is with Elliot, he's very sneaky. We've only just started to realise what a hard time he's been giving you.'

Mary-Anne added in. 'Make sure you come and talk to any of us if there's more trouble. We can't do much about it but we can support you.' She waved her hand around the group. 'You can trust all of us. There's plenty of staff that you can't, but us lot, we stick together. Most of us have no option but to stay. Mortgages, family commitments and partners who also work in the area. Stick with us. It won't solve everything but it might help.'

She relaxed. It was so good to be with other teachers who understood the predicament she was in. 'Thank you all so much. Elliot has constantly harassed me,' she said. 'I thought department policy said that first-year teachers would get a lighter load, some extra spares, and mentoring from an experienced teacher.'

They all laughed. 'Mentoring? What's that?' Barney said. 'He'll tell them he's mentoring you or even worse some of us have had to suffer good old, Eliza Tuls. How could you call her a mentor. But it lets Elliot off the hook. There will be a form. Tick, tick, tick. That's all he has to do. Mentored! Completed! Who's going to check on anything out here.'

By the time they pulled up at the pub the woes of school had been left behind. The group from her staff room were a mixed bunch but they were supportive and now it seemed, also enjoyed quite a few drinks on a Friday afternoon.

* * *

Their table was loud and boisterous and as she sipped a large beer she soaked in the relaxed pub atmosphere. This was what she'd been looking for when she applied for the job. A small country school with a bit of fun and adventure on the side. Plenty of opportunities to develop her teaching skills and start her career, as well as make new friends.

One of the other girls from the staffroom, Laura, kept buying Amy drinks. 'Here's to Amy, may she survive the term and year.' Laura toasted her and they all clinked their glass together.

'May she survive Elliot,' Jason said.

'And the nefarious Gwen,' someone else added.

Laura wrapped her arm around her. 'We'll look after you. This is your mentoring session.'

Amy smiled and watched as Laura spotted someone across the room. Laura was a glamorous looking blonde girl and heads had turned when she entered the bar. She was also a local. 'Lived all my life, here. Went to school at Matfield and now look at me, back here teaching. All I need now is to marry a local man with a big property and shitloads of money, have a couple of kids and kick back. Home is here for me.'

She elbowed Amy and nodded towards a long bench full of men who looked like they'd come in for a beer after working out in the paddocks. 'Number one. Check out the tall fella with the blonde hair. Macka. Single. No kids and from one of the biggest family companies in the shire. They own all the stockyards and meatworks as well as thousands of acres of land. Never married. She took a long sip of her beer before continuing. 'Two. Beast. Yes, that's his name but he's not a beast, but rather the softest hearted, kindest man you'd ever meet. They reckon he's gay but I think I could turn him.'

She laughed. 'Just joking. He's not gay just uber shy. Three. Angus Carmody. Skip him. Rough and ready and a tarnished background. Four, Well, now. I'd say that would be my pick. Mellick Maloney. Tall, strong and built like, well, you know. Look at those muscles. Oh my God, he's looking over here.'

Laura stood up and waved, rewarded with a wave back from Mellick. She bent down and whispered in Amy's ear. 'He's just come back from five years of working overseas. It's been a while, but he and I go way back. He was my first kiss down behind the shopping centre when I was thirteen. He had bumfluff and pimples on his face, scrawny legs and braces back then.' She adjusted her dress and licked her lips. 'Look at him now though. This could be my lucky day.'

With that, she put her drink down, adjusted her very short dress again and sauntered over towards Mellick. They met halfway and it was plain to see that he was keen to see her also. When he bent down and kissed Laura on the cheek, the group of men he'd been sitting with cheered and clapped, a couple of them calling out. The two of them headed up to the bar together, a large beer each soon in front of them, as they continued their conversation away from the others.

Amy watched them for a moment before looking back to the group of men who had turned back around and continued their conversations. Angus sat with them. He was facing her and he lifted his hand and gave her a wave.

She waved back, pleased to see him again. What a shame he wasn't what he appeared to be. Even Laura hadn't had anything good to say about him. She turned back to the conversation at the table, laughing when Barney did an impression of Elliot, Jason adding in with the high-pitched pious voice of Gwen. Thank goodness she had good people around her. She would survive school. Now she just had to survive her date with Edwin.

CHAPTER 14

*S*everal different outfits were spread across her bed. Should she wear shorts, jeans, or a dress? It would be hot in the afternoon and the temperature didn't drop much at night. With no breeze or sign of a cool change it would be sensible to dress for comfort. A mid-length skirt and strappy shirt matched with sandals looked okay, she thought, as she twirled in front of the full-length mirror. Her hair was going up though. It was too hot to wear it down and she wound it around her fingers, coiling it up in a messy bun on the top of her head. Nerves swirled in her stomach. What was Edwin chasing? Was it just a one-off date because he'd felt sorry for her, or had she, as he said, had some sort of effect on him?

A warm feeling filled her when she thought of how he looked after his children by himself and what a great job he'd done. It was sometimes harder for a man to bring up kids as a single parent. They often didn't have the support networks that women did. She adjusted her hair. Edwin hadn't been at the pub with the others. Poor guy, he was probably too busy looking after his kids and managing a household to get out to socialise.

When he knocked at the door she had been ready, her nerves unsettling more as the minutes ticked past. He was ten minutes late but she decided that was acceptable. Dark blue jeans and a white collared shirt made him look more handsome than ever and when he looked her up and down there were flutters in her stomach. Get a grip, she reminded herself. This was what happened when you hadn't dated for a long time.

'Wow.' He leaned in and kissed her on the cheek. 'You always look amazing.'

She stuttered, his warm lips on her cheek and now his hand on her arm unsettling her. 'Thank, thanks, thank you. You look nice also. I wasn't sure what to wear. It's so hot.'

Still holding her arm he led her to the car, holding the door open for her. 'You'll get used to the heat once you've been here for a while.'

He talked a lot as they drove out through the town and onto the main road that would take them to the next small town of Hillview. Perhaps he was also tense because he seemed to talk more than usual. Although it was difficult to think that a man like him would be nervous. He was, after all, very confident and even a bit self-important when he spoke. By the time they pulled up at a park near the Hillview River, she'd heard a long string of details about his life. He'd also told her a lot more about his ex-wife, particularly all the things she'd done wrong.

Amy listened patiently, the conversation continuing as they sat on the picnic blanket that he'd brought with him.

It was a beautiful spot by the river with large weeping gum trees lining the sides, their sparse leaves providing some shade from the relentless heat. The riverbed was dry and sandy, lizards and even a long black snake making their way across the open ground to shelter in the rocks on the other side. 'I'm sorry to go on so much about all my troubles over the years,' Edwin said as he poured her a large glass of chilled champagne. 'It's just been so long since I've had a woman to talk to. You're only young but you seem very mature. I can't tell you how much it means to me that you're here today.'

That had made her giggle, both from the effects of the drink and his comment. All her life she'd been told she was immature and needed to wisen up. 'You're nearly twenty-five,' had been her mother's words to her as she was leaving. 'I'd had you by that age and a house and mortgage. You need to settle down and stop acting like you're still eighteen.'

Her father had been more understanding. 'Do what you want, Amy. You're only young once. Our generation was brought up differently. Marriage, house, and kids. Luckily we're comfortable enough to do what we want now.'

She thought of her parents as she sat under a blistering blue sky on the edge of a dry river surrounded by dry plains and desert that stretched as far as the eye could see. She was supposed to be having an adventure by teaching in such a remote town, doing something different and moving out of the ordinary. Settling down was the last thing on her mind.

'Thanks, Edwin. No one ever tells me that.'

They talked for a bit more and she added in when he

discussed the children. 'My mum said she'd look after them today,' he said. 'I didn't tell her who I was taking out. I don't want everyone to know my business. There's a lot of gossip that flies around this town.'

'Yes, I've noticed that.'

Edwin lay back and looked up into the trees. 'Sometimes I love this land but other times I feel like something is missing. There's a gap in my life.' He sounded sad and she didn't know what to say.

When he sat up he moved closer to her, taking the drink from her hand and putting it down on the ground beside them. 'I feel like you've come here for a reason.' When he leaned forward and kissed her she was shocked at his forwardness, they'd only met a few times, but his lips were soft and she kissed him back. Pulling her closer he caressed the back of her neck, their bodies touching. When the kisses became a bit rougher and his arms drew her in tight, she pulled away, sitting up straight and trying to think rationally. 'Let's not rush anything, Edwin. I've only just met you.'

He touched her cheek. 'I know. I couldn't help it. You're so beautiful and I love talking to you. I agree. Let's take it slowly.'

Something didn't sit right with Amy. There was a tone in his voice that was strange, almost like he had practised the words or that he wasn't being genuine. He'd gone to a lot of trouble with the picnic and drinks and she wondered if she wasn't the first girl he'd brought here. He also didn't ask her what she wanted to do, it was like he gave instructions and she should just follow them. She needed to be careful and not get drawn into something she might not want.

CHAPTER 15

The rest of the afternoon passed quickly and Edwin had been the perfect gentleman. Thankfully he carried most of the conversation, talking about what he did on the property and what his plans were for the future. 'It's a family business,' he told her, 'but my father has a larger part of the holdings than some of the others. There are plenty in my family who aren't interested so I'm already going through legal proceedings to make sure most of Dad's section comes to me. It's worth a lot of money.' He glanced at her as they drove towards Hillview. 'I'm worth a fortune.'

He paused for a long while, waiting for her to respond. The trouble was she was already tired of answering his statements and agreeing with him about how successful he'd already been. Large properties were like big houses and people who had lots of money; these meant nothing to her. She knew that social and family status was important out here. That had been obvious from the first week she had arrived. In these small towns and surrounding areas, there were successions of relatives, dynasties, and generational families who owned large corporations and properties that spanned thousands of kilometres, with businesses that operated in the six figures and more realm. Who you were married to and what you did was important. 'That's great,' was all she could come up with.

'I'll be one of the richest men in the district once ....' The sound of his voice started to drone into a background noise and she concentrated on the scenery out the window. She'd driven this way when she first arrived but she'd been so intent on getting to Matfield that she hadn't taken in too much of the landscape. Now as a passenger she could survey all the different areas on either side of the road. The landscape to the eastern side of the town was different again and she looked in awe as they drove through an area scattered with large boulders, the red dust covering their surfaces. Plains that stretched to the north were endless with no hills to border them, just a hazy blur on the horizon that blended in with the sky. The sun was starting to drop in the west and colours of golden orange flooded the expanse.

She spoke out loud. 'It's beautiful. The colours at this time of the day.'

Edwin pulled up beside another rocky outcrop and they climbed up on a large boulder. He took her hand to help her up and she noticed he didn't let go even when they were safely at the top. She pulled it away to shade her eyes from the setting sun, the brilliant pinks and reds searing across the last of the darkening blue sky. When the sun sunk below the horizon, thousands of tiny birds rose from the bushes at the base of the rocky outcrop.

They blackened the sky as they flew overhead, bound for where they settled down for the night.

'Budgerigars. A bloody pest. Shoot them all,' Edwin said. 'C'mon, we'll miss the movie if we don't get going.'

She would have preferred to have watched the last of the sunset display but she didn't say anything, instead she followed him back to the car. 'Right, movies are next,' he said as he put his foot down, the car speeding towards their next destination. Edwin drove too fast for Amy's liking and she held her breath a few times when he narrowly avoided some kangaroos feeding by the edge of the road. 'More bloody pests. Shoot the lot of them,' he muttered.

* * *

They'd grabbed a burger at the café on the main street of the small town. 'Everyone will be at a park concert at the footy club,' Edwin said, as he passed her a large burger and drink. 'No one to see me and take the gossip back home.' He shook his head and put on a sad voice. 'It's been really hard since the kid's mother left. I can't tell you how much I'm enjoying being with you today.'

His look was intense and she thanked him for the burger and the day so far. 'It's been lovely, thank you. It's good to get away from town and be somewhere different.'

He leaned up and pushed a strand of hair away from her face. 'I'm glad you've had a nice time.'

The movie was one she'd seen before but she had been truthful when she said it was nice to be out. For a while she forgot about Elliot and the problems at school. Even though she had no intentions of going out with Edwin again, she could still enjoy the night.

Driving home after the movie, Edwin had been quieter then he'd been during the day. She'd tried to talk but he'd only grunted in reply. Perhaps he was all talked out. He definitely drove with a heavy foot on the accelerator though and she was relieved to see the lights of Matfield ahead. He glanced over at her. 'I was going to take you up to the lookout, but I guess like you said we should take it slow.'

She held her breath, concerned that he might ask her tricky questions about another date. When they pulled up outside her apartment she grabbed her bag and got out of the car as quickly as she could. When he came around to where she was, he stood in front of her, blocking the way. He took one of her hands. 'I really like you, Amy. I hope you'll let me take you out again.'

Just as she went to reply, the door next to her apartment opened. Eliza's apartment. It was dark and Amy couldn't see who had come out through the doorway until the person got into the car near to where they were standing. It was Elliot. He looked at them through his open car window and even in the dim light she could see a smirk cross his face. 'Evening, Edwin,' he said, his wincing voice cutting through Amy like a piece of chalk drawn across a blackboard. 'Nice to see the little lady is making friends.'

Edwin dropped her hand like it was on fire, puffing his chest out and moving towards Elliot's car. 'Evening, Elliot. Were you here fixing something?'

Elliot mumbled as he looked away from them and started the engine.

'Fixing something alright,' Edwin said to Amy as he returned to where she was standing. 'I wonder if his wife knows where he is. The only reason I didn't smack him in the head right now was because you asked me not to intervene. Someone needs to mess him up real good.'

Amy was lost for words as she watched Elliot's car pull out of the car park and drive up the road. She fumbled in her bag for her key. When she pulled it out Edwin took it from her hand. 'Allow me,' he said as he unlocked and opened her front door, waiting for her to enter, the key still in his hand.

She held out her hand. 'Thanks, Edwin, it was a lovely day.'

He leaned against the doorframe, swinging her key in the air. 'What, you're not going to ask me in? Just for a drink maybe?'

When she went to take the key from him he held it up higher. 'Whoa, you're not getting away that easy. You and I have a real connection.'

Her mind whirled. All she wanted to do was to go inside. 'I'm tired. Thank you again, but I just want to go inside.'

His face changed and he scowled, before smiling at her again. 'Are you sure? You look like you could do with a good shoulder massage. You're stressed about Elliot and school. It would do you good to talk to me about it. Maybe I can help. He's a wimp. All I'd need to do is threaten him or tell him to watch his back. He'd crumble. He's piss-weak.'

She held her hand out for the key. 'I'm tired so I'd prefer if we called it a night. Maybe another time.' She wished that she hadn't mentioned seeing him again, but it was all she could think of to get him to leave. 'I need to go to sleep.'

He leaned across and kissed her firmly on the lips, grabbing her arm roughly and pulling her in towards him. When she pulled away, he laughed. 'Think about that when you go to bed. I have a good feeling you and I will be seeing each other again.'

Holding back her words she took the key he now offered. 'Night, beautiful,' he said as he turned and sauntered back to his car. She clenched her fists as he started the car, leaned out the window and blew her a kiss.

'Not a chance,' she muttered under her breath, turning and closing the door behind her.

CHAPTER 16

*M*onday's staff meeting was her priority this morning and she made sure she was at school before it started. As the staff trickled in she watched Elliot down the front, full of self-importance and pacing up and down as he talked on his phone. Laura sat down next to her, a bundle of marking in her hands. 'This is supposed to be done to hand back at the first lesson,' Laura muttered, 'but I had a big weekend. Seemed good at the time but now I'll pay for it.' She wrinkled her nose up. 'Look at Gwen, strutting around like she runs the show. I reckon she's on with him. Check out how they look at each other.'

'But he's married isn't he?' Amy said, her thoughts crossing to Elliot's visits to her neighbour's apartment. Now as she watched Elliot and Gwen interacting, she tried not to giggle at the way Gwen marched up and down as if she was the most important person in the room.

Laura made a loud tutting noise, before dropping her

voice to a whisper. 'Married, that don't mean a thing to Elliot. His wife Penelope is a regular bridge player down at the pub on a Wednesday. My mum plays also. The word is Penelope is having an affair with one of the big bosses who works in the mine to the south of here. They meet up in the city every month. She's only staying here in town until their son is finished school. Then she and the kid are moving to the city.'

Amy didn't want to add fuel to the fire. Gwen was obviously not the only woman Elliot was having an affair with if his presence at Eliza's place was anything to go by. As if Elliot knew they were talking about him he looked directly at both of them. His face was blotchy and red, his nose bulbous and his sparse hair slicked back to hide the bare patch in the middle of his head.

'Gotta love a comb-over,' Mary-Anne said as she leaned over from the seat behind her. 'He's giving you the evil eye, Amy.'

Her voice held a bitter note. 'He hates me. Told me so. Beginning teacher.'

Elliot scowled, waiting for the group of teachers to be quiet. A thin smile edged his lips and he nodded politely as Mrs Turvey, the Home Economics teacher waddled in. Amy looked at the time. Five minutes late.

Mary-Anne whispered, 'That's Gwen's sister. Can't do any wrong.'

Elliot's voice boomed through the hall. 'Quiet, please.' He glared at Amy. 'I know some of you are new but manners should be something that are practised by every-one.' He waited; a typical teacher long pause. 'Right, now that I have your full attention.'

Amy tried to focus as he went through a long list of

things that must be done before the week was out. The paperwork was never-ending. There were forms to fill out about what personal development courses you had to attend, emails that must be sent out to parents, daily, weekly, and monthly, planners for the next term to be submitted as well as a million other things that needed to be done by five pm on Friday.

As she scribbled the list in her diary, her head started to swirl. How was she going to fit all of this in, mark her maths exams, prepare her music lessons, attend three meetings this week, answer the twenty or more emails she received a day and ring nine parents whose kids were at risk of failing? Oh, and then the very minor detail of, teaching.

Elliot's tone had changed and she felt like he was staring directly at her. 'I have in my hand here a document about the code of conduct. I think some of you need reminding about what is allowed and what is not, particularly when it comes to fraternising with parents of students.' He paused again and she held her breath. 'And....' There was another long pause. 'That includes parents of students from the primary school.'

Clasping her hands together she forced back the impulse to put her hand up and ask him if that included married staff fraternising with other staff to who they might not be married. She bit her lip. It was almost too much. Over the years she'd worked in a variety of jobs, both when she travelled and while she was at university. But Matfield was certainly something else. The other ridiculous point was that every person in town over a certain age had a kid going to one of the schools. There were no other options. Surely this was an Elliot rule, not a department one. He seemed to make rules up as he went along.

One of the older teachers, Kerry, filed out next to her. She bent down and murmured in Amy's ear. 'Keep your head down, your mouth shut and don't get involved in anything. Don't say anything bad about anyone, or anything. Just focus on the good and concentrate on your classes.' She looked up and peered over her glasses at Amy, her twinkling green eyes set deep in a face lined with creases of wisdom. 'It's the only way you'll survive out here.'

With that she strode off, her long green skirt and vivid white shirt, fresh and fashionable in the sea of boring greys, blacks and browns that teachers seemed to favour.

CHAPTER 17

*O*f course, she could have guessed, by ten o'clock that day there was an email from Elliot. *Attend a mandatory meeting in my office at 3.30 this afternoon. Not optional.*

Damn, she thought, she'd promised herself to do some swimming training at the local pool this afternoon. They also ran a fitness class that looked good. She hadn't had time to get there yet, and this was supposed to be her first. Now there was no chance of making it.

***

Elliot and Gwen were waiting in exactly the same places as the last meeting.

'This is getting to be a habit, Miss Coops,' Elliot said as he shut the door behind her.

Amy was tired. Monday was her busiest day and once again she hadn't had time to eat anything other than an apple while she was walking around doing playground duty.

When Elliot sat down behind his desk she noticed his face was redder than usual. Perhaps that had something to do with the teacher who had stormed out before she came in. Another young teacher who had only been at the school a couple of years longer than herself.

'Right, I'll get straight to the point. It has been reported that you were out with Mr Edwin Carmody who is also a parent of children at the primary school. This is in breach of policy number, um, Gwen, the number, do you have the paperwork there?'

Gwen passed him a bundle of papers. 'It's all in here. All the details,' he said. 'Because of this latest incident I have had no option but to report another, might I repeat, another code of conduct against your name.'

She went to say something but he talked over the top of her. 'There's no use trying to defend the allegations. Miss Tuls has given me permission to say that she has reported you for let us say, sexual overtures, or dating events that took place on Saturday night. She has given a detailed description of you both kissing in full view of her.' He held his hand up to stop her from talking. 'Don't say a word, Miss Coops. There's nothing to add. Miss Tuls is the one reporting this. I have nothing to do with it as it's her report and I need to hand it over to the department. I will say it again. This has nothing to do with me. It has all been witnessed by Eliza Tuls.'

Gwen chipped in as she passed the document to Amy. 'It's all typed up for you and you need to read the last part carefully, because you have already had a code of conduct, are late to classes, and so on and so on, future referrals could lead to, diminished work performance and that means less pay for you, Miss Coops.'

A thought crossed Amy's mind, that she was already on the lowest scale of pay. She took the documents and stood up. 'Thank you so much.' With that, she turned and walked quickly towards the door. She opened it and then slammed it behind her as she exited. The office ladies all looked up as she came out of the office, their eyes wide. Linda Crosby, who was always nice to her, stood up and called out. She followed Amy out, calling her name as she walked back towards her staffroom. 'Amy, Amy, stop and talk to me.'

When she stopped, Linda put her arm around her shoulders. 'Don't let them beat you. We all know you're doing a good job. He's a nasty little man who has decided to make life hard for you.'

Tears threatened to spill and she blinked several times, refusing to cry. 'I've done everything I'm supposed to. I've gone the extra and the kids have been working well for me. I have students lined up wanting to join the music classes. I don't know what more I can do.' She waved the papers in the air, 'This is a code of conduct for disrespectful behaviour in a community setting. I went out with Edwin Carmody on Saturday night. Picnic, movies and something to eat. It was just a date. He kissed me when he dropped me home.' She stopped talking when she saw the look of horror on Linda's face. 'I know, don't panic, he's not my type. It was a one-off. He kissed me, I didn't kiss him. Eliza Tuls lives next door to me and Elliot happened to be visiting her.' She rolled her eyes. 'He saw me and Edwin together but the report says nothing about him. It's all been reported by Eliza, which gets him off the hook for being somewhere he shouldn't have been.'

A savage look crossed Linda's face. 'She's a snake. They're meant for each other. What a mongrel he is. I bet neither Gwen nor his wife, Penelope, know that he was visiting Eliza.'

'No, nothing was said about him being there and he made it very clear that the incident and report had nothing to do with him, rather it had all been brought about by Eliza.'

Linda crossed her arms and shook her head. 'Don't let it get you down. You're not the first one he's taken a dislike to.'

'I won't. I don't have a choice anyway. My contract is until the end of term two. I'll see it out, but then I'll have to think about my career choices.'

'Don't talk like that. The kids love you and I want my Sandy to be in your class next year. He's in year six and he's already saying he wants you as a teacher. We need bright young teachers like you. Go home and have a drink. Elliot's a nobody.'

*I*t had taken Amy a while to complete some other work she needed to finish when she got back to the staffroom. By the time she drove out through the school gate it was five-thirty. She remembered that she had brought her swimming gear with her to work. By now the fitness class would be finished, but she could still go and do some laps. It was too hot to do anything else and exercise might help her forget about the run of events and the threat of diminished work performance. She threw the folder with the papers Gwen had given her on the back seat of the car. She'd look at them later. For now, she wanted to do something that wasn't related to education.

The pool was quiet, with only a few other swimmers going up and down in their respective lanes. Hopefully, there weren't any students there or anyone else she knew. Her black one-piece was respectable at least. She clenched her teeth. Being respectful and respectable were unwritten ethics in her own personal code of conduct. They should be everyone's, she thought, no one should need to be told how to practice them, including Elliot.

Code of conduct, she thought as she dived in, the water streaming from her hair. What about the fact that Elliot used the school golf buggy on the weekend or that he sent the janitor over to his rentals to do maintenance during school times? There was a list of dodgy things she could write down as long as her arm. What was the use though? The regional director, as Elliot had told her, was a long-time friend of his. They'd gone to school together. Anyone who made complaints about him had been transferred to another area and the more you antagonised him the heavier and more difficult your timetable became.

As she pushed off from the edge of the pool she concentrated on her stroke, making sure to be strong in her movements and push any thoughts of work to the side.

She'd always loved swimming. It was something she and her dad had done together. He'd been a national champion in his day and a photo collage of him at the Commonwealth Games took pride of place on her cabinet. There were a couple of other photos alongside. Her sister, Kailee's, wedding, with all the family posing with wide smiles on either side of her and her new husband Graham. A photo of her mum holding Amy when she was a baby and the one she loved the most, a photo of her mum and dad, Kailee and Amy, when they travelled around Australia for two years. Their home had been an old blue Kombi van, with a popup top and travel stickers on the side. She smiled at the thought, remembering her mum buying a new sticker from each new town they pulled into. Dad would put it with the others on the back or side of the car, making sure there were no bubbles in it. They'd all stand back and look at the colourful collection, that over time faded. The stickers were a sign of how far you'd travelled and by the time the family finished their trip there was hardly room for any more.

She turned at the end of the pool, gliding through the water to start another lap. Her family would be horrified at the way she was being treated. When she was a teenager her mum and dad had run the local pool and she couldn't remember a time when either of them had been rude to either their employees or customers. Her boss at the skincare shop she'd worked at had been a lovely, kind person who had treated her as a trusted employee and paid her extra at times, giving praise and friendship in reciprocation for Amy's good work ethic. It was how she had been brought up. Manners. It was all about manners, loyalty and hard work. That's what had always been drummed into her.

* * *

She kicked harder, aware that the swimmer in the adjacent lane was going stroke for stroke with her. Her times had never matched her dad's but she'd been to state finals and broken records when she was a teenager. Although she'd stopped swimming competitively when she went to uni, she had always kept training. Even though she was only here today to improve her fitness and push any thoughts of Elliot or school from her mind, she wasn't about to let someone else go faster than she was. Picking up her pace she pushed harder, turning faster and ploughing through the water. Taking a side-ways glance, she noticed the other swimmer continued to keep up with her, their strokes clean and firm as they stretched out beside her. For another ten laps they swam beside each other. Her competitive streak kicked in though and she finally pulled out in front, maintaining her speed and even picking up a bit more as the other swimmer fell further and further behind her.

The other swimmer had stopped, the water in the lane next to her now empty. As she went back and forth, completing another ten laps she wondered who it was. Thoughts of school and Elliot crept back into her mind, and she remembered that she had a heap of work to do tonight before tomorrow's lessons, and, she pulled up as she reached the end of the pool, there was the code of conduct paperwork to go through.

As she pulled off her goggles she noticed someone standing at the end of her lane. Tanned feet and legs; legs that were very muscly and strong. Standing up she looked up at the swimmer's face, the wide smile of Angus making her laugh out loud.

'Oh, my goodness. Was that you?' She laughed louder before sinking back under the water. When she came up she pushed her hair back before accepting his outstretched hand. He pulled her out of the pool and soon she stood beside him, the water running down her back and legs. The sun was still scorching hot although her body was cool and refreshed as a slight breeze pushed across where they stood.

He crossed his arms. 'I had to stop to get my breath. You nearly killed me. It wasn't until I got out that I realised it was you. You're a really good swimmer.'

'Under 16, State champion for 400 metres, three years in a row.'

'No wonder I couldn't catch you,' Angus said. 'I only started swimming in my twenties to fill in time. My stroke probably needs some work.'

They stood looking at each other and she was reminded how good-looking he was. He wore board shorts and she couldn't help but notice his muscular chest and well-toned body.

'It's good to see you again,' he said. 'I haven't noticed you here before. I come a few afternoons a week, after most people have left, to do my laps.'

She wound her hair up in a bun. 'I was supposed to do a fitness class this afternoon, but I was held up at work.'

Her face must have shown her feelings. 'How's that going?' he asked.

'To be honest, not great.'

'I hope you're getting some support from some of the other staff.'

'Yes. There have been quite a few of them who have been helpful and let me know to come and see them whenever I need help. I don't feel quite so alone at work.'

They'd chatted a bit longer. 'Thank goodness, someone is looking out for you,' he said. 'Hopefully, it will improve.'

'I have my doubts about that. I've made friends and the music program is going well, but I'm not sure that teaching is what I want to do.'

'You'll have to keep me updated.'

She would have liked to have talked longer, but the owner of the pool called out that they were about to close.

Angus walked with her out to her car. 'I'll see you

around,' he said, as he opened her car door for her. 'Good to see you.'

She pulled a face when she saw him look down at the shoes scattered near the accelerator. 'I'm moving them. Just about to put them on the other side,' she said as she bent down and threw them over the seat into the back. 'Done. See. No more shoes under my feet.'

He'd shaken his head. 'See you again, Amy. I'll be checking your car when I see it in the carpark here. No shoes near the pedals.'

'She laughed, waving to him as she drove out of the carpark. It had been good to see him again and she wished they could had stayed longer and talked. Perhaps she'd run into him at the pool some other days. Edwin's words came back to her. 'Murdered, he murdered someone.' She needed to be careful. First, there was Edwin who she would not be going out with again and now there was his cousin who she had been drawn to from the first moment she'd met him. Both good looking and friendly. Different in nature but similar in looks. Both single. Her brows knitted together. Both from a small town where gossip ran rife and everyone knew exactly what everyone else was up to. Best to steer clear. Of them both.

CHAPTER 19

*A*s the weeks passed Amy settled more and more into the life of a teacher in a small country town. By now she knew many of the parents and it was difficult to go anywhere without someone stopping her to talk about how their child was going or ask how she was liking her new school. As the term neared its end she decided to stay in town rather than go back to the coast for the two-week holiday. Her parents were away in Melbourne and there wasn't anyone else she particularly wanted to visit. Besides that, she had loads of schoolwork to do over the holidays.

Elliot had been away for a couple of weeks so the pressure was less with fewer emails and her days at school had been a bit more peaceful. The school hummed along better without Elliot and at least she didn't risk running into him when he came to visit Eliza.

Most things in her life were going somewhat smoothly, apart from Edwin, who had tried numerous times to get her to agree to another date. He was persistent and she'd tried every excuse there was to avoid his advances. Several times he'd turned up on her doorstep, always with some excuse that he had some extra fruit from the markets, or he had just happened to grow too many pumpkins and she might like one. He was of course always charming, but he'd also started to get a bit pushy and kept insisting that she owed him a night out.

'I thought you'd take me out somewhere,' he said. 'You know a payback for when I took you out. This time it will be your choice of where we go.' Even though she was firm in her replies, he was persistent. There was no way she was going to give in though. Surely, soon he'd work out that she just wasn't interested in him.

CHAPTER 20

*A*ngus was well aware of his cousin's feelings for Amy. Edwin had made sure of that. A couple of times he'd spotted Edwin's car as it glided into the street where Amy lived. He'd also overheard him telling some of his mates that Amy was a sure thing for him. 'She's busy at the moment with schoolwork but she's keen on me. Young and sweet, just what I like.'

Edwin was at the pub having a beer when Angus called in to pick up a bottle of wine. There was no way to avoid him and Angus pulled his shoulders back and nodded as he greeted some of the other men. Edwin smirked and looked him up and down. 'Well, well, here comes our young Angus. Come and have a beer with us, mate, or are you still off the grog? Scared to wet your thirst?'

Angus hadn't even bothered to reply. He'd only come in to pick up a bottle of wine for Nana. He kept his eyes down and didn't stop to chat. He only socialised on a rare occasion, a special event, or like the other day when he'd

come in for a mate's birthday. That had been the afternoon he had seen Amy there with the other teachers.

Once he had bought the wine he slipped out through a
side door to avoid Edwin and his group of friends. No
doubt his cousin was talking about him or spreading
rumours about someone else who annoyed him. Not that
he cared. It was easy for him to stay out of discussions
about other people. Small town gossip was the last thing
he wanted to be part of. There wasn't much that
happened around town that wasn't talked about and Nana
had mentioned to him that Edwin had taken the pretty
teacher that they'd given a lift to, out on a date. He
wondered what Amy saw in Edwin. She'd seemed too
smart to be fooled by his arrogant nature but then again,
he hardly knew her. Perhaps that was the type of man she
liked.

Just because he thought of her sometimes, especially
after he saw her at the pool each week, didn't mean
anything. Their training sessions had become a regular
meet up and during the day he'd hope that she'd be there
in the afternoon. An image of her kept recurring. It was
the first day he'd seen her at the pool and helped her out.
Standing in the sunshine, the light glinting off her wet
arms and legs, the water running down her body that was
clad in the most flattering black swimsuit he'd ever laid
eyes on, was a picture that was etched in his mind.

She never mentioned anything about Edwin when
they spoke, but he never asked her too much about
personal matters or if she was going out with anyone. It
wasn't any of his business and their conversations were
usually about swimming or what she was doing to try and
stay out of Elliot's way.

Sometimes they stood in the carpark long after their swimming was done and the pool office had closed. At times she'd cut the conversation short and hurry off, almost as if she wanted to say something but then didn't. Now it made sense. When they'd talked about the swimming hole out at the boulders and Angus offered to take her there, he'd sensed a sign of panic in her answer. At the time he couldn't quite work it out. All he'd done was offer to go for a drive and a swim. Just a friend taking a friend for an outing.

He shook his head. If she was involved with Edwin she wouldn't want to be seen driving anywhere with Angus. Edwin had a jealous streak and she might already be aware of it. What a shame. Amy was the first girl in as long as he could remember who interested him. Maybe not romantically, but just to talk to and spend time together. He drew a deep harsh breath. Perhaps it was for the best anyway. The events of the past still weighed upon him and he wondered if there would ever be a time when guilt didn't plague him or when dreams of regret stopped tormenting his sleep at night. Sometimes he thought it had been a mistake to return to where everyone knew his past, but the property and family had drawn him back.

Besides, his therapist said, it was better to confront the past head-on. Plunge in and get it over and done with and then get on with life. But in a place like Matfield, no one ever forgot the past and with cousins like Edwin to goad him at every turn, everyday life was not made any easier.

It had been eighteen years since his mate Billy had died. Eighteen long years where he'd paid time and time again for the mistakes he'd made that had led to his death.

As he went to shut the gate to Nana's property he

thought about that night. The memories never left him and little things like the rusty latch on the gate that reminded him of the colour of Billy's hair jumped out when he least expected it. The motorbike that he'd passed earlier as he drove home with the bottle of wine had been the same model as the one Billy had bought the year before he died and the young guy sitting outside the pub had the same lanky legs. Shaking his head, he looked down the road, trying to rid the visions that haunted him.

A cloud of dust following a ute that was hurtling along the road brought him back to reality. The driver was going way too fast and as the vehicle approached where he stood outside the gate, he recognised it as Edwin's orange Falcon. As usual he was speeding, but he slowed as he approached and to Angus's surprise pulled up right next to where he stood. He must have come from the pub and from the way he walked and called out it was obvious that he'd had too much to drink. What an idiot, driving when he'd been drinking. At least he didn't have the kids with him.

Pushing his hat further down on his face Angus held onto the gate, continuing what he was doing and ignoring the fact that Edwin had come right up beside him.

'Are you right?' Angus said as Edwin leaned over him. Edwin had always been taller and bigger. Even when they were little he'd loved nothing more than to push Angus around, sneaking around and saying mean things to him when no one was near, picking on him any chance he had.

Edwin's breath smelled like rum and there was a dangerous glint in his eyes. His words were harsh. 'I'm good, but you need to stay away from her.'

'Stay away from who?'

'You know who I'm talking about.'

'I have no idea what you're on about.' He went to say he didn't think Edwin should be driving but the irate tone in his cousin's voice made him wary and from past experiences he knew it didn't take much to trigger his aggression.

'Stay away from Amy. She's mine,' Edwin growled.

It was probably the worst reaction Angus could have shown, but it came naturally, a loud laugh as he looked with mirth into the angry eyes of Edwin. 'I didn't realise that a woman belonged to someone. How exactly does she belong to you?'

Edwin's curled-up hand came up fast, the blow hitting Angus squarely in the eye. He staggered backward, the gate saving him from falling completely to the ground. Edwin leered over him. 'This is just a warning. I've been told you're stalking her, following her to the pool and back to her car. I'm telling you, stay away.'

Angus held his hand to his cheek. He'd been in plenty of fights before. There had been lots of times in his youth when he'd hung with the wrong crowd and he'd had to defend himself against bigger men. Usually, he'd been full of grog though and stupid enough to get into bad situations. This time he hadn't moved quick enough, the blow catching him off-guard. His eye stung and when he put his hand up to it, blood covered his fingers.

By the time he righted himself and wiped the blood away from his face, Edwin had moved away from him. He watched him get in his car, the dust flying out from behind it as he took off up the road. For a long while Angus stood in the same spot, staring up the dirt road in the direction the car had gone. The thought of fighting back and getting revenge was not an option and long ago he'd learned to take the knocks and stay out of the way of men who liked to exert their dominance. One day Edwin would get what was coming to him, but it wouldn't be from Angus. That instinct to hit back had left him long ago.

* * *

That night he held an ice pack against his eye, the pain throbbing through his face. Luckily Nana had been in the shower when he stopped by and dropped the bottle of wine off. She was leaving for Brisbane in the morning with his aunty, so at least he had avoided her questions and wouldn't have to explain what had happened. A pressing urge to warn Amy about Edwin nagged at him. Did she realise that Edwin was an aggressive, nasty person, who had a temper that had driven his first wife away and several girlfriends that came after her? Filling Amy in on local gossip wasn't up to him though. If she and Edwin were an item, then she'd made her own choice. Who was he to break up a relationship?

CHAPTER 21

*A*ngus saw Amy a few days later. He'd waited until later in the afternoon to go to the pool but she was still there, doing her laps. No one else was around and he chose a lane further away from her. It was best they both do their own thing.

She'd spotted him though and swam over to do her strokes in the lane next to him. As usual she picked up the pace and he used every bit of strength to keep up with her. This time he did better, the training must be paying off. As they turned together at the end of the pool he glimpsed her body, the usual black one-piece flashing through the water next to him. The beautiful image of her must have broken his concentration because suddenly she surged ahead, the splashing from her feet blocking his vision as he lagged behind. Darn, he thought, she's got me again.

When he stopped at the end, he stood up, gasping for breath. Today was the hardest he'd pushed himself and his lungs ached for air, his legs throbbing from the exertion.

She sat on the edge of the pool, her legs dangling in the water as she stared at him. The concerned look on her face reminded him that he had a large bruise around his eye.

'G'day,' he said as he gave her a grin. She was beautiful, her arms and face tanned from spending time in the pool, her shapely legs and slender feet right near where he stood in the water.

She squinted as she stared hard. 'What happened? Your eye. It looks terrible.'

'Walked into a door. It's nothing. Looks worse than what it is.'

She frowned. 'Strange bruise from walking into something.' She twisted her hair and wrung the water out of it. 'I haven't seen you this week. I've missed talking to you.'

He wanted to reach out and touch her, to push the tendrils of hair back that hung down the side of her face. His heart beat fast, but this time not from the swimming and he dipped under the water, coming back up to find she was still staring at him.

'I've been busy.' He wanted to add that he'd missed her too and that all week he'd thought of nothing except her.

'Have you been out to the boulders yet?' she asked.

'No.'

'The holidays will be over soon. I thought about your suggestion. I'd like to go with you.'

He straightened up and ran his hands through his hair. 'Look, Amy. I really like you but I know that you're going out with Edwin, and I don't think it would be fair if I took you out when you're with him.'

A look of horror crossed her face, her eyes narrowing. 'What? I am not going out with Edwin. I went out with him once and I'll say this to you because I trust you, I won't be going out with him again. He's pestered me so much this week that I'm going to have to tell him that if he doesn't stop I'm going to report him.'

'Report him to who? His mates, the coppers. I wouldn't do that if I was you.' He looked around. There was no one else in the pool but the owners would be inside waiting to close up. 'I think you and I need to talk because Edwin seems to think you two are an item.'

She stood up and he couldn't help but stare at her legs and slim body. Leaning over, she offered him her hand. He held his up and she pulled him out, both laughing as he put one foot up on the edge and jumped up into a standing position beside her. 'Edwin and I are definitely not an item. That is something I couldn't be surer about, and do you know what, Angus, I'd really like the chance to talk to you properly. With no one else around.'

He thought hard. 'Most of the family are going to Rocky for the weekend. There's a family reunion, but I'm not going.' Hesitating for a moment, he finally took the plunge. 'Would you like to come camping for a night? No strings attached. I have two swags and all the gear. I could show you the best swimming hole in the region and there's a walk we could do late in the afternoon. You'd love the sunset and scenery.' She hesitated. 'You can trust me, Amy. Nothing serious, just as friends. Perhaps it would be best to not ever let Edwin know though. Even if you aren't with him, he thinks otherwise.' He lifted his hand to his eye and rubbed it.

Amy's eyes widened. 'He did that didn't he?' Did he say something about me?'

'Someone told him that I was stalking you, here at the pool.'

Her eyes narrowed and she wrapped a towel around her waist. A hint of anger flashed across her face. 'What time will you pick me up?'

Grinning broadly, he shook his head, tiny droplets of water from his hair scattering everywhere. 'Four o'clock, Saturday morning. We can be at the campsite and set up before it's too hot. You'll love it. Only a few people know about it and there won't be anyone else there. It's on Nana's property.'

CHAPTER 22

A quiet rage came over Amy that night. How dare Edwin say she was going out with him. The situation couldn't be further from the truth. The couple of times she had been with him or spoken to him over the phone she'd always got a strange feeling about the way he talked to her. Like she was a kid or someone who he could manipulate or control. The last time he'd rung he had been angry and she'd also glimpsed that side of him that cautioned her that he probably had a temper. There were lots of warning signs. Now she just had to get him to stop ringing her.

* * *

Angus parked up the road a bit and messaged to tell her to meet him there. She knew why. Eliza would hear his car and before Amy was even out of the street everyone in town would know that Angus Carmody had picked her up. She didn't want to sneak around but for the moment it was for the best, both for her and Angus. Elliot would also be back at school after the holidays so better not to poke the bear any more than she needed. A sigh caught in her throat. How had she got into these situations without even doing anything wrong?

***

Excitement rippled through her body as she threw her bag into the back of Angus's four-wheel drive and jumped in the front with him. 'I feel like a kid sneaking out,' she giggled, turning to him as he grinned back.

'It's a good feeling. I feel the same. Off on an adventure.' He started the car up. 'Just you and me and we're going to do some walking and exploring.'

'That's what's been missing for me lately,' she told him as they drove out through the outskirts of town. 'It's all just been about work since I arrived here. I miss doing spontaneous exciting things.'

Only a few houses had lights on, the streets deserted, apart from the usual few mangy dogs fighting in the middle of the road. The dogs scattered when the ute neared them and Amy looked back at him, the two of them like conspirators, sneaking out before anyone noticed. She added, 'I've just turned twenty-five, I need more than just work and more work.'

'I'm five years older than you but I'm the same. I love living with Nana and helping her, but most days are just about work. That's why I love swimming. I do it for me and it frees my mind.'

They talked the entire way out to the boulders and Angus pointed out the different landmarks on the way. He'd taken the main road out of town, but then turned off, opening a gate and making his way onto Nana's property from a side entrance. 'The family property wraps around the town. It's quicker to get to this place by the main road and then out through here. It's isolated and there's no reception out further but I have a satellite phone so there are no problems if we were to break down or something went wrong.'

A worried look crossed her face. 'Don't worry,' he said. 'Nothing will go wrong. I've spent a lot of time out here. Once I stayed out here by myself for six months. I only came in for supplies once a month.' He tried to keep the melancholy out of his voice but he knew he'd failed. It had been one of the lowest times of his life and several times he'd been tempted to just stay out there and never come back to reality again.

'Why?' she asked.

Taking a deep breath, he closed his eyes for a second, that heavy feeling that pressed down threatening to engulf him. He never talked about those years and it was only because he was driving out to this area for the first time in a long while that he'd spoken out loud. 'Just needed some space.'

She laughed as she looked out through her window. 'Well, plenty of that out here.'

* * *

Amy had a subtle way of changing the subject and lightening the mood. It was as if she sensed there was something deep in his past but didn't want to pry and he was thankful for her intuition not to push him to talk about events he didn't want to. Before long he was laughing along with her as she relayed her stories about Elliot and Gwen and the crazy antics that went on at school. There were enough stories to keep them both amused and entertained, and between the kids, teachers, Matfield High School, and Elliot, it seemed there was never a dull moment. No wonder she was keen to get away.

As the track narrowed, he drove slower. 'We'll stop here and stretch our legs. The sun is about to come up behind us.'

He was pleased to see that Amy had dressed for the conditions and the usual white sandals she often wore were replaced with hardy riding boots. She wore denim shorts and a strappy red singlet, her body toned and tanned, her hair pulled up in a ponytail. 'Oh no, I've forgotten my hat,' she said as she searched in her bag. 'I've left it on the table back home.'

Angus rummaged through the back of the ute, holding a ragged Akubra hat in his hand. He dusted it off on his jeans. 'I have a spare, it's dusty but it will do the job.' He placed it on her head and was rewarded with a glowing smile. 'You look like a local now,' he quipped.

As they sat on a couple of camp chairs he'd pulled from the back of the ute, they sipped a cup of tea and watched the sun rise over the distant horizon. The dusty browns of the earth morphed into a glow of red, and sunlight filtered across the vast plains. Tiny animals ran back and forth between the sparse tufts of spinifex grass and a bird sounded its eerie call from a bush nearby.

It was still and peaceful and Amy spoke quietly. 'I love the early morning sounds in the bush. I've heard it before. When I was a kid, my parents and my sister Kailee and I travelled around Australia in a van. We were away for three years.'

'Wow, that would have been something special.'

They'd talked more about their families and he'd asked her about her parents and sister. It sounded like they were all close and he could tell that she missed them, even though she wanted to do her own thing. 'I think it's because of the hard time Elliot has given me. I usually don't miss them that much, but I must admit I've felt isolated out here without them. It hasn't been an easy year so far. He's a bully.'

'I've heard that. He's not from around here so I don't know him that well but there's been a large number of staff go through that school. A lot of them don't stick around, which is a shame for the kids. The primary school does a lot better at keeping their staff. She's supposed to be nice, the principal there.'

'Oh, she is,' Amy said. 'I've met her several times.' She sipped the last of her tea, watching the sky as it turned from a dark blue to a lighter shade, the colours of the landscape changing once again making for a spectacular sunrise. 'I don't think I've made the right decision coming to Matfield. I'm not usually a quitter but I can't see me lasting. I shouldn't have to put up with being treated the way I am, plus Edwin is also annoying me.'

Angus stood up, the mention of Edwin's name reminding him of his own annoyances. 'I know that feeling when someone is making life hard for you. It's usually a sign that something is lacking in their own life. I also understand that feeling of wanting to leave the problems behind.' He put the chairs back in his ute. 'We'd best get going. Sounds like you have some decisions to make.'

CHAPTER 23

*I*t had taken another two hours to get to their destination. Amy found it hard to imagine that there were any boulders or waterholes nearby when as far as the eye could see there were only wide stretches of red dirt with tufts of dried-up grass doing their best to survive. Occasionally they crossed a dry creek bed, a few head of cattle standing in the shade of the trees, the leaves dried and only just hanging on. 'She's dry,' Angus said. 'We're in desperate need of rain.'

'We get so much wet weather where I'm from on the coast. It's a pity we can't send it this way.'

'I spent some time at the Sunshine Coast. There's a lot of it I haven't seen though. The beaches were beautiful.'

'Yes, I think my time out here has made me realise I'm a coastal dweller. I mean,' she waved her hand in the air, gesturing to the scenery they drove through, 'this is amazing and there's nothing in the world like it, but I need to be near the salt water. I miss putting my feet in the sand and swimming in the ocean.'

The bushes around them thickened and Amy was surprised to see a cluster of rocks and hills rising on the horizon to the south. 'There it is,' Angus pointed to their destination. 'I haven't been here for a long while. Even though we're in drought there should still be water in the waterholes. It never dries out.'

He'd navigated the ute through narrow tracks, the paths invisible to her eye, but it was obvious he knew exactly where he was going. Eventually they came to an area where Angus slowed and then eventually stopped. 'This is where I've camped before. We'll set up here.'

A small clearing under some low gum trees was the perfect camping spot and she helped him unpack what they needed from the ute. They'd stayed away from the larger trees, many of them with thick branches and dead limbs hanging precariously, looking as if they would come down at any moment.

In the middle of the camp area was a fire pit, the circle of rocks around it covered by dirt that flew around when the wind picked up. 'It doesn't look like anyone has been here since I was here a few years ago,' he said. 'That's good. I hope no one ever does come here. I like to think of it as my special place.'

As she shaded her eyes with her hand she looked around. The white of the gum trees was stark against the red of the earth and the vivid blue of the sky. Dull green leaves hung on stoically to the branches, providing a small shady area. It was an incredible landscape and she constantly stopped to look at it as she helped Angus set up the table and chairs, as well as the two separate swags, ready for them to sleep in at night. Angus dug a hole in the sandy part down near the creek bed for her to use as a toilet. He wrapped a tarp around some branches to provide privacy for when she needed to use it. 'Watch for snakes though. It's a long way back to a doctor,' he said.

Amy had slipped straight back into her camping habits from when she was a kid. She hadn't travelled that much after those years. Her parents had gone from an old van to a large house overlooking the ocean. They'd managed the local swimming pool and she'd spent most of her time either in the ocean or swimming laps of the pool. Her music had also kept her busy and any spare time had been spent with friends and family, gazing over the ocean, watching the whales as they migrated north, or sipping lattes in the many cafes there were in the area. When her parents retired and moved to an old timber house on the Maroochy River she'd moved with them. Her job at Noosa was nearby and everything she wanted was within a short distance.

Camping reminded her of childhood and years of carefree travelling. She hadn't thought about it for a long time and the memories that came back made her relax even more.

'I love this,' she said, pushing back strands of hair from her face.

'Love what?' Angus asked as he pushed a sturdy stick under the handle of the billy, balancing it carefully as he held the bottom and poured them both a cup of tea.

'Camping. Sitting in the dirt with nothing but nature around you.'

'Wait until tonight. The stars are amazing.'

'Thanks so much for asking me to come here. It's like every bit of stress has already left my body.'

Angus passed her a cup of tea. 'I know the feeling. It's why I've always come to this place.'

* * *

As soon as it was cool enough they walked from the camping area and headed towards the rocky outcrops that were dotted throughout the hills. Angus led the way and she wondered how he knew where he was going. There was no path visible but he never wavered or stopped to check where they were going. As they climbed higher the gap between the rocks narrowed and a couple of times she had to squeeze through a narrow opening or clamber over a boulder that blocked their path. At one stage Angus waited for her and held out his hand to help her over an area littered with large boulders, their surfaces smooth and hot under her hands. 'Not much further,' he said. 'It's hard climbing but well worth it. We're nearly there.'

A few straggly trees clung to a cluster of rocks and she heaved herself up and over, standing up beside Angus who had stopped and was looking in front of them. 'This is the rockpool,' he said. 'Nothing has changed. It never does.' A well-worn path wound its way around rocks and bushes, and she was amazed that anything could grow in the dry and rugged conditions. In front of them was a circular rockpool, the dark water still, but clear.

As she got closer she could see the bottom and the smaller smooth boulders that formed the edges under the water. The small pool was mesmerising and she marvelled at the cool oasis, hidden amongst the rocks in a deep gully, situated in some of the driest land in the country.

'It's fed by a natural spring,' Angus said. 'If you look up

here, there are some rock paintings. Aboriginal people used this place for water and celebrations. I have all the history written down at home. One of the local elders, Ernie, is in his nineties and he lived in this area for much of his early life. He brought me here when I was a kid and then came back out with me in later years. That was after I'd been away for a while. He told me the story of this place. They used to bring sick people here, or relatives with problems. He told me it's a healing place.'

She turned to him, detecting once again a sadness and tender emotion in his words. Her words were quiet. 'And is it?'

He turned to her, looking into her eyes, his chest rising as he took a deep breath. 'Yes, it is.'

* * *

They'd swum together in the pool, the cool water pressing against their bodies. Her usual black one-piece had been replaced by a yellow bikini. No school kids out here to see her. She could be herself and any inhibitions were lost. When they finally got out, they lay on their backs on the smooth boulders, talking and laughing like two kids. They made up stories about the shapes of the clouds that scuttled overhead and took turns calling out cooee, their noises echoing up through the canyons that cut through the steep cliffs behind the pool.

A rocky ledge just above the pool was a good place to sit and look out across the plains. Amy's skin tingled from the warmth of the sun after the icy water and she felt the best she had since she'd arrived at Matfield. 'You can feel something here,' she said. 'I can't explain it, there's something spiritual. As if we've stepped back in time and there's no one else on the planet.'

Angus passed her a sandwich from his backpack. 'It is an ancient land. I've never brought anyone else here and you aren't to tell anyone about it, especially those paintings. When Nana split up her land this part was given to my parents. The deeds were drawn up years ago. No one else wanted this section anyway, it's too dry and hardly holds any stock. It suited Mum and Dad, although last year they signed it over to me. I don't have any siblings. That means I can protect it.' He gazed around the area. 'In my mind, no one owns this part anyway. It belongs to the first people who were here. Ernie and his mob. It's their sacred land.'

She took the sandwich and gazed up at the boulders behind them. 'How special that you can make sure it's always protected. I promise I won't tell anyone. I feel privileged that you've brought me here.' They sat and ate together, washing the sandwich down with the water that Angus had brought with him. 'You're super organised,' she said. 'It's a long while since I've camped. I'm out of practice.'

'I've spent plenty of time in my swag and away from everyone. I'm good at being organised. Routine, food, work, sleep. That's my life and I don't mind it that way.'

Sometimes what Angus said confused her. Was he happy with the way his life was, or was he deep down searching for something else? Perhaps there was a piece of happiness that eluded him at the moment. There were also his comments about his past to contemplate. Why would he have camped out here for so long by himself?

He was a deep thinker and she remembered what Edwin had said about him spending time in jail.

He must have noticed her trying to read his face. She had been staring. 'Right,' he said, standing up. 'We need to get going if we want to see the sunset.'

* * *

When they reached their destination they perched on a wide rock, looking out over the western plains. Behind them in the east a full moon rose slowly, its bulbous shape floating in a sky that darkened as the sun sank below the opposite horizon. Angus pointed to the west. 'Those clouds we were watching from the rockpool should give us some colour when the last of the sun's rays hit them.'

She drew in the last light of the day, the vivid colours starting to appear the lower the sun sank. A string of clouds hovered above the plains, their puffy shapes now tinted with bright flashes of red and orange. A dark pink filled the gap between the earth and the clouds, the ground glowing from the display above.

Neither of them spoke, the scene so incredible it took Amy's breath away. They watched until the vivid colours faded, the red and oranges transforming into dull tones until they too paled into the waning light of the evening. Stars began to appear high above them, and Angus pointed to them and named them. 'They kept me company when I was out here by myself.'

In the dim light of the evening, she sensed his loneliness and she wanted to wrap her arms around him and tell him whatever it was she understood. Did she though? Could you really know a person from just a few chats over the previous few months, a man she'd swum next to but still didn't know very much about?

* * *

They'd returned to the camp using the last of the light to guide them. She busied herself while Angus prepared the fire and it didn't take long before they were ready to eat. Dinner was scrumptious. A pre-prepared Spaghetti Bolognese and a crusty damper cooked in the coals had seemed like the best food in the world. 'You're a good cook,' she said. 'This is the best meal I've ever tasted.'

He spooned some more into her bowl, turning the left-over damper still warming next to the coals. The fire flickered when he stirred it, sparks spiralling up into the night sky. 'I think you're exaggerating. You must be hungry.'

'I am starving and this food is the best. Walking and swimming in the waterhole has energised me.'

He looked at her and a smile played around his lips when she held out her tin cup—that was filled with lemonade—and clinked the sides with his. She admired his rugged face and was drawn in by his big dark eyes fringed by long eyelashes. Leaning back in his chair, he crossed his legs at the ankles, his well-worn riding boots glowing in the firelight. A bruise still showed on his cheek and dark stubble covered his chin. 'Your phone must get reception here, I keep hearing it beep,' he said.

She let out a long breath and also leaned back in her chair. 'It's your mate, Edwin. He's persistent.'

'I'm glad you worked him out. I wanted to warn you about his controlling nature but it's not my place to do that and from what he said I thought you were going out with him.'

'I picked up on it straight away. I haven't had that many boyfriends, but none of them have been like that. They've been the opposite and on equal terms with me. I'm not used to men like him, or Elliot, with their bullying ways. I guess I'll learn a few life skills out here.'

Angus ran his hand through his dark curls. 'Edwin's always hated me, right from when we were little kids. He's like a dog with a bone and won't let go of the past. It's a shame because I love his kids, but I don't see them that much because of him.'

'No wonder his wife left.'

'Yes, Kathy was lovely but she had to get away from him. He's had other girlfriends since her, but I notice he's extra keen on you.'

She laughed. 'He'll soon get the message. I'm not interested. Besides, like I said before, I'm not sure I'm going to hang around in Matfield.' Staring into the fire she tried to keep her voice even. 'I've been miserable since I started at the school. This is the best day I've had since I arrived.'

'I'm glad you came.' He wrapped his hands around his cup. 'I hope you don't mind that I didn't bring beers or wine. I don't drink alcohol.'

'I wondered about that.' When she looked up at the stars she wished that she could ask him more about his past. But really, it was none of her business. There were so many aspects about him that she didn't understand, almost like an entire chunk of his life was missing or hidden.

He stared hard at her. 'What are you thinking about?'

Swivelling in her chair, she took off her boots and

tucked her feet under her bottom. 'Can I ask you some-thing and you don't have to tell me if you don't want.'

His eyes narrowed. 'Ask away.'

'Edwin told me you had murdered someone and that you went to jail. I know that's a strange question to ask someone when I'm out here by myself with you, a million miles from anywhere, but I've always felt a closeness to you, and,' she smiled reassuringly at him, 'I trust you. Also, your nana said we needed to be friends.'

He let out a chuckle and she waited for a moment before continuing.

'What Edwin said keeps popping into my mind and I want to know if he made that up because he was jealous of you. I've told you so much about myself, but I'm picking up there's something you're leaving out of your story. Maybe a problem. Like I said, just tell me to butt out if you don't want to talk about whatever it is.'

Angus shook his head. 'Edwin is half my problem. Like I said before, he won't let go. I'm surprised no one else has filled you in on my younger years. They love to gossip in this town and there's still some who hold a grudge against me.'

'I haven't asked anyone and it's only Edwin who has said a few things. You're the only one I'd believe anyway. Is there any truth in what he said?'

As he hopped up to stir the fire and put the billy on for more tea, she watched him. The sleeves of his blue shirt were rolled up, the length of his shirt hanging over his jeans. He passed her another piece of damper and she spread butter on it and then a large dollop of jam.

She wondered if she'd gone too far or appeared nosey. 'You don't have to tell me. It's rude of me to ask. I have things that have happened in my past that I don't often share.'

When he sat back down his shoulders slumped and she wished she hadn't brought it up. She was taken aback when he spoke. 'I have been in jail.' She stared hard and her body tensed as she tried to act as if what he'd said was just normal conversation.

'Can you please pass me some more of the jam,' she replied.

'Do you know what, Amy, for the first time in my life I want to tell someone the truth. You make me want to talk about what happened, to get it off my chest and I want you to know what my story is; what makes me quiet sometimes and why I like to be by myself.'

Suddenly she wanted to backpedal with her questions. Was what he wanted to tell her going to change her opinion of him? Maybe the gap in his life was better left unshared. She put her hand on his arm, the touch of his skin sending a quiver through her fingers. 'It's okay, you don't have to.' When she pulled her hand away he was staring at her and she was sure there were tears in his eyes when he started talking.

'No, I want to. If we're going to be friends it's better you hear it from me. It all happened a long time ago but when you live in a small town, people don't forget.' He leaned forward and poked the fire again, his voice uneven when he started to talk. 'I was wild as a teenager. We all were. There was a group of six of us who all hung around together. Mick was my best mate.' He stopped and took a long sip of his tea. 'He was lanky and tall with ginger hair. We used to call him Ginger Mick. We were all the same at that age. Loved our footy, going out with the girls and drinking as much grog as we could lay our hands on. Small town and nothing else to do.'

He leaned back, his eyes focussed on the fire. 'One Saturday we'd been drinking all day, since about ten in the morning. It was the usual thing to do on the weekend. We were camped out on the river on the eastern side of town. It was a regular hangout for us kids and all sorts of things happened out there. Like I said before, we were wild and none of us had a brain in our head. It's true what they say, at that age you think you're invincible, or rather you don't think about anything at all. You just do it because you can, and it's a challenge or it's something that gives you an adrenaline rush. Mick was right into pot. Loved it and constantly had a smoke hanging out of his mouth. I didn't ever get into it. I guess I was so addicted to beer that there wasn't room for anything else.'

He looked towards her. 'You might not understand any of this, I'm not sure what your upbringing was like.'

She scrunched her mouth up. 'I understand completely. It was the same on the coast. We were all drinking and smoking way too young. My swimming and being involved with musical groups probably kept me from doing too much damage with any of that. Pure luck that's all. There aren't too many at that age that think or act clearly.'

He stoked the fire and stared into its depths. 'We all had our licences by then and everyone was obsessed with their cars. On weekends we'd tinker with them and add extras that made them go faster or sound louder. Mick got bored with that though. He always liked the action part. The faster he could go the better and the more dangerous the stunt, the wilder and crazier he became. I hadn't been with the rest of them, sitting around a fire talking and drinking. I was actually under a car trying to fix a part on the chassis. I nearly had it finished. I can remember Mick kicking my feet and when I pulled myself out, he poured some beer on my face. We wrestled in the dirt. You know play fighting. We were like brothers. He had two sisters and I was an only child and at that age it's your mates who you're closest to.'

Amy sat still, listening and watching the embers rise up and then disappear into the night sky. The gum trees were silhouetted as the moon rose higher in the sky and she waited for Angus to continue.

He cleared his throat. 'Mick wanted to drive out further and do burnouts in a paddock that we often went to.' He stopped talking and stared for a long while at the fire. 'He kept telling me to stop working on the car and to go for a spin instead. I wanted to go home. The next day was Nana's birthday and there was a big surprise party organised. I told him that and even threw all my gear in my car ready to leave, but he kept at me. I'd been drinking but had stopped a while before. I'd been working on the other car for a couple of hours so I hadn't been drinking during that time. Mick had been smoking the entire day. He was stoned out of his head and he said if I didn't take him out there he'd drive himself. Eventually, I gave in. A couple of others came with us and we all piled in Mick's car. I didn't want to drive, even though I'd stopped for a while, I had been drinking most of the day before that. The others threw beer cans at me and I remember Mick putting his arm around my neck and urging me to hurry up. He said I was the only sober one there and he went on and on about being a good mate, I was his brother, we were all brothers and I was letting everyone down who wanted to have a bit of fun. He said it would be a great way to finish off the day.'

'Peer pressure.' She closed her eyes for a moment, a tightness in her chest reminding her of past events she had witnessed. She had a fair idea of what Angus was going to tell her next. 'I've seen similar happen when I was growing up.'

'Yep, all those lectures your parents give you when you're a teenager, all those talks about how life can change in one split second because of a bad decision and how you can't go back on something stupid you do.'

His eyes were sad when he looked at her and she wanted to wrap her arms around him and tell him it was okay, she understood and he didn't need to tell her anymore. But he held his hand up. 'Don't feel sorry for me. I can see that look in your eyes and I don't want sympathy for what I'm going to tell you. I don't want sympathy ever. I just want you to know the real story.'

She whispered, 'Go on. What happened?'

'I drove out to the spare block. There were three other mates in the back of the car. No one had seat belts on and everyone was either stoned or drunk. They were all yelling at me from the back and going crazy, telling me to put my foot down, that I was being soft and driving like a girl. Sorry, their words, not mine. They were right, I wasn't going fast, I was just trying to placate them by swinging the wheel back and forth a bit. Mick started going crazy, he was in the passenger side in the front next to me. I think he'd had something other than pot because he was out of his mind. He stood on the car seat and balanced out the window, hanging onto the top of the car.

He was yelling out and waving a can of beer in the air. I slowed down, intending to come to a standstill, at the same time yelling at him to sit down as I tried to drag him back into the car.

'The rest is a bit of a blur, but over the years I've put the run of events into order. Plenty of time to do that when you're locked up for three years.'

Her eyes were wide and she looked straight at him. 'What happened?'

'The car hit a hole full of bulldust and I lost control for a minute. I hit the brakes but the car still had movement. The hole was deep and it flicked the car one way, jerking it around. I still can't believe it. We weren't going that fast and I'd been careful. The ride was just a pathetic attempt to shut him up.'

'Oh, my goodness. He was flung out, wasn't he?'

'He was. Everyone else was okay except Mick, who was still hanging out the window yelling like a wild man when it happened. He lost his grip and fell. There must have been a large rock right where he landed and he hit his head. We all jumped out and tried to help him but he slipped away.'

Angus put his head between his hands. Amy had no words. Where she had grown up similar accidents had happened. Teenagers had been killed and others carried injuries for the rest of their lives. She put her hand on his arm again and squeezed it. They sat silently for a long while until he finally sat up and turned to her. 'Thanks for listening. I haven't told many people that story since it happened, apart from the police that is.'

She was horrified. 'You went to jail for that?'

'Yep, I did my time. Mick's father was the local solicitor and another relative was a high-up judge in the city. They made sure I paid. To tell you the truth I'm glad I did go to jail, the guilt was unbearable and at least I felt like I gave my dues over the three years. The point is nothing will ever bring Mick back.'

She took a deep breath. 'I also lost friends in my teens. Stupid accidents, sometimes with no one to blame, although there was always someone who copped the brunt of it. The point is you were all in that together. Everyone was as much to blame as each other and at that age you think you're invincible.'

'When I was in jail, Mick's two older sisters visited me every week. They lived in Rockhampton and never missed seeing me.'

'Really? That says something.'

'They didn't blame me. They knew what Mick was like and they'd been wild in their day also. They fell out with their father after the court case and don't speak to him to this day. They still keep in touch with me. They tell me that Mick wouldn't have wanted me to be punished. They know what really happened.'

Suddenly the moon appeared over the top of the bushes, lighting up the area where they sat. 'Thanks for telling me the story,' Amy said. 'I feel like I understand you now. Where you've come from and what you've been through.'

He stared at her for a long while, sadness reflected in his eyes.

Finally, she broke the silence. 'I lost a best mate also. He was the passenger. Similar situation. All young and stupid. Drugs, alcohol and fast cars. He was my first real boyfriend and I should have been in the car with them, but we'd had an argument and I walked out and went home from the party where we were. His name was Mario. He was Italian, his parents owned the flashiest restaurant in town. But he was wild too and that night he was angry with me for leaving the party. I've always felt like it was my fault. His parents still live near my home. Sort of added to my reasons for moving away.' She stopped talking, her chest tight and the tears welling in her eyes. 'It could have been any of us. If you made it through those years unscathed you were lucky.'

Angus looked at the ground when he replied. 'It's hard to work out how to move on. Coming back here hasn't been easy but I'm sick of running away from it.'

'You've done well to return.'

'I'm glad I did for Nana and Grandpa, but I'm not sure it's where I want to be.'

As they gazed up at the moon she wondered if it was where she wanted to be either, but then where would she go if she left Matfield? She pondered another question but left it unspoken. Where was he going? What next for Angus Carmody?

CHAPTER 24

A weight lifted from Angus's shoulders. When he talked about the accident it felt like it had happened only yesterday, not twelve years ago. Over the years he'd thought about it so much it had been all-consuming, the guilt and loss hanging like a lead weight in his mind and heart. Now as an adult the guilt was still there, but even though he had been the one holding the steering wheel and therefore held responsible, he had finally accepted that it wasn't entirely his fault.

His other mates who had been in the car had long ago moved away and started their lives in a different area. They'd kept in contact with him when he was in jail and still called him a couple of times every year. They also carried the guilt and perhaps they were the only ones who understood what had happened that night.

He'd been comforted by Amy's words and her ability to listen without judgement and it felt special that she'd shared her sorrow and guilt about Mario. She knew the pain and grief of losing someone at such a young age.

When she rested her hand on his arm he knew that this weekend a true connection had been forged. She understood.

* * *

By the time they left on Sunday afternoon their friendship was cemented. With the radio blaring out random seventy's songs and the car windows down, letting the wind whip in through the car, Amy felt like she was a teenager again. She sang at the top of her voice, one of her dad's favourites, *Children of the Revolution*, vibrating noisily from the ute's speakers. Angus laughed at her, her feet up on the dashboard, her fingers poking his arm until he also sang along with the next song, a Meatloaf classic.

'My parents brainwashed Kailee and me with this music when we travelled around Australia. I know all the words to every song from the seventies and eighties.'

* * *

As they got closer to town a familiar angst filled her and she stopped singing and wound the window up. Tomorrow was the first day of the new term and although she had everything ready, for sure there would be more she needed to do. Because it was Monday she'd also need to be early for the meeting.

'You've gone quiet,' Angus said. 'You're not thinking about work are you?'

'I am. I actually feel sick.'

'It's just a job, Amy. Don't get so worked up about it.'

'I like to do a good job and I know that I do. The other

teachers in my staff room tell me that I'm doing great and the students and parents seem to like me. The kids are all passing and learning. They love their music classes and even their behaviour is better compared to when I started. I feel like I'm making a difference.'

'It's Elliot isn't it?'

'It's difficult to work under those conditions. I feel like I'm walking on eggshells all the time. Terrified in case I do anything wrong.'

'What would be the worst thing he could do to you?'

'Sack me.'

'And is that such a drama?'

'At this stage, probably not.'

'Wouldn't you just pack up and go somewhere else? I thought they needed teachers everywhere.'

She sat up. 'They do.'

'Maybe you need to take a different approach. Stand up for yourself. Don't worry about being sacked. If that happened it might be a good thing.'

'You know, you're right. We're independent children of the revolution.' She laughed. 'Although I think that was meant for those born in the fifties. But you're right, I should stand up for myself. If he sacks me, he sacks me. C'est la vie!'

'Yes. C'est la vie! Just do your best and don't go overboard with the hours you're putting in. If he threatens you, walk away from him. If he gives you more things to do that you can't possibly fit in tell him they are on your list of things to do. Make a list and show him if you need to. Don't go straight away when he calls you up for meetings. Walk to the beat of your own drum.'

'Wow. I like it!'

'It's worked for me. I suppose I did learn a few things from being inside all those years.'

'Okay. A new beginning. A new me.' She giggled as they pulled into her street. 'Pull up right outside my apartment please and make as much noise as you want. I don't care about anything anymore.'

He grinned broadly at her when he spoke. 'Not even Eliza Tuls! Bloody hell, I've created a monster.'

*T*heir timing was perfect and Eliza was sweeping the path outside her apartment when they pulled into the carpark. Amy had tiny shorts on and a midriff singlet, her feet bare, her hair wild and tangled from the wind. She jumped out of the car and called out loudly, 'Eliza, how are you? Good to see you.' Waving and cavorting around the car Amy hoisted her pillow under her arm and ushered Angus inside.

Laughing, he put her bag down, whispering as he looked back out through the front window. 'Did you see the look on her face? She nearly turned purple. I thought she was going to pass out.'

Amy threw her pillow on the lounge. 'Look what you've done to me. I don't care about anything anymore. This really is the new me.'

* * *

Angus stayed and made them both a coffee. They laughed and talked about everything they'd done and seen on the weekend. When he went to leave she wanted him to stay for longer, but work loomed for them both tomorrow and she needed to get some lessons ready for the week.

She hugged him, loving the feel of his arm around her as he hugged her back. 'Thank you, Angus, that was the best weekend ever. I feel like I know you a bit better now and I'm glad we talked about everything. Maybe we're both a bit lighter for sharing.'

He gave her a gentle squeeze. 'I'm rejuvenated also. Like a new person. That's what that campsite does for you though. It's a magical place. We'll go there again.'

'I promise I won't tell anyone about it. I'll see you at the pool tomorrow afternoon.'

'Five o'clock,' he replied. 'I'll be there. You want to watch out, I'm getting faster. By the end of the term I'll be beating you.'

* * *

She wished she could have maintained the carefree attitude and light feeling she'd got from that weekend. Sometimes it only took someone to point out the obvious and give you a few tips on how to deal with tricky situations. Angus was good at reading her and was also able to point her in the right direction. When he suggested what she could do to avoid certain situations, suddenly solutions became clearer and she could see a clear path to take. On Monday morning she'd been confident and carefree, organised, and ready to begin the term.

By the end of the day however, she felt frazzled. The

air-conditioning in her classroom had broken, most likely the wiring eaten by rats over the holidays. The internet was not working either, another wiring problem the technicians had said was probably the same glitch as the air con. If there was no internet she had no way of getting her emails. She'd left her phone in the staffroom, the constant messages from Edwin today almost too much to bear.

When the internet worked for a bit during the morning she'd managed to read some of the emails. The first one was from Elliot, who replied to her email about the wiring problem. He said she needed to try not to complain so much and a school rule was to have your phone on you at all times. Angus's advice sounded in her head and she did manage to put the problems to the back of her mind and focus on her students. When the rest of her emails came through at three in the afternoon, her inbox had flooded with messages from the office, particularly from Elliot. Most of them were generic and had been sent to all staff, however there was, she peered closer—of course there was—one addressed directly to her. The usual, URGENT, glaring at her in the heading. She read the rest of it quickly.

Please come to the office at four o'clock to explain why your attendance certificates for workplace health and safety as well as code of conduct courses have not been uploaded to the main folder. Gwen is waiting for them. This is an URGENT matter.

Her fingers flew across the keyboard. *Thank you for your email, Mr Garranto. Unfortunately, I have a prior appointment this afternoon so I cannot attend your meeting. I am available Wednesday afternoon at four. Thank you, Miss Coops.*

With that she hit send, closed her computer, packed up her bag and headed for her car. A new Amy. A new beginning.

* * *

It was a relief to get home early for once and she'd have time to do some things before going to the pool. No sooner had she shut the door and sat down than she heard a car pull up outside. A loud knock on the door startled her and she looked through the window to see who it was. Edwin's orange car was parked right outside her door. It was as good a time as any to tell him exactly what she needed to. She was tired and cranky. Perfect!

He leaned on the door frame, his aftershave wafting across her room as he looked her up and down. 'After-noon, beautiful, I've missed you. You're home early.'

She stood in front of him. 'I am. What can I do for you? I'm really tired and not in the mood for talking.'

He ran his hand through his hair. 'I've missed you. You haven't answered my calls. Are you going to ask me in? We haven't seen each other in ages.'

She stood in his way as he tried to walk in. 'Let's get something straight, Edwin. I went out with you once and that's all. I don't want to go on any more dates and to be honest I don't want to talk to you or see you. I have too many other things to do and you're just not my type. Nothing personal but that's how it is. Please stop ringing and pestering me.'

He growled. 'I don't know who you think you are. You're hanging around with that Angus, aren't you? I'm not stupid. Both of you weren't in town all weekend. I bet you were sleazing around together in the motel on the highway. That'd be about his standard.'

She crossed her arms. 'It's none of your business what I do but no, I wasn't there. What I do has nothing to do with you. Move on.'

His demeanour had changed completely and if it wasn't broad daylight and Gwen wasn't next door hanging out the window listening to every word, she would have been frightened. He had a dangerous look in his eye and his hands were clenched tightly by his side.

Venomous words flew from his mouth. 'You deserve each other. If you lay down with dogs you'll get their fleas. You two are much the same. Sleep around with whoever comes your way.' He leaned into her, his words spat out. 'I wouldn't touch you with a ten-foot pole. The word around town is that you're a hussy. Getting it on with half the teachers at school.'

'Where the hell do you get that garbage from? Leave now and do not ring me or message me again.'

'You're going to be sorry. I have a lot of sway with your school.' He threw her a sickly smile. 'If you thought it was tough going before now, then you ain't seen anything yet. I'm mates with half the staff there. Elliot might not be my friend but when I talk he'll have to act. Wait until they hear who you've been sleeping with. Angus Carmody. Convicted murderer and jailbird.'

She took a step back and slammed the door in his face, quickly locking it and pulling the barrel bolts firmly across. Just in case.

CHAPTER 26

*E*dwin left Amy's place and went straight to Angus's workshop. Angus had been under a car, working on the engine when he noticed Edwin's distinct clean leather boots standing firmly next to him. He lay on his back on a trolley and quickly pushed himself out from under the car. This time he was ready for whatever was to come.

There wasn't a violent bone in Angus's body but there was no way he was getting another black eye. Although he hated fighting, time in jail had taught him how to defend himself and he knew if Edwin came for him, this time he'd be quicker.

He didn't need to take any action though because when he stood up, his boss, Marcello, came from behind the counter. Edwin must have thought that Angus was there by himself and a look of shock crossed his face when he saw Marcello. Marcello was a third-generation mechanic of Italian stock and directly related to some of the mafia families in Sicily.

Marcello's brother-in-law had been in the same prison as Angus and when Marcello visited, he always booked extra visiting time to spend with Angus. Coming from the same small town and knowing the full story of the accident he had ensured that Angus was well looked after while he did his time. He talked him into completing a mechanic's course while he was on the inside and treated him like he was his own family. After all, Angus's Nana was a family friend and Angus's grandfather and him had been best mates. Why wouldn't he help him?

'You boys are all the same,' he'd said during one visit. 'Not a brain between you and that Mick, God bless his soul.' He crossed himself. 'He was the worst out of all you. It might well have been him in here for me to visit and you resting in the ground. Don't dwell on it, son, just do your time and when you need help, I'll be there.'

The day that Angus walked out of jail, Marcello had been there to pick him up and pay for his accommodation in Rockhampton. He'd bought him clothes and other items he needed, pushed his business card into Angus's pocket and told him whatever he needed was just a phone call away. Marcello had been true to his word and when Angus finally decided to return and live with Nana he'd worked as a mechanic for Marcello who badly needed staff.

Now the huge Sicilian man stood with his arms crossed, staring down at Edwin who suddenly looked very uncomfortable. 'What can we do for you, Mister Edwin?' Marcello said. 'Are you here to apologise for the black eye,' he tilted his head towards Angus. 'You're lucky he didn't hit you back.'

Edwin tried to remain confident but he knew he stood

on dangerous ground. 'This piece of shit needs to stay out of my way.'

Angus stood up and came closer to Edwin. 'Suits me. You stay out of mine and you stay away from Amy. Don't think I won't come for you, Edwin. Jail wasn't great but I learned how to survive and fight back.'

Marcello edged closer to Edwin. 'I got plenty of mates also. Some in Sicily but plenty here. They love a new challenge.'

Edwin backed out. 'Just stay out of my way,' he mumbled as he turned and disappeared around the corner.

The two men watched him as he drove out of the carpark. Marcello shook his head. 'He's got bad blood that one. I don't know how he fits into your family. Now, son, are you still intent on leaving at the end of this month?'

Angus patted Marcello fondly on his back. 'Yeah, only another few weeks. I've just got to tidy some things up at home before I leave.'

'I'll be sorry to see you go. You're the best worker I've had and you're like my own son. But I understand. I was the same at your age. Lucky I have those two grandsons coming in.'

'Thanks Marcello, I'll be sorry to leave here and I'm not sure where I am going, but yeah it's time to go.'

CHAPTER 27

*E*lliot had been relentless in his pursuit of Amy. The emails never stopped and although she maintained the attitude of not caring and trying to prioritise her workload, it still wasn't easy. A couple of times she was so tired she had fallen asleep on the lounge when she got home from work. Angus had missed her at swimming and one day she'd woken to his knocking at her door.

At first she was worried it was Edwin but she heard Angus call her name. When she let him in she burst into tears, his worried face peering into hers as he led her to the lounge.

'I'm going to go down there and sort Elliot out. This is ridiculous. You're so nice to everyone. Even Marcello my boss talks about you. His grandsons are in your class. They love you and say you make English interesting.'

She sniffled, blowing her nose with a tissue he passed her. 'They're both leaving in a couple of weeks. They hate school.'

'They do, but he says they love you. They're both going to do apprenticeships with Marcello anyway. It's a better option than staying at school and getting into trouble. Don't doubt yourself it's not you, it's bloody Elliot.'

'Please don't get involved. I should be able to look after myself. I'm getting to breaking point though.' She blew her nose again. 'I guess that's obvious. I'm seriously considering leaving. I have only a few boxes of belongings and a couple of pieces of furniture. It would be easy to pack it up and move back to the coast. I can't take much more of school. The only good thing is that Edwin has stopped annoying me. Thank goodness. I'm not sure why but there has been nothing, no message or calls. I even passed him in the main street the other day and he didn't even look sideways at me.'

'At least that's something. I tell you what, why don't I take you out to the boulders this weekend? We can hike and swim and I'll show you some other caves and paintings out there that are much bigger than the other ones we saw.'

'I have so much work to do.'

'Stuff it. C'mon, you're only young once, you can't be working every weekend.'

She sat up and dried her eyes. 'Thanks, Angus. I have to mark this weekend and we're expected to be at school for the concert on Sunday. I've been allotted to stand in the toilets in the breaks and make sure the kids aren't doing anything they shouldn't be.'

He wrinkled his nose. 'Yuck. How did you get that job?'

'Just lucky I guess. I'm not sure how I'm going to get from the stage to the toilets in the allotted time but everyone has got a list of jobs to do. Maybe we could camp again in a few weeks.'

A sheepish look crossed his face and he looked down. His words came out quiet and she wasn't sure she'd heard him right. 'I wanted to talk to you. I'm finishing up my job soon. I'm going to move away.'

She blinked several times. Her immediate response was to burst into tears again but she held them back. 'Really? Where are you going?'

When he looked up his gaze held hers. 'I don't know yet. Not sure. I just need to be away from here.'

'Wow. That's a big decision. I'll miss you.'

'Sounds like you won't be here much longer yourself.'

She wanted to say that he was the only stable person in her life who was worth staying in the town for, but she held her emotions in check. He wanted freedom and she obviously wasn't too high up on his list of reasons for staying. 'I understand.' She bit her lip to steady her emotions. 'I truly understand but I will miss you.'

* * *

The next week dragged and she hardly slept. If she was going to leave she would need to start looking for another job somewhere else. The idea of going back to the coast was not appealing and she scoured the internet, pouring over maps and thinking about where she'd like to work. There were hundreds of teacher vacancies from one end of Australia to the other. Remote, city, private, public, wherever she wanted to go. Nothing called out to her though and she spent the nights tossing and turning, thinking about what to do.

On Thursday afternoon she went to the pool. Angus hadn't been there all week and an emptiness filled her. The look on his face when he'd told her he was leaving; those dark thoughtful eyes that she might never see again. She was on her third lap when she noticed him dive into the water and swim alongside her. Stretching her arms out and kicking hard she quickly outpaced him, her powerful strokes driven by an anger at how nothing had worked out for her in Matfield.

The sun was low when she stood up and pulled herself out of the water. She hadn't even noticed when he'd left the pool, she'd been so transfixed with her laps. Her muscles ached and the cool of the water was refreshing after the taxing bite of the relentless heat. It was nearly winter but the days were still hot, the sky clear without a promise of any rain to come. Angus was still there and he walked out from the changeroom and passed her a towel. 'Wow. You're on fire. That was fast. There was no way I could keep up with you today.'

She gave him a small smile. There was no use pretending that she was happy, everything felt dull, useless and with no direction.

'You seem down.'

She shrugged. 'Maybe. We're not supposed to be happy all the time are we.'

They stood staring at each other. When he put his hand on her arm she knew it was goodbye and she felt the tears threatening to spill. Wiping her face with her towel she looked back at him.

'When do you leave?'

'I was going to leave next week. How many more weeks of school do you have left before the holidays?'

'Two, if I make it.'

'Have you thought about what you're going to do?'

'I'm leaving. I haven't told any of the students yet but I'm not coming back after the holidays. There are plenty of jobs out there, and,' she hesitated and looked down at her feet, 'I might get out of education. Maybe teaching is not for me.'

'Hey,' he gently squeezed her arm, forcing her to look up. 'Don't do that to yourself, you're a great teacher.'

Her body felt heavy and she folded her arms. 'I'll work it out.'

He shuffled his feet and ran his hand through his hair. 'Actually, I came here today hoping that you'd be here. Will you come out to my place for dinner? I've mostly packed up but I've still got some food there.'

A heavy sadness pressed down and she went to reply but Angus interrupted. 'I won't take the excuse that you have work to do. I want to show you something before I go. Please, Amy, I'd really like you to come out home.'

* * *

It hadn't taken her long to go home and get changed. She pulled on a summery floral dress that came to just above her knees. Her hair had grown longer since she'd moved here and it was now down past her waist. She clipped it back on one side and threw on her sandals. When she looked in the mirror her face was despondent and she turned quickly away. Twenty-five years old now, her birthday had come and gone last week, and no-one had even known. The only consolation had been a long phone call with her sister and parents. There was no direction in her life. Her dreams of a fulfilling career had not worked out. Maybe the next job and town would be better.

* * *

Angus had gone to a lot of trouble and a small table was set up under the lean-to on the side of his cottage. He'd borrowed some elegant China plates and cups from Nana, trying hard to avoid her questions. 'We're just friends, Nana. Remember, that was your idea and it's worked out. We're good mates. I wanted to do something nice for Amy before I go.' Nana yelled out to him from where she was bringing in washing from the clothesline. He called back loudly, making sure she could hear. 'Yeah, I know, she's a nice girl and yes I might try and stay in contact with her. I have also given your suggestion some consideration. We both have our own things we want to do. It's just dinner Nana, nothing else.'

* * *

Amy laughed when she saw the table. 'How lovely is this. Is this how you eat every night?'

'I thought it would be a nice way to say goodbye.'

Her face fell when he said that and he quickly changed the subject, talking instead about the weather. Angus had prepared crumbed fish and salad. 'I'm not a great cook but I love making salads. There're two different sorts here and hang on, I have a potato bake I need to get out of the oven.'

He'd watched Amy from inside as he lifted the dish from the oven. She was quiet and he knew she was trying to make decisions, much the same as he was, about which direction to go next.

When they'd finished dinner they both sat back and looked up at the stars. 'I'm going to miss this,' she said. 'I'll miss you and I'll miss the night sky. I'm not sure I'll miss anything else though.'

'You sound definite that you're leaving.'

'Yes, I've decided. I've let a few of my friends at work know, but no one else at this stage. I haven't been offered a contract for next term anyway, so I'm under no obligation to let Elliot know. If he had any decency he would have told me that he wasn't going to offer me any more work. I've emailed and asked but there has been no response so I take it that my contract will end this term.'

They'd talked for a bit longer and he could tell she had no idea what she was going to do or where she was going to move to. He stood up. 'Come with me. I want to show you something.'

She followed him to one of his sheds, waiting as he swung open the large wooden barn doors. An owl flew out and she squealed as it brushed past her face, its large eyes staring straight at her. He fumbled around in the darkness until he found the light switch. With one flick the entire shed lit up, large fluoro bulbs hanging from the ceiling casting their glow throughout the massive shed.

In centre place was his grandfather's old red truck and Amy ran her hand over the bonnet. 'Thank goodness you came along that first day I met you,' she said. 'I'd still be stuck out there.'

He walked towards the back of the shed. 'Come back here, I want to show you my latest purchase. She's a beauty and I've spent a long time getting it to where I want it.'

* * *

Amy hadn't known what to expect when she followed Angus into the shed. She suspected he may have bought a new tractor or a motorbike. She would never have guessed the vehicle that he was showing her now. A blue and white VW Kombi van, with a canvas pop-up top, a sliding door and roof racks was in front of her. She ran her hand over its surface, automatically grasping the handle and sliding the door open. Angus leaned in beside her and flicked a light switch on that lit up the back of the van.

Inside the van was very much like the one she had travelled around Australia in with her parents when she was a kid. There was a small table with bench seats, a gas stove and a sink. The wood panelling on the walls was the same and the floral curtains hanging in front of the small windows brought back childhood memories.

'Wow. This is very similar to the one my parents had. Remember I told you we travelled around in it.'

'Yes, I do remember that. I'd had my eye on this one for a while. A mate of mine on the coast travelled in it last year and I'd told him if he ever wanted to get rid of it to let me know. I've spent a few months revamping it and fixing up the engine. She's a beauty.'

'It is,' she said, sitting down on the bench seat inside. 'I love the curtains. They look like the original ones from the sixties.'

'Nana made them. She had the material in her sewing box. She covered the cushions for me also.'

He sat down opposite her, his eyes looking over the interior. I've fixed up the pop-up top. The canvas was broken but I've spent some money on that to make sure it's right and won't leak.'

'Is this what you're going to leave in?'

'Yep. This is it.'

'What day are you going?'

He stood up and she followed him back out. The door slid across and he clicked it shut. She stood with her arms crossed, waiting for him to answer.

'I was going to leave on Friday. I've still got quite a bit to do and get into order before going though.'

'This might be the last time I see you then. I also have a lot to do before I leave the week after.' She ran her hand over the blue paint, her words getting stuck in her throat. 'I hope you, well I guess you'll, you know, have a great time. Wherever you go.'

His dark eyes looked straight into hers. 'I wondered if you'd be interested in coming with me?'

She blinked several times. Did he mean coming for a drive before he went? 'What do you mean?'

'Come with me. I want to know if you're interested in joining me. I can wait to leave until the week after. I'm taking the swags so you could sleep in the van and I'll be outside in the swag. Just friends, no strings attached.'

'Are you seriously asking me to go with you?'

His lips curled into a smile. 'Yes. Why not? Come with me. On an adventure.'

She narrowed her eyes, looking from him and then to the van and back again. 'That would be a very impulsive thing to do and not normally something I would jump into. Also, I have just completed four years of university, I'm trying to begin a teaching career and have a rather large uni fee bill to pay.'

He grinned back at her. 'Yep. Impulsive, spontaneous, something out of the ordinary.'

She looked back over the van. 'Where are you going?'

He held his hand up and pointed out through the open shed door. 'Left.'

'Left, where?'

'Just, left, at this stage.'

'You really want me to come with you?'

'Yes, I do. I wouldn't ask you otherwise. We get on great, you want something different and both of us are leaving here and looking for who knows what. I want to do this while I'm young and there's nothing except Nana to keep me here. She's happy for me to go. She understands. I hadn't said anything to you before now because I wasn't sure when I was going to leave, but now that you're certain you're going to look for something else,' he paused, a wide grin across his face, 'It's perfect timing. If it doesn't work out we can go our separate ways. Nothing ventured, nothing gained, as Nana would say.'

Amy's heart thumped hard and suddenly she was excited about the time ahead. Angus's offer had come completely out of the blue, but in that moment she was up for something different. 'I'd have to leave my car somewhere.'

'You can store it in here,' he waved his arms around. 'There's plenty of room, or we can leave it at my work and they'll sell it for you.'

'Would your nana mind if I left it here? Do you have a time limit on how long you're going for?'

'I have no idea how long. Maybe if I, or we, if you come with me, find somewhere that we love, well who knows. I'm keeping an open mind on how long or where to eventually end up. That's part of the adventure, not knowing how the journey ends or if it ever does. And as for Nana minding,' he chuckled, 'she suggested the idea to me, saying that perhaps you might be interested in doing some travelling considering you weren't happy at the school.'

'She's quick to pick up on things. I ran into her the other afternoon. She was in town collecting her mail. We had a cup of tea together at the café. She didn't have long as she had a hairdresser appointment but we sat for an hour or so and talked. She's a bit sneaky because she never said anything to me about you going away and she must have known.'

'I did ask her not to say anything to anyone. I didn't want to explain to the others in the family why I'm going.'

'Aha. You know she did ask me a few questions about where I'd travelled and what my plans were. I mentioned I was thinking of quitting and going elsewhere. The more I think about it, I can now see where her questions were going. She looked like she was having fun. Obviously she was storing all that information and then had ammunition when she suggested me going with you.'

'Once she said it, I loved the idea. I'm not sure I would have asked you otherwise. It didn't enter my head that you might be interested in coming. As soon as Nana said it though, I thought that perhaps you might. We'll have a great time and it will be cheap living. That's if you decide to join me.'

'That's the other thing, I don't have much money behind me.'

'We can pick fruit or I'll get mechanic work and you could even do some relief teaching. There's work everywhere on the road and we won't need much money. It will be simple living.'

Her head spun. This was not in her plans and not even something she had ever thought of doing. But her mind whirled, it would be an adventure. She followed him out of the shed. 'Think about it,' he said. 'Go home and work out if you'd like to come.' His face was alight with enthusiasm. 'We'd be great together. Friends, we're good friends.'

She stopped in her tracks, her arms once again crossed. He turned and came back to her. 'Is that all?' she asked. 'Is that all you want, just friends.'

He took a deep breath and she could tell he was thinking hard. 'Just friends, for now. I'm not looking for a relationship, but... I'll be honest, I love spending time with you. You've become my soul mate. Let's see how we go, take it as it comes.'

CHAPTER 28

They'd talked until late in the night. Amy wanted to make sure if she went with Angus they would go halves in everything and share the decisions. 'I don't want to be just tagging along. It would be better for me if our ideas were equal,' she said.

'Of course. That's why we work well together. We're even.'

He was very relaxed about the direction they would travel; the, *turn left*, plan. 'You can decide where we go if you like,' he said. 'I've looked at a map but everywhere seems good. I'm happy to talk about where you want to go and work it out together.'

She shrugged. 'I don't care. I like your idea of, *left*.'

* * *

By the time she got home, her head was spinning with ideas. It would be easy to pack up her boxes and furniture and send them back to her parents. She'd just need to work out what clothes to take on the trip and what to get rid of. The savings she had, would do her for a long while if she was careful with how she spent. From her childhood she knew that camping life was simple and there was little need for possessions. The best part was now she had a plan after leaving Matfield. No more school, no more meetings, and no more Elliot.

It probably wasn't the best move to make for her career but teaching was always something she could go back to at any time. It was okay to take a break and besides, if they had treated her better she would have stayed. The students were manageable, and most of the staff were great, but the overriding bullying of Elliot and his crew were intolerable and it was time to draw a line in the sand, or, she giggled, a line in the dust.

When she unlocked and went into her apartment, she closed the door and leaned back on the wall, closing her eyes. Travelling in a Kombi van to who knew where, and with Angus. She pulled out her phone and messaged him. He'd asked her to let him know when she was safely home. 'I'M HOME AND I'M COMING WITH YOU. LEFT, IS FINE WITH ME.'

*E*lliot's face coloured a shade of purple when she handed him her letter to officially state that she would be leaving at the end of the term. 'But that's just next week,' he spluttered. 'Gwen has a new contract drawn up for you that will see you teach here until the end of the year. It's impossible to get teachers, particularly music and maths teachers. The situation is even worse than when we first employed you. You can't leave, we've put so much work into your training. We've given you so much help and what we're looking for is stability in our teaching staff.'

Gwen pursed her lips and looked at Amy over the top of her glasses. 'I have your new contract here. It's drawn up, ready for you to sign.' She passed it to Amy. 'You can't leave with such short notice. We won't be able to find someone else now. It's only a couple of weeks and the new term begins. Sign on the line there, thanks.'

Amy stood firm. 'I asked several times about the renewal of my contract but no one ever got back to me.'

She turned to Elliot. 'If you remember I came to your office a couple of weeks ago and said that I needed to know if my contract was going to be extended. You told me I would have to just wait and see. That new teachers were at the bottom of the list.'

Elliot mumbled under his breath before replying. 'I had to consider student numbers and other teaching staff. You absolutely cannot leave. You're leaving a burden for other teachers if we can't fill your position plus, think of your students. If you have no loyalty to the school or staff then perhaps consider the impact on the students.'

'I have considered it but I have made my mind up and I will be leaving.'

Gwen's face had turned a shade of red. 'You can't.'

'I can and I am. I've already checked with the department and I'm in my full rights as I was only on a six-month contract. Perhaps if you'd been more supportive I might have stayed. It's also nearly the end of term and you've never once talked to me about what I needed to plan for next term or what was going to happen.'

'That's what we're doing now. We have your timetable ready; maths, English and music,' Elliot said as he handed her a piece of paper, her timetable for next term printed on it.

She scanned the timetable. 'I can see that it's similar to this term and you've done the same and have Mrs Beets on some of the music classes when she isn't a music teacher. I understand that sometimes that happens in schools however Mrs Beets has been on leave the entire time I have been here and I am aware that she is also on leave next term. That means that a relief teacher takes the class or they are supervised in an area near another class and rarely if ever get to participate in an actual music lesson. As you know, I have had parents email me and ask for me to take those classes.'

Elliot growled and stood up behind his desk. 'You have plenty of music students. You need to learn to teach what you're given. As a junior teacher don't ever think you'll get the classes you want.' He pushed his hand through his oily strands of hair, the perspiration starting to run down his face even though the air conditioning was on and the room was cool.

'Wouldn't it make sense if it is consistency that you are after, to have me on the music classes instead of a relief teacher? It makes it very difficult to run a full music program, including band and choir, for the school when half the students aren't even being taught the basics in their music classes. I have raised this and several other issues with you on numerous times, however to no avail. These problems have added to the reasons for me leaving.'

Elliot's voice was raised when he replied. 'You will teach maths.'

'I will not teach maths. I am leaving.'

'You won't get a reference from me if you do go. No consistency or loyalty. Where do you think you are going to get another job? Wherever it is, the first thing they'll do is ring me and I'll tell them exactly how much trouble you've been. You're late for everything, can't follow basic instructions and think that you have the right to question my authority. Where the hell do you think you will go from here?'

A pause of silence filled the room and both Elliot and Gwen stared at her, no doubt hoping to intimidate her and get her to change her mind. Neither had ever shown her any respect or care and she looked from one to the other, before throwing her most endearing smile their way. 'Thank you both for your time.' She held out her resignation letter, waiting for Elliot to take it from her. Neither of them moved though, their faces stony, their arms folded.

Taking a step forward she placed it on Elliot's desk. 'I don't care what you think and as to where I'm going. Left. I'm going, left.'

CHAPTER 30

School had ended for the term and for Amy, her career, was also finished. No more lessons, students or classes, until who knew when. The desk she had sat at for the last six months was now empty, the shelves no longer stacked with books and marking, and her timetable and name badge had been thrown in the bin. The teachers in her staffroom gathered around, some of them also preparing to leave by the end of the year. They had kept her sane over the last two terms and she hugged them back, promising to keep in touch and fill them in on her travels.

As she drove out the gate for the last time a weight lifted from her shoulders. Now all there was left to do was to clean out the apartment. Most of the boxes had been picked up by the couriers and tonight she would pack her bags and take her car to Angus's place.

They'd talked on the phone twice a day since she'd made her decision and he'd come over several times to help her pack and clean out the rooms.

There was an air of excitement as she looked at the empty rooms. Done. Everything was sorted.

* * *

That night she left her car at Angus's place. She'd leave it in the shed and then after a while when she knew how long she'd be away, she'd work out what to do with it.

They'd positioned it in the corner and stacked some of her other belongings near it. 'Not that anyone else will be in here anyway,' Angus said. 'But at least it's all out of the way. Nana had been waiting on her front steps to say goodbye and Amy gave her a hug, always in awe of how sprightly and energetic the old lady was. 'Well, my dear, the end of another chapter for you,' Nana said.

'It is. It really is and I'm excited to start the next stage.' She turned to Angus. 'Who knows where we'll end up or what we'll see.'

'Angus leaned on the verandah post. 'It should work out okay because we both like hiking and exploring different places. I told Amy that you suggested it.'

Nana gave a little smile and her blue eyes sparkled with mischief. 'I said right from the start that you two would be great friends. I could tell it from the moment I met you, Amy. It makes sense to go away together. Now, remember to look after each other and I'll be looking after both of you in my thoughts. A postcard now and then would be nice.'

'I'm not sure they have postcards anymore, Nana,' Angus said. 'I can easily ring and have a chat every so often. That way you'll know where we are and what's happening.'

'Well, anyway, keep in touch and both of you remember that...' she gave a little cough and smiled sweetly before continuing, 'remember, well, even friends have to make compromises and get used to each other's ways.' She put her hand on her heart. 'You're both young and with your whole life in front of you. Enjoy, enjoy, enjoy.'

'I hope you're okay here without Angus,' Amy said as she hugged Nana again.

'Oh, I'll be fine. One of my great-nieces is moving into the house here with me next weekend. She's seventeen and is keen to come and live here and do some work with Grandpa's cattle. It's going to work out perfectly. Besides I'm never alone, Grandpa is always with me.' She looked up at the sky. 'He's always just nearby, taking care of me.'

When Angus dropped her home Amy felt like the adventure had already begun. There was just a bit of cleaning to do tonight and a few last things to pack up and then she was ready. Ready to hit the road.

CHAPTER 31

*A*ngus had also spent the night cleaning up his cottage and packing a couple of last items in the van. Nana's excitement was contagious and he couldn't wait for the trip to begin. Amy would be good company and add an exciting dimension to the trip he had planned. For once he didn't want to be by himself and sit alone at night. Now he had the urge to be able to share the experience, to talk about what was to come and most of all—he stopped what he was doing and took a deep breath—he had to admit to himself that he was the happiest when he was with Amy. It was like a breath of fresh air listening to her and he loved trying to help her work out problems or make suggestions that would help. Although she was independent and headstrong, sometimes a bit of a nudge or a word from him saw her change direction and put things into perspective. They were going to make a good travelling team.

* * *

Nana emptied her teapot over the back verandah of her house. An owl called out from a dilapidated wooden building not far from where she was. She squinted and picked out the bird's dark shape on the roof. The small building had once been their only toilet, the outhouse, and she smiled, recalling how Angus used to hate going out there by himself once it was dark. Now it was only used to store old farm equipment and hadn't been used for many years; decades even. Angus had also moved on and the worries that she had for him for so many years after the accident were finally leaving her. Even though there were moments where he was a bit quiet or down, mostly he seemed at peace these days.

Time moved quickly and the older she got the faster it seemed to travel. The moon shone across the yard and she noticed another owl sitting on her clothesline, its eyes glinting in the light from the moon. A slight breeze blew across her face and the air of the outback swirled around her. The familiar smells of dust, cow manure, and a slight tang of eucalyptus leaves from a tree nearby, filled her senses. She would miss Angus. He had been there when Grandpa needed help and then helped nurse him when he was sick. But now, just like Grandpa, he was going to leave the small town again. This time it was on a happier note and she sent a silent prayer up to Grandpa to look after him and Amy as they went.

As always Grandpa spoke back to her, his words in her mind making her nod and smile. He had been quite a romantic and she knew he would delight in Angus travelling with such a lovely young girl. 'They say just friends, Grandpa,' she whispered into the dark. 'We will see.'

* * *

The next morning, Angus arrived at Amy's place just before the sun came up. He helped her carry her two bags to the van, sliding the door open and putting them on the floor at the back. When he opened the front door for her and held her hand as she hopped up into the passenger's seat, they grinned at each other. They were still wearing the same smiles on their face as he started the engine and they slowly rumbled out of her carpark.

'Which way?' he asked, looking up and down the road. 'Left?'

'Sounds great,' she replied. 'Head left.'

CHAPTER 32

*N*either spoke until they reached the first intersection south of the town. Angus noted that Amy was unusually quiet and he let it be. It was a good start for both to think quietly about the travels ahead and he was still impressed that she had made such a big decision so spontaneously. For him, although it was exhilarating to finally be on the road, he'd had a long time to plan the time away and think about what a nomadic lifestyle might bring. He frowned. Was he running again? Was this the easy way to get away from Edwin and the small town where he could sometimes still feel the nasty jibes and unspoken whispers?

'Penny for your thoughts,' Amy said as he slowed and then stopped by the side of the road.

He ignored her statement which he knew was more of a question to try and work out what he was thinking about. But he wasn't used to sharing too much and he wasn't about to start, particularly in the morning. Working out your own problems and getting over them was his motto. He wasn't sure it always worked, but that's what he intended to stick with.

They both peered through the windscreen of the van, a thick ball of red dust coming from the south, throwing a hazy tinge over the road in that direction. 'That'll be the trucks coming in ready for the auction tomorrow. It's a big day. Nana has some of her mob going there. They should fetch a high price. Those fellas take them back to the coast, to the saleyards there.'

He wound up his window, waiting for the truck to pass. The driver gave them a wave as he looked down at them.

They sat and waited until the dust had cleared. 'I'm surprised you didn't hang around until after the auction,' Amy said.

'No. Nana wouldn't have it. I asked, but she wanted me to leave when I had planned. Otherwise, she said I'd never end up going.'

'True, I suppose. Sometimes it's better to not think too hard and just do it.' She giggled, revealing the dimple in her cheek.

'Yeah, look at you. Pretty big decision.'

'I know. I don't think the reality has set in yet. Doesn't seem quite real. Your Nana seemed pleased that we were travelling together when I spoke to her last night.'

'Oh, she was pleased alright. She got her way. She told me, fate is a funny thing.'

'It is and it's even weirder to think that Elliot set it in motion by telling me to take the wrong road the day of the funeral.'

'I've never thought of it like that. Maybe we would have found each other and become friends anyway.'

The dust cleared and the road ahead was now visible. If they continued straight they would be heading in a southern direction which would take them through a few small towns until finally reaching the New South Wales border. On the left were two roads, one that would lead to the eastern coastline and the other pointing more to the north. Amy pulled a comical face at him. 'Two choices to the left. Which one Angus?'

Holding the steering wheel with both hands he leaned over it and looked up through the windscreen and then sideways. Back and forth. Back and forth.

'You choose,' he finally said.

'What. No way. The first decision is yours.'

He hesitated while he thought. 'I tell you what. If we take this second one on the left that leads to the coast, we could go and visit your family. You talk about them a lot. How about we camp along the coast a bit, go and visit them and they can meet the person you're going to be travelling with. Then we can go from there.'

She sat upright, her eyes alight. 'Really? You'd really do that? I would love to see them before we take off to who knows where and ...' she grimaced, 'my mother has been ringing me constantly, trying to find holes in my plans, or should I say, non-plans. I don't think they're very happy with me throwing in my job and they don't know you—as they told me over the phone—from a bar of soap.'

'I figured as much. Nana has also been in my ear that she thought it would be the right thing to do. I think it's only fair. That way they won't worry about you once we leave there.'

Nana had suggested the idea, reminding him that Amy's parents would probably worry about her firstly leaving her job and then also going away with someone she had not long known and who they didn't know at all. He promised her he'd do the right thing.

'Okay then.' Amy pointed ahead. Take the second one on the left. Oh, my goodness, Mum and Dad will be beside themselves, not to mention my sister. Seriously, they all think I've lost my mind; especially Dad. He can't understand that I did all that study and now I'm just throwing it away. I mean they're great about me doing my own thing and all for trying something new. They just worry that's all.'

Angus steered back onto the road, the van taking a while to get back to speed. He'd put a new motor in it and gone over everything with a fine toothcomb but it was an old vehicle so the speed it travelled at wasn't quite up to the modern cars. They both settled back in their seats. 'I get your dad's point of view,' Angus said. 'You have done a lot of study. I'd say you'll go back to teaching one day. I mean you might have a break, but it would be a shame to write it off when you've only been at that one school.'

She shook her head. 'No. I've decided to put it all behind me. It's just not for me. The system, the bureaucracy and people like Elliot.'

'Not everywhere would be like Matfield. I'm sure most places would be run better and treat the staff well.'

'I'm not going to find out. That's the second part of my getaway. No more teaching. Ever. I've been looking and there's heaps of fruit picking and other casual work. It doesn't seem to matter where you go.'

'Up to you, I guess,' Angus said, leaving the conversation at that. He understood why Amy had left the school but it was a waste of a good teacher. He'd seen her working with the choir and interacting with some of the other students the day of the funeral. They loved her. She was a natural.'

'Do you think we'll get work?' she said, changing the subject.

'Without a doubt. Every little town is screaming out for workers. You'll see as we go. Different jobs everywhere.'

They'd camped that first night in one of the national parks. There was only one other tent that was a fair distance away from where they were, so they felt like they had the place to themselves. Angus pulled out two chairs and set up a small fold out table next to the van. They'd camped near the riverbank, a cluster of twisted paperbark trees providing them with some shade. 'There's no rain in sight,' Angus said. 'I wouldn't camp here if there was, because...' he swept his hand across the plains stretched in front of them, 'this whole area goes under when it floods.'

'Really,' Amy said, her eyes wide. 'It's so dry you wouldn't think it would ever see that much water out here.'

She was stretched out in one of the chairs, her feet up on a tree stump that had been useful for resting her drink on when they'd had dinner. He'd given in and let her cook. A tasty meal she had whipped up in no time. While they'd been driving they'd worked out their finances and how they would split the bills. Both had good savings that would last for a while, until they found places to work along the way.

Everything would be halved. Fuel, food, and although he'd tried to change her mind, she was also adamant if there were repairs to the car she would also pay half.

'It's only fair that I pay for half the parts of whatever is needed. You'll be fixing it for free so I need to contribute.'

Lesson one for him today. She was stubborn and as much as he'd tried to win the argument, he had given in. He glance at her out of the corner of his eye. Her legs were stretched out in front of her and she looked upwards at the sky, its expanse covered in stars that filled the dark void. She was dressed much the same as he was. Shorts and a t-shirt, and he smiled, riding boots on her feet. He wondered if she'd packed any of her white sandals in the bag that she'd brought, stacked in the back of the van with his. Tomorrow they'd have to work out where they were going to put their clothes. There were only a couple of small drawers and he was happy to leave his belongings in either a box or his bag.

She turned to him, pushing her hair back behind her ears, her face lit with the glow of the campfire. Pulling out a packet from behind her back, she giggled, holding the packet in the air and shaking it.

Now she had his full attention. He sat up straight, pulling his feet down from where they rested on the same stump as hers were. 'Marshmallows. Are you kidding me. I told you I'd organise the food to begin with and not to bring anything.'

She shook the packet, using her other hand to pull out two long sticks she had also hidden behind her. 'So, you don't want any?'

Her eyes teased and he grinned, feeling like he was a kid again. 'Maybe not.'

'Don't like marshmallows?'

'I never said that.' He went to grab the bag but she pulled her hand away. 'Say, please.'

'Please. Please Miss Amy, may I have a marshmallow?'

'I'm not a teacher anymore.'

He leaned sideways towards her, flashing her his best smile. 'Please Amy, I would love some marshmallows.'

The night had turned into a feast of roasted marshmallows and hot cocoa. When neither of them could eat any more and agreed that it was time to turn in for their first night, Amy had taken a torch and gone to use the bathroom facilities. They had checked out the amenities earlier and they were clean and spacious, with solar hot water supplied if needed.

Today had been a perfect start and he was pleased that she seemed happy with the arrangements and provisions so far. It had all been part of the planning when she'd agreed to travel with him. He was already well equipped for the trip ahead and there was no need to take excess. After all there was limited room in the van and the lighter and simpler they travelled the better. It would be interesting to see how she went though. They were only supplied with limited basic items and sooner or later most people wanted more.

Angus liked life simple. He gazed up at the stars, a satellite tracking from west to east catching his eye. This was going to be an interesting trip. Like the light above that travelled alone, moving across clusters or constellations of stars, he too was used to moving across the path of others without stopping. Always going forward, but alone. Now however he had the company of Amy, a friend to enjoy and share with whatever came next.

* * *

When Amy returned from her shower she snuggled back in her chair, the fire drawing her to sit back down in front of its warmth. She was so tired from the day of travel, as well as the weeks leading up to leaving, that after a short while she fell asleep. Angus nudged her gently on her shoulder. 'Hey, mate. Crawl into the back of the van. Your bed's made up.'

She stood up, still half asleep. The fire was now glowing embers and she looked to the side of it. Angus had set up his swag, a small lantern in front of it giving off some light. He steered her towards the van and she noticed a towel over his shoulder. 'The showers are great,' she managed to say before crawling across the bed and laying her head on the pillow.

He grinned at her through the open door. 'All okay?'

She lifted her head a little to smile back at him. 'Perfect. Thankyou.'

'See you in the morning,' he replied, before sliding the door across.

She snuggled into the comfy bed, taking one last glimpse out the side window at the stars, before falling into a deep sleep.

CHAPTER 33

*W*hen she woke the next morning it took her a while to work out where she was. She must have got hot during the night because she'd kicked off the blankets and even the sheet. She searched the bed. Even the baggy t-shirt she usually wore to bed had been tossed off and she quickly found it and pulled it over her head.

The sun was just making its way over the top of the shrubs that grew next to where they were parked. Lying on her back she took a good look around the back of the van. Where she had slept was enough for two people to sleep and it could also turn into a table and bench seat, handy for when it was wet weather and you couldn't sit outside. There was a tiny sink and gas stove along one side which Angus had said they probably wouldn't use. He didn't want to cook inside and it was easier to use the tub and gas stove he had set up for outside. From the back door of the van, you could access the storage, their bags and boxes with other essentials stacked neatly in that area. She could see why he had said to only bring the absolute minimum. There wasn't much room for anything that wasn't essential.

She sat up again and pulled on her shorts. Bathroom visit first and then she'd see if Angus was awake. There was no sign of life from the swag so she headed to the facilities to freshen up. It felt so right to be travelling with Angus and she was pleased they had talked about and agreed that theirs was a friendship relationship rather than delving into a romance. Her feelings for him were all over the place and travelling in a small van and being together most of the time would let her see sides of him that perhaps she hadn't encountered before.

Although he came across confident and friendly she had also glimpsed a different side of his personality. There were times when he seemed to shut down and avoid certain topics. It usually happened when the conversation became deep and meaningful.

* * *

By the time she returned to the campsite he had stoked the fire, a billy hanging over it, the steam just starting to filter out from under the tin lid. She had so much to tell him, and she launched into a conversation about how good the showers were and how clean the amenities were. He nodded and smiled back at her, reclining back in the chair, a cup of tea in his hand.

Making her way to the van she threw her towel and clothes on the bed before grabbing a cup and making her way back to where he sat. She rambled on, going over the events of the previous day and asking questions about where they were going that day. It took her a while to realise he was just nodding politely in reply, but so far had hardly spoken a word since she returned from the showers. He got up and adjusted the billy which was now boiling. She held her mug out and he filled her cup before sitting back down.

'Would you like me to make you some toast?' she asked. 'I'm going to make some for myself.'

'No thanks,' he answered.

She scrunched up her face. He seemed angry or upset about something. 'Is everything alright.?

'Yep.'

'Didn't you sleep well? If you like I can sleep in the swag and you sleep in the back of the van. I don't mind.'

He didn't answer and she racked her brain for something she might have said or done last night that might have upset him. She'd never seen him so quiet. 'It's okay. I'll move my stuff off the bed and swap you for the swag. That way you'll get a good night's sleep. I can sleep anywhere.'

As she went to stand up he turned to her. 'It's okay, Amy. We're not swapping.'

By now she was really perplexed. He was upset about something. Was he regretting asking her to join him? Had the fact that his planned trip was no longer being taken alone just sunk in.?

As if he read her thoughts he answered her doubts. 'The sleeping arrangements are perfect.'

'Well, what's wrong? Something is obviously bothering you. I'm sorry, Angus, but I'm not a mind reader and if you don't like the way I've done something or you're starting to have regrets about asking me on this trip then you had better say something now. I'm not used to beating around the bush and playing mind games. Let me have it. Just say if you've changed your mind. It's not too late. You could leave me at Mum and Dad's, I'll …'

He looked at the ground and shook his head. 'Sorry Amy. There isn't anything wrong. This is just me in the morning.' Looking up at her he gave her a half-smile. 'I don't function or speak usually until I've had my morning coffee and sorted my thoughts for the day.'

'Oh. Okay. Are you sure that's all it is because it seems like there is something wrong and that you are cranky with me?'

He stood up and picked up the billy, bringing it over to her to fill up her cup. 'I promise there isn't anything wrong. I'm not a morning person. You can ask Nana. They all know to leave me alone most mornings until morning tea time. I can tell you're not like that.'

'Hmph,' she said, scowling at him. 'That's a bit boring. The morning is when I have most of my energy. I like to talk about what I've thought of during the night or what my plans are for the day. This is when I like to thrash out different ideas and bounce ideas off whoever is with me. I can see that's not going to happen. That's a shame because I've missed those early morning conversations with someone while living by myself.'

* * *

Angus stifled a chuckle. She was way more talkative than usual and she couldn't sit still, moving from her chair over to the table to get something to eat and then back to the fire to put a log on. It was a well-known fact in his family that he was grumpy until about ten o'clock most days. Anyone he lived with had come to accept it and left him alone until he was ready to join in or talk. It also hadn't been helped by his time in jail. The mornings had been a good time to say even less and keep your head down. He'd always kept his mouth shut, even when he'd been pushed so hard that he could have fought back. But he'd only been a small fry in the big scheme of prison life and luckily his skills in the mechanics' section of the workshop had kept him out of harm's way.

Now as he looked at Amy who had jumped up to retrieve her hat from the back of the van, he wondered how she would cope with his 'moods' as Nana liked to call them. It didn't always make him the easiest person to live with. He hadn't wanted to say too much about them before she joined him. Everyone had their own faults and he was sure there would be things about her that would annoy him. They'd just have to learn to live with each other's little quirks and personality traits.

She stood at a distance away from where he sat and he admired how fresh and bright she appeared in the morning. He always dragged himself out, no matter where he slept and as he ran his hand through his hair he wondered how he looked. Once he woke up properly he'd go and have a shower but until then she'd have to take him as he was. Amy on the other hand looked amazing and he took advantage of the fact that she had her back to him as she brushed her hair and looked out across the campsite. She had on tiny denim shorts that showed off her legs, a yellow singlet, bright against her tanned skin, and her hair hung loose and shiny in the morning sunlight. How could anyone look so good when they were camping, he wondered, as he filled up his coffee mug again. Usually, he didn't bother about his appearance unless he was going out, but perhaps he'd make an effort, considering how good she looked. At least he should try and look some-what respectable.

'There are a big mob of kangaroos over there,' she said as she stood on her tiptoes peering over the bushes nearby. 'They're looking straight at me. Oh, there they go. Wow, they're huge and there are about fifty of them. Quick come and have a look.'

Obviously she hadn't understood when he said he didn't come alive until mid-morning. Her face fell when he stayed seated, so with a loud sigh he stood up and went over to where she was. The morning light filtered across the plains, green tufts of grass the kangaroos had been feeding on the only colour apart from the red earth. He shaded his eyes, and a strong feeling of connection to the land came over him. 'It's a beautiful country,' he said. 'Takes your breath away.'

They stood beside each other and for a while neither spoke. He could tell the beauty of the landscape had a similar effect on her. 'We're going to see so much, travel-ling. This land around here is familiar to me but it still moves me in a way that's hard to describe,' he said.

Amy closed her eyes and lifted her face to the sky. 'Smells like freedom to me. Wide, open country, just waiting to be explored.'

Tipping the last of his coffee out onto the dust he took one last look. 'I'm going for a shower. Will you be ready to go when I get back?'

'I will. Ready to go wherever the wind blows.'

He laughed as they turned and made their way back to the van. This trip was going to be an adventure and Amy's company was already uplifting. It made for a change. They'd get along fine, he thought, as long as she didn't talk too much in the mornings.

CHAPTER 34

*B*y the time they reached the next town it was ten o'clock and Angus had started to come to life. He told her he had travelled the same road many times and pointed out different roads that led to the north and south. 'Plenty of different directions to go.'

When he glanced at her she smiled. 'So glad to see you're in the land of the living,' she said to him. 'I didn't quite know what to make of you this morning.'

She hoped she hadn't overstepped the boundaries of friendship with her remarks, but she'd already decided that she was going to say what she felt from now on. Hadn't the last term at school taught her that much? No more keeping quiet and going along with everyone else just to keep the peace. This trip was another direction for her and if she started confident and in control then hopefully next time she came across another Mr Gantarro, she'd be quicker to put a stop to any nonsense or bullying. She shivered when she thought of the school and toxic work environment she had been thrown into.

That was something else she had learned, no more teaching jobs. There were plenty of other options out there.

'What were you thinking of then?' Angus asked. 'It's like you were trying to shake something off and, yes, to answer your concerns, this is what I'm like in the mornings. Lucky for you I'm outside the van and you're inside at that time. Separate spaces and our own peace and quiet in the mornings.

'You're going to die with me around. I'm the opposite, however I'm not unused to the inability of people to communicate in the morning. My dad is much the same, and my sister also. Neither of them like talking in the morning. Mum and I would always leave them sitting inside and we'd go out on the verandah with our breakfast. She and I would talk the entire time we were eating.'

He frowned. 'It's not a bad trait if you ask me. It gives you time to wake up properly and gather your thoughts, without,' he stressed the without, 'without, anyone interrupting you or talking in your ear when you've just woken up.'

He slowed the van as they neared a petrol station on the outskirts of town. She wriggled in her seat. 'Can I play music in the morning? I like to put it on and you know, sort of dance around to it, get the body moving, the blood running.'

He groaned and rolled his eyes.

'Right. Okay. I get it. No noise for the grumpy old man before ten in the morning.'

'Maybe instead of worrying about your music you could sort out your clothes and fix up the back of the van, ready for when we move on.' He looked back over his shoulder at the unmade bed behind them. 'That's a mess in there and it's only day one.'

She turned quickly around, surveying the back of the van. 'Oh, sorry. Yes, of course. I should have fixed that up. I was so excited about the day ahead that I forgot.'

He laughed as he pulled up next to the petrol bowser. 'You're messy, aren't you? Just from what I've seen of you, I'm getting the idea that you aren't very tidy.'

She twisted her mouth. 'Okay, we're even. You're a grump in the morning and I'm just a tad untidy.'

'This is going to be interesting, because I'm the opposite when it comes to being neat and organised. This van is only small, and everything has to be in its place otherwise you won't be able to find what you need. Mess will drive me crazy. You'll have to pick up after yourself and keep everything in its place.'

She saluted him like a soldier. 'Yes, Sir. Will do.'

He shook his head at her as she jumped out of the van. 'I'm just going to use the toilets. You won't drive off without me, will you?' she asked.

He grinned back at her but didn't reply.

CHAPTER 35

By the time she returned to the van, Angus was in full conversation with the man who ran the petrol station. He was a tall, thickset man of about forty and he held out his hand for Amy to shake. 'Name's Beatle. Beatle Dickworth.' Beatle wore what most workers wore out in these parts. Blue thick cotton shorts with a fluoro orange long-sleeved shirt that his large stomach pushed against, straining the buttons down the front to their utmost.

She shook his hand, grimacing at his tight strong grip. 'Pleased to meet you, Beatle.' He grinned broadly. 'You too. Your boyfriend here needs to ask you something.'

She went to correct him but Angus spoke before she could. 'Beatle is after a mechanic for a couple of days. Are you okay if we camp here for a bit?'

Beatle pointed to a grassy paddock behind the garage, a large fig tree with sprawling branches offering a shady place to park. There's a toilet and shower block there you can use. There might be a couple of other campers pull in but you're more than likely to have the place to yourself. I'll shout dinner at the pub across the way. I'm desperate to get this truck fixed and, my man here,' he thumped Angus on the back, 'is perfect for the job.'

'Beatle's a mate of Marcello. We've met before.'

'Your timing is perfect. My son is the mechanic but he's had to take his wife to Brisbane for a medical appointment. A farmer out further needs his truck fixed this week. He's got stock to move for a shipment.' Beatle looked hard at Amy. 'You can't answer emails and order stock via email can you? If I gave you a list and the suppliers, would you be able to do some bookwork for me? The missus had to go down south to the daughter's place. She's having a baby.' He chuckled loudly. 'That's the daughter having the baby, not the missus. Gawd love us if that was the case.' He ran his hand through what little hair he had. 'Left me they have, the lot of them. The missus packed her bag before she'd evened finished telling me what was going on. Babies! I love 'em too but ... if I didn't know better I'd think the missus just wanted a break. You know, she's going where there are shops, cafes and no work.'

Amy smiled at him. She could tell he was fond of his wife but had been left in the lurch.

He continued, using his most endearing voice. 'I'm bloody useless on that computer. What do you say, Amy? Are you up for some emailing? I'll pay you well. You look like a capable young girl who could run a business.'

She answered without hesitation, the idea of making some money other than being in a classroom, very appealing. 'Yes, sure. I can do that. Sounds good.'

'What? You're serious.' Beatle wrapped one of his arms

around her and squeezed hard. 'What a girl. Thank you from the bottom of my big heart.'

Beatle shook their hands again and Amy winced at his strong grip. They had obviously come along at the right time and what a perfect way to start the trip with some work for them both.

* * *

That night after they came back from the pub they'd sat together in front of the fire, their stomachs full from the huge steak and veggie meal, that had been complemented by the largest slice of pavlova she'd ever seen. Beatle had told the pub that anything they wanted was on the tab and she'd enjoyed a glass of white wine that washed everything down nicely.

Now she was full though. 'Pub meals are enough for three people. I feel like I won't need to eat for a week,' she said.

'That was bigger than usual,' Angus replied.

'You didn't seem to have any trouble getting through it.'

He patted his stomach. 'You never know when the next feed will come from. Talking about food, we need to work out how this kitty is going to work. We did say that we would put in the same amount and that will pay for food, fuel and camp costs.'

'Sounds good to me. What we have left over we put in our savings.'

'Although, if I make more, I'm happy to pay for everything,' Angus said. 'We might not always get work like this together.'

'Yes, well that works the same if I have work and you don't,' she added.

They'd sat for a bit longer and worked out some of the other details of travelling. Angus was a non-fuss person and it was easy to find options they agreed on.

She'd gone to bed that night, content, and had even folded some of her clothes, making neat piles in the plastic box he'd given her to use as storage. She could be tidy if she wanted to, she'd just have to work at it. Angus was right. There was limited space and thank goodness she'd only brought the necessities and sent nearly all her belongings back home. The way the van was set up gave her everything she needed. As she lay watching him through the window get into his swag for the night she thought how relaxed she felt. They were only two days into their travels and already the stress of the past months had lifted, that nagging panicky feeling she often experienced when thinking about what needed to be done for the days ahead at school had disappeared and in its place a slow calm sensation descended. Even though she was working tomorrow she didn't need to think about it until then. She closed her eyes. They'd both said they'd start work at six in the morning when it was a bit cooler. Time now for sleep.

CHAPTER 36

They had ended up camping next to the garage and working for Beatle for a week. Luckily she hadn't let her parents know they were going to call in, so there was no need to rush. Beatle found her one job after the other and by the time Angus finished working on the truck she felt like she had the bookkeeping up to date and the office back to shape. There had been efficient systems in place and she could tell that usually it was well-organised. That had made it easy to get into the swing of what needed to be done.

Now the van was packed and ready to go and they stood saying their farewells. Beatle had tried to get them to stay longer but they'd been adamant they wanted to get moving.

'The missus has been flat strap with family and she has a few health problems of her own. She'll be tickled pink that everything is back in order,' he told them. 'She arrives back tomorrow. It's a shame she won't get to meet you and Angus.'

They shook hands with him, Amy knowing him well enough now to warn him not to break her hand. 'Sorry luv, the missus always says I've got a bear grip.' He gently shook her hand, before turning to Angus. 'She's a keeper, this one. I know you both tell me you're just friends but you work well together. Like a team. I bet by the time you call in here again, maybe on your way back in a year or so it will be a different story.' He winked at Amy. 'You could do worse than young Angus here. Just think, you'd always have someone to fix your vehicles.'

* * *

They waved back at him through the van windows, grateful for the work he'd given them and his generosity, but they were also eager to get on the road.

'That was a handy start,' Angus said, putting his foot down and picking up speed as they turned off onto the open road. 'It's good to get some money in the bank account but it's also great to get back on track.'

'Perfect timing for both of us. I felt a bit guilty getting paid for what I did. Answering phones and emails, sorting out the office, and a bit of bookwork. Beats teaching any day. Beatle pays well also.' She looked at the road ahead, a blue cloudless sky stretching above the horizon. 'We haven't travelled very far from Matfield.'

'Yeah, I thought we'd get a lot further than that. You have to take work when you can though. We might go weeks without any. Who knows. No stopping now though. We should be on the east coast in two days. Sun, surf and beach. I'm looking forward to a swim.'

'It will be good to see the family but I'm also keen to start travelling. I'm just starting to get used to the setup,' Amy replied.

'Plenty of time. We don't have any deadlines.'

'I know. I've got itchy feet now. That's your fault. You started all of this.'

Amy did feel a tinge of nostalgia as they travelled across the green rolling hills of the hinterland that sprawled out behind the Sunshine Coast. Maleny, Montville and Palmwoods. They were all familiar places to her. Small towns that her parents had taken her and her sister to on many occasions. Nestled in amongst the hills were running creeks where you could lie on blow up mattresses and float with the currents. The water was cold enough to chill your drinks in and often they'd put their camp chairs and a table in the middle of a shallow stream so they could cool down and relax. The area was vastly different from the region they'd left last week and she thought about how large the state of Queensland was and how many different landscapes it offered.

'Not far from your home now,' Angus said as he changed gears, the van moving slowly up a steep hill. They'd driven in from the west and when the van finally made it to the top of the range they gained glimpses of the coastline, the prominent Glasshouse Mountains poking up from the valley floor, and the glistening waters of the Pacific Ocean further in the distance. It would always be home, but when she'd left only six months ago she had thought she would be gone for years. A new career, a new town and a new school. She looked out her side window. It was like admitting defeat coming back home so soon.

* * *

Angus could tell from Amy's silence and the look on her face that even though she was looking forward to seeing her parents, coming back to the coast so soon was not what she had expected when she'd left to begin her teaching career. 'You've done the right thing, Amy. You couldn't have put up with working there any longer,' he said, watching her out of the corner of his eye.

'I'm not a quitter, usually.'

'You put up with too much as it was. Look at what Beatle said when you told him what had happened. He reckoned you should have complained to the higher authorities.'

'Beatle doesn't understand the system. There's no use. I'm just a first year, well not even a first year because I didn't get that far, but a new teacher. What would I know.'

'They sapped your confidence, didn't they.' He watched as she took a deep breath and for a moment he thought he saw tears in her eyes.

'They did.'

He didn't push the point. Maybe her parents would convince her that it was just a bad start and a bit of a break away travelling might be just the thing. 'Okay, now you need to direct me. There is a large black pole up there with red, green and amber lights on it. It's been a while since I've seen one of them.'

She smiled at him and he wanted to reach over and pat

her arm. She was fiercely independent and he loved that, but there was also a tenderness in her spirit and it was a shame that her first teaching experience had taken the wind out of her sails. There was nothing for it but to get on with it. He knew that better than anyone. Now to meet her parents.

CHAPTER 37

*A*my had only rung her parents when they were less than an hour away from home. It was a Saturday night and she had guessed correctly that they would be home. 'They don't go out that much at night. You watch, when we get there they will be sitting out on their back deck overlooking the Maroochy River. Mum will be drinking red wine and Dad a beer. The dog will be there with them and Dad will have music on.' She turned to him. 'Thanks for suggesting we visit. It means a lot to me and it will put them at ease once they meet you.'

* * *

Yvonne and Chris, Amy's parents, had been exactly where she had said. The house was an old Queenslander, nestled on the banks of the river. 'High enough to escape any floods,' Amy told him as she opened the front door and ushered him in.

Her parents jumped up and greeted them warmly. He

took to them straight away. In fact, they were so much like his parents it was uncanny. When Angus said that they reminded him of his parents, Chris made jokes about their year being a good vintage, just the same as Angus's father would have. Yvonne even looked like his mother, she drank the same wine and asked the same questions.

Over dinner they'd laughed and told stories about their own camping experiences. Yvonne dragged out large photo albums and embarrassed Amy as she showed Angus photos of the family camping in a variety of places throughout Australia. 'Look at her. She was just the sweetest little girl,' Yvonne said as she pointed to a photo of Amy and her sister playing in the mud in Western Australia.

'I love your flairs and striped T-shirt. Wow, definitely a trendsetter,' he said, trying to stifle his laughter.

'Mum, really. I think Angus has seen enough photos.'

'No, I'd love to see more,' he added, as Yvonne turned more pages, revealing a very young Chris with the two girls hanging off his shoulders.

'We had good times. The four of us.' Chris said. 'Are you sure you don't want a beer, Angus, or maybe a glass of wine? I have spirits inside if that's more to your taste.'

'Dad, Angus doesn't drink. He said that before when you tried to coerce him.'

'Okay, okay. I'm just asking.'

Yvonne closed the albums up and put them to the side. 'So, let me ask this again. You two are just friends? Did I hear that right? Travelling together, sitting here looking and talking like a couple, but just friends. Hmmm.'

Angus turned to Amy. He'd let her answer. 'Yes, Mum. Just friends. We're travelling companions.'

Yvonne turned to Chris and raised her eyebrows. 'Okay, if that's what you reckon. We'll go along with it.'

Amy offered Angus the fruit her mum had put out to finish the meal. 'We called in so you could meet me and know who Amy was travelling with,' Angus said, plucking grapes from the plate Amy held.

'And what about your job, Amy,' Yvonne continued, 'I know you've explained the situation but that's a big decision to throw in your career when you've only just started.'

'I know you're both disappointed but I had no choice. I couldn't stay any longer.'

'I'll vouch for Amy,' Angus said. 'I could see what was going on. It's hard to explain how bad it was but it wasn't just your usual politics of a workplace. The principal was out to get her and he made her life hell. It's tough in those little towns when everyone knows each other. The locals loved Amy and I know my nieces and nephews adored her. But the hierarchy rules the roost and he's mates with the others above him. She did the right thing getting out.'

Chris sat up straight and stared hard at Amy. 'But you will go back to teaching. You're just going to travel for a while aren't you, and then find another school to teach music at?'

'No. I'm not going back to teaching. I'm going to do something else. It's not for me.'

A long silence followed her statement. Eventually her mother muttered, 'And when our Amy says she's not going to do something, then she won't.' She blew Amy a kiss. 'Love you darling, but you're the most stubborn person I know.

'And where would she get that from?' Chris quipped

back, the mood lightening as her parents bantered back and forth, laughter soon breaking the questioning time and letting Amy relax once again.

Angus stiffened though when Chris turned to him, the other two quiet as he asked, 'And what's your story, Angus. Amy said you're a mechanic. Is that what you did when you left school?'

Angus's jaw tightened and under the table he clenched his fists. It always came to this, the awkward questions, particularly from people who didn't come from around home and know his story. Usually, he skirted around the time he'd spent in jail. It was easy to leave it out. But Yvonne and Chris were nice people, he was travelling with their daughter and he didn't want to lie.

Amy looked down into her cup of tea as he looked to her for support. He was on his own. His decision. Amy looked up when Chris laughed out loud. 'You're not a murderer or something are you? You both look like there's something you're not telling us.'

'Dad, stop.' Amy's words came out loud and Chris and Yvonne both turned to Angus.

'It's okay, Amy,' Angus said.

He took a deep breath. 'Actually, Chris it's not that funny that you've said that because I just want to get this out of the way. Amy and I are going to be travelling together and I'd hate you to hear second-hand gossip about my past.' He noticed Yvonne's eyes widen and she glanced at her husband as he continued. 'I spent three years in jail for a stupid incident that involved teenage boys and fast cars. I was the driver and,' he was surprised how choked up he was getting as he talked. This was not as easy to tell as he had anticipated. 'Well, my mate Mick, well, he... he was killed. We were all in the car together but I was the driver and his family, well mainly his parents made sure I paid for my stupid actions that night.' An ache in his chest made him sit up straighter and he gripped his hands together, his knuckles turning white from the pressure. 'We were all stupid kids and I paid the consequences. I don't usually talk about it but the past follows me wherever I go so I'd rather that you know.'

Yvonne got up out of her seat and came beside him. She wrapped her arms around his shoulders and squeezed him tight, her actions bringing tears to his eyes. Her words were gentle, the kindness in her voice overwhelming. 'We understand and you don't need to explain. I'm sure Amy and you have discussed this and she would have told you we had similar incidents occur here in our community. We've seen it all before. Sometimes it is the driver's fault, but sometimes not.'

Chris leaned over the table, his elbows resting on the surface as he twisted his hands together. 'Lost a few of my own mates in accidents. Could have been me. We've all done things we regret in our younger years. Put it behind you and move on. You're only young and you've paid your dues. I'm sorry about my comments.'

Angus wiped his eyes. 'Thank you. You weren't to know and it means a lot that you understand. It's hardest in the town where I come from. There's still some there who blame me.'

Amy nodded and their eyes locked. She always seemed to understand him and be there for support. They were a good team. 'Mick's sisters have always helped Angus through everything,' Amy added. 'They knew what happened and believed Angus shouldn't have gone to jail.'

Chris lifted his glass in the air. 'Well, young man, you have our trust in travelling with Amy. Calling in to see us before you head off has made our day. Neither of us will worry about her now. In fact, I'm a bit jealous of the freedom and that you'll be on the road and can go wherever the wind blows.

Yvonne returned to her seat. 'Maybe we should hitch the van up and go on a trip ourselves. Nothing is keeping us here at the moment.'

Chris nodded. 'Perhaps we will.' He looked towards Amy. 'Don't worry we'll go a different direction. And, perhaps Angus, you can work on our daughter returning to school one day to revive her love of teaching music to kids. Maybe she'll listen to you.'

'Where are you going to go?' Yvonne asked. 'There's so much to see.'

Angus and Amy looked at each other and smiled like conspirators. They spoke in unison. 'Turn left.'

Amy laughed and finished the directions. 'We'll head away from the coast, back over the ranges and in a western direction to begin with. When we're not sure where we want to go, we'll turn left.'

CHAPTER 38

*A*nother few days with Amy's parents left Angus feeling secure and welcome and even though it was only a short visit they'd made him feel like he was part of the family. They couldn't have been more hospitable and when he met Amy's sister, Kailee, and husband, Graham, the pieces of her background came together and he recognised that some of her traits that were similar to others in her family. By the time they were ready to leave, a stronger bond had developed between him and Amy. He'd even offered to stay longer, after all, there was no hurry. They could spend extra time with her family. 'No way,' she said, adamant she was ready to leave. 'I'm keen to get on the road and see what's next.'

As the van pulled out of her home street and they waved goodbye to Chris and Yvonne, a sense of freedom and excitement filled him. Her parents hadn't judged him for his past and had instantly understood that events from years ago still haunted him. It had been easy to talk to them. Maybe because they were disconnected from his hometown or perhaps because they were from the same era as his parents. Another step had been taken, another move for his mindset, and in the right direction.

'Where to now?' Amy asked as they drove back out through the hinterland and headed west.

'There's a road coming up on our left. It's bitumen,' he replied as he slowed, waiting for her decision.

'Looks good. Turn.'

They laughed as the van swung left, Amy resting her feet on the dashboard as she turned the radio up louder. 'I love Cat Stevens,' she said as she swayed back and forth to the tune blasting from the speakers. 'And might I add, that was a lot of words coming from you so early in the morning.'

He ignored her last statement and focussed on the road ahead which was narrow and windy. He figured if they headed this way, sooner or later they'd cross the ranges and be able to go in the general direction of west. They'd be south of Matfield, almost like they had zig-zagged to the coast and back. There were plenty of small country towns scattered across the outback regions. Some he had been to and others he hadn't. It didn't matter because there should be work wherever they headed and hopefully by nightfall they'd find a good spot to camp where they could reassess their plans and work out where to go next.

He glanced at Amy who was still jigging around in her seat and singing at the top of her voice. She swayed one way. 'I'm being followed by a moon shadow.' She swayed back his way. 'Moon shadow, moon shadow.' Her arms waved in the air and she criss-crossed her legs on the seat. 'Leaping and hopping like a moon shadow.' Turning the radio up louder she winked at him. 'Moon shadow, moon shadow.'

He shook his head and turned his focus to the road. So much energy and enthusiasm so early in the morning. The weather had started to cool and although she still wore her favourite tiny denim shorts, she'd thrown a flannelette shirt over her t-shirt. Her hair was loose and he doubted that she'd brushed it. It hadn't taken her long to throw off the restrictions of getting dressed formally each day for teaching and to relax into the gypsy lifestyle of living in a small van and roaming whichever direction they wanted. He turned the radio down a little, ignoring the look she threw his way. Hopefully the music and singing would keep her occupied for a while and stop her talking.

CHAPTER 39

That afternoon they pulled into a camping area adjacent to a lagoon. Yvonne had given them a ready-cooked meal of spaghetti carbonara. Angus prepared a fire to cook over. Once it was hot enough Amy used it to heat the spaghetti in a saucepan. She'd offered to help collect some wood. 'No, that's my job,' he answered. 'I love having a look around once we've stopped. Besides you wouldn't offer to help if you had seen the black snake that I nearly stood on next to that fallen tree. A good reminder to watch out for them.'

She tucked her feet up under her on the chair. 'I don't mind snakes, but not black ones or those horrible deadly browns. Make sure you keep that swag zipped up.' She turned to look at the van, for a moment wondering if snakes could crawl up into it. Surely not, she thought. Hopefully with the noise that they both made moving around, the snakes would have taken off in the other direction.

'The fire will keep them away from the campsite,'

Angus said. 'They love those old logs in the bush, plus they'll hang around nearer the water.'

They both looked across to the lagoon, half of its surface covered in large lily pads with pink flowers flashing a hazy colour in the late afternoon light. The sun sank behind the gum trees on the other side, knee-high grass and small shrubs testament to the rain the area had received the month prior.

Angus pointed to one of the trees and they watched as a kingfisher flitted from a branch down onto one of the lily pads. The light was fading and it was difficult to see if the bird caught anything. Amy watched it dart off into the darkness of trees further around the lagoon. There was no breeze and as the sun disappeared a cool night air filled the area.

'It will get cold out here tonight,' Angus said as he added more wood to the fire. 'I hope you brought some warm gear as well as your summer attire.'

'That's very posh. Attire. I guess my favourite denim shorts could be classed as that.'

Angus passed her a mug of tea. 'I'm surprised to see how quickly you've settled into van life. I don't see any doubts about leaving the school or running away with me to who knows where.'

'Couldn't be happier,' she said, before winding spaghetti around her fork and putting it into her mouth. 'Mum sure makes a good spaghetti. Easy dinner tonight.'

They'd sat for a bit longer and talked. Conversation, as long as it wasn't in the morning, came easily between the two of them. He'd dragged his chair closer to the fire and she followed with hers as the cold of the night began to settle in. The embers threw a warm golden glow across where they sat, and she watched him as he stoked the fire. There were no showers at the campsite so he'd set up an outdoor shower with a bucket full of warm water and a small hand pump with a shower nozzle on the end. She'd been surprised at how far the small amount of water had gone and she'd managed to have a reasonable shower that removed all the dust and dirt that had collected from the day of travelling.

A small pop-up shower tent had provided privacy although she realised after she'd finished that her silhouette was probably visible due to the lamp that hung from the wall of the tent, shedding light inside the enclosure. She wondered if he'd noticed or if he had been too busy tending the fire. If he had noticed, he hadn't said anything. She'd have to check next time he had a shower. She glanced at him, his eyes cast to the night sky. Tonight, he looked different. A dark stubble grew on his face and his hair was tousled and unbrushed. Instead of his usual shorts and t-shirt, he wore jeans and a zipped-up hoodie. Cuddly, she thought. Like a soft cushion you could snuggle into. Stop, she reprimanded herself. Friends. Nothing more. There was a lot of travel to cover without any complications.

He smiled at her as if he could read her mind. 'What?' she asked.

'Oh, nothing. You were staring into space.'

'Just thinking about tomorrow.'

He looked at her as she pulled a blanket over her legs. 'You should be warm in the van tonight. I put an extra blanket on the bed for you.'

'Thank you,' she replied. 'As long as you're warm enough in the swag.'

A few times she had brought up the subject that it was a bit unfair that she always got to sleep in the comfort and warmth of the van each night. But he had been adamant. He loved sleeping in the swag. It suited him fine and he probably would have slept in it even if she hadn't joined him on the trip. 'No more discussion about it,' he said. 'The arrangements suit us both.'

He was the perfect gentleman and for the hundredth time she thought about how lucky she was that he had invited her to come with him. This beat teaching any day. She went to tell him how much she appreciated his friendship, but then stopped. He wasn't great at taking compliments and she could tell it made him uncomfortable. Being kind came naturally to him.

CHAPTER 40

The lovely thoughts she'd had about Angus the previous night had gone out the window the next morning. Kind, friendly and generous were not the first traits that came to her mind when she tried to get some sort of response to her questions. Her questions came naturally. They just burst out of her mouth and she was not about to stop asking when she was curious about so many things. As she sat and ate her breakfast, different types of birds flew across the lagoon before settling in the trees. There were hundreds of them and their noisy calls filled the morning stillness. They were brown hen-like birds that she hadn't seen before. She plied him with questions as she walked around the campsite, looking up into the trees before walking back and forth to the lagoon. A couple of times his replies had been more than two words but mainly he just shrugged his shoulders and stared down into the fire instead of talking to her and trying to work out what the birds were.

She'd stormed off after he'd ignored her questions and

started to walk around the other side of the lagoon. Although she had her boots on, the grass was long and it hadn't taken long for her to spot her first snake of the day. It was long and black and slithered quickly away in the other direction as she neared it. Her nerves were on edge though. Where there was one snake there was bound to be more. Something else moved in the grass beside her and she jumped, her eyes scanning the track in front. Snakes made her nervous and she didn't feel like walking around the lagoon by herself. It was time to return to the campsite and, a grumpy Angus.

* * *

Most of the gear was packed away by the time she returned. He didn't ask any questions about her walk so she took on a code of silence also. Two could play at this game, she thought.

When she opened the passenger's side of the van to climb in, a neat pile of different items was stacked on her seat. A hairbrush and some hair ties. Okay, so she'd left them and her toothbrush on a stump next to the fire last night. A sock and, her blue bra were also there and she tried to remember where she may have left them. Perhaps in the shower tent last night. 'Oh, my bracelet. You found it,' she exclaimed as she pushed her silver bracelet over her hand. 'It's been missing since the first day. Where was it?'

Had he heard her question or was he just ignoring her? It was hard to tell. She feigned a nonchalant look before shoving all the items left on the seat into her bag at her feet. 'Thank you. Quite a collection. I can't believe you found my bracelet. My sister gave me that. I don't usually take it off but I must have. Lucky you found it.' She turned and gave him a grin before turning the radio on as he started the van.

She started singing, 'Just the Two of us, we'll always be together just the two of us.' As the van swung out of the campsite and onto the road she sang louder, not stopping until the song finished. 'Dad's favourite,' she exclaimed at the end of the song, hoping that her singing and talking were annoying him as much as he was annoying her.

CHAPTER 41

That day they'd covered long distances, the scenery becoming more remote and drier the further west they went. The only other traffic on the road were long cattle trains and work utes, their yellow stickers and numbers on the side showing they were part of the mining industries that were the lifelines of the small towns and communities out this way.

'Where we're headed is mining territory,' Angus said. 'Not much else out here apart from mining and cattle. I've always wanted to visit these places.'

She peered out the window, the road running in a straight line in front of them. On either side, wide open plains stretched in every direction. 'It's so flat and dry,' she commented.

'It is. There's a small town up further going by that last sign. Gowrie. We might stop there the night if we can find somewhere to camp.'

They neared the outskirts of town just as the light was beginning to fade. To the side of the road was a wooden sign hanging by two chains from a fence: Gowrie Caravan Park. Previously they had talked about not staying in caravan parks if they could help it. The bush camps and national parks were what they intended to aim for. But, after the long drive, a place with proper amenities was enticing.

'What do you think?' Angus asked as he slowed and then stopped in front of the sign.

'It would be nice to have a proper shower tonight.'

'Okay. We'll stay here. It doesn't look like it's booked out.'

They both looked across the grounds of the park, a few vans situated further to the back. Apart from that there didn't seem to be anyone else set up. She stretched her legs in front of her, ready to get out after sitting all day. Lights popped on in the office block as they parked in front of it, and a man appeared through the door as soon as they got out of the van.

He shook their hands. 'Pleased to meet you. Name's Barney and the wife is Betty. She's inside getting my dinner ready. After a campsite?'

'Yes. Just for one or two nights at this stage, although we might stay longer if there's a bit to see,' Angus replied.

Barney laughed. 'There's plenty to see. Depends on what you want. Toilets, showers and washing machines are all here for your use. You're the only guests so far, so make yourself at home. They used to have some of the mine workers stay here but that only happens now when everything else is full up. I have another couple of vans booked in, but they won't be here until tomorrow. They're both here for a week. Grey nomads.'

What would you do here for a week, Amy thought as

she looked around. Everything was brown. The Besser brick amenities block was tinged with an orangey-brown shade as were the rocks and gardens. Not that you could really call them gardens, rather just dry bushes and dead pot plants. There were a few old vans in a row down the back of the park, but other than that it didn't appear that anyone else ever stayed here. The vans looked empty although one of them had Christmas lights still strung around the exterior. The caretaker must have followed her gaze.

'It's dry at the moment. They say there's some rain on the way but that could be months away.'

'Right,' she replied.

She hadn't felt like talking that much that night and Angus had noticed. 'Are you okay?'

'Yeah, I'm fine. It's just very dusty out here. And in the middle of nowhere.'

'Don't judge the town by the caravan park. They don't have the water to keep these places looking good when it's this dry and the bore water discolours the bricks and rocks. We might stay for a couple of days and have a good look around. How about tomorrow night we go into town to the pub.'

'There's a pub here?'

'There's always a pub. The town's up the road a bit further. Barney said it does a good feed. We'll go in the afternoon and have a look around and then have something to eat. My shout.'

'Oh, you should have said that first. Sure, sounds good.'

* * *

Angus walked with her when she went for a shower. The park was isolated and the office lights had been turned off. When she looked up into the night sky a million stars blinked back at her. 'It's so dark out here,' she whispered, as she followed him toward the amenities block.

'No moon tonight. Watch where you walk. You don't want to step on anything.'

She trod carefully, grabbing his arm when something rustled in the bushes beside where they walked. 'What was that?'

He chuckled. 'Probably just a rat or possum.'

'Maybe we should have parked closer. I'm okay with bugs and some other wildlife but snakes are not my thing.'

'Usually, they will get out of your way before you get near them. You just have to keep an eye out for them.'

They stopped outside the ladies' amenities. 'You go in and have a shower. I'll be right next door in the men's. I'll wait outside for you when I'm finished so you don't have to walk back by yourself.'

She clutched her towel and clothes in her hands, peering back out into the darkness. 'Sounds good. Don't go back without me.'

The shower was refreshing and Amy enjoyed the full flow of water pouring over her body. She closed her eyes and tilted her head back, letting the water run over her. A shower at the end of the day was always refreshing and tonight was a bit more luxuriant compared to the short showers they usually had. It was exciting to be camping somewhere different and she relaxed under the warm water, the steam filling the cubicle and heating the small space.

It took a minute to register that suddenly she was starting to feel a different sensation other than the water. Her body froze as something slithered over her foot. When she looked down, a dark brown snake moved across her foot. It flicked its tongue menacingly, its eyes focussed on her for a moment before moving away from the water. The rest of its body emerged from the drain-pipe and she screamed as it slid across the tiles, its entire body now visible as it lay stretched out, just out of the water's reach.

She screamed again and cowered in the corner close to the taps, the snake moving a little more before curling most of its body up, looking like it had settled in on the floor between Amy, her towel and the door. She yelled as loud as she could. 'Angus. There's a snake in the shower.'

He must have already started moving when he first heard her scream as he answered her from the other side of the shower door. 'What colour is it?'

'Black. Dark Brown.'

'Can you get out.'

'No. It's between me and the door.'

'Don't move and don't startle it. Is it blocking your way?'

Her voice was hysterical. 'Yes!'

'You're going to have to climb out over the top. If I try and come in and get it, or try and chase it out, it might not be happy and it will likely come towards you and away from me.'

'It's just lying there and every now and again it puts its head up and looks straight at me. It knows I'm in here.'

'Is there a bench or chair, anything in there that you can stand up on to get out of its way?'

'No, there are only hooks for the clothes. There isn't anything.'

She quickly surveyed the shower cubicle. The walls ran down to the floor, the only other opening, a gap under the door. She jumped as the snake flicked its head in the air, its tongue flicking in and out again, almost as if it was trying to work out where she was. She looked up. The walls did not run right to the ceiling and if she could hang onto the top she should be able to get her foot onto one of the taps and hoist herself over the top and into the shower cubicle next to hers.

The snake moved a little, its head moving in her direction, its body curling up once again as it moved a little closer. 'Angus, it just moved closer. It's like it's trying to get closer to me but doesn't want to get under the water.'

'You need to get out of there. I looked under the door and it does look like a brown. Do you think you can climb over the top?'

'Yes. But Angus.' She found it hard to keep talking, her body was shaking and her limbs felt like they wouldn't move where she wanted them to. The water continued to stream down, as she kept watching the snake.

'What?'

'I can't get to my clothes. They're the other side of the snake.'

'Forget your clothes. Just get out. I'll pass a towel to you if you're worried. I'll look the other way. I have seen a naked woman before you know.' He chuckled and she felt a surge of anger jolt through her body. Did he really just laugh? Did he think this was funny?

'This is not the time to make jokes.' She let out another short shriek. 'Shit, it just moved again. I think it wants to go back down the drainpipe where it came up from, but I'm in the way and there's not enough room for the two of us.'

Angus moved to the cubicle next to hers, his hand passing a towel over the top. She tried to wrap it around herself, knotting it at the side and hoping it would hold. 'Look the other way, because this towel is not going to work and I'm getting out now.'

She hung onto the top of the dividing wall, a surge of strength and panic allowing her to get her foot onto the tap and then push herself onto the top of the wall so that she could get one leg over. The towel scrunched up under her body; at least it took the roughness away from the narrow edge she was scrambling over. Now she could see Angus, who glanced quickly at her before turning his back.

'Are you okay?' he said. 'Don't fall. You look like you're panicking a bit. Take it slow. You don't want to break anything.'

'Of course I'm bloody panicking. A very large deadly snake just came up through the drainpipe and crawled across my foot before guarding the entrance to the doorway.' She pushed her other leg over and levered herself down onto the floor, her towel falling at her feet. She quickly picked it up and wrapped it around herself, just as Angus turned around, his face covered in a wide grin.

'You okay?'

She blinked hard, her body trembling from the shock and exertion of levering herself over the wall. 'Are you laughing?'

'Well, it is sort of funny. What are your chances of a snake coming into the shower with you? Lucky you're fit and able to do what you just did.'

She glared at him. 'What are my chances? Well obviously bloody good.'

Hanging onto the top of the wall he jumped up and peered over the top. 'Geez, Amy. That looks like a brown.' He looked again. 'Bloody hell. I reckon it's actually a taipan. Race up and get the caretakers. I'll stay here and watch in case it goes into one of the other cubicles. There are small drains that run under the walls. It might change location.'

'But my clothes.'

'Forget them. Wrap the towel around you. Quick. Go get someone.'

Wrapping the towel tightly around her body she ran barefoot through the dust up to the park office. Luckily there was a light on the verandah of the building, its glow giving her some light to see where she was going. If there was a snake in the shower there were likely to be a million of them, probably warming themselves on the dusty track where she ran. Her feet hardly touched the ground and her hand clutched at the towel, keeping it in place. She jumped up the three stairs and stood outside the screen door, looking straight in at Barney and Betty who were sitting just inside at a small table, both enjoying a cup of tea as they watched the news.

Barney looked like he had showered, cleaned up, and was ready to relax for the night. The only thing he wore was a pair of jocks that were nearly invisible, due to his large stomach that hung down over the top of them, and she thought, thank goodness over the top of anything else in that direction. Betty at least had a cotton nightie on, her hair up in curlers, and a cigarette in her hand. 'Gawd. Is everything alright,' Betty said as she jumped up and opened the door.

Barney was right behind Betty and Amy focussed on his face when he spoke. 'Blimey, love. What's happened?'

'There's a snake in the shower. It came up through the drainpipe and I had to climb over the top to get out. Angus is watching it to make sure it doesn't go elsewhere in the shower block. He said it's a Taipan.'

Barney's eyes widened. 'Hang on love, I'll just pull on my trousers.' He turned around and she got a full view of his large muscly legs, his calf muscles like bulging tyres that bowed out under the pressure of his large body.

Betty opened the door wider. 'Oh, you poor thing. I hate snakes and we get some doozies around here. It's not the first time one's come up through the drainpipe. They're after the water.' Betty crossed her arms, a faint smile crossing her face as she drew back on her cigarette. 'Were the two of you in there together? Nice balmy night for making love.'

'For goodness sakes,' Amy said as she adjusted her towel. 'No, we weren't. We're just friends.'

Betty smiled and raised her eyebrows. 'Sure. Sure. That's okay. Barney will get a shovel or he's got a thick stick there with a chain on it that he uses for those snakes. Here he comes.'

Barney re-emerged, this time with shorts on and a navy-blue singlet. He'd even tucked the single into his shorts. She blushed when he looked her up and down, obviously noting that she was only clad in a towel. 'Oh, I see. You two were in the same shower.' He winked at

Betty. 'Good night for it. Lucky young Angus was there to save the day. Let's get to it. The only good snake is a dead snake. Also, if it is a taipan it will hang around. There's been a few rats around. I keep meaning to set traps for them. It'll be after them. We're used to snakes coming up through the drains. That's a regular occurrence but usually they're just your common, red-bellied blacks or a tree snake, not a bloody taipan.'

She walked quickly beside Barney as they made their way back to the shower block. Her feet were now covered in a brown sooty dirt, her skin clammy and hot from the activities of the night. So much for her shower, she thought. 'The Taipan is lethal, isn't it?' she asked.

'Sure is, one of our deadliest. Strange though, they usually stay away from human activity and shelter for most of the day. Maybe it had been taking cover in the drains.'

* * *

By the time they reached the showers, Angus had pulled a plastic chair into the cubicle next to where the snake was and he hopped down as Barney entered the cubicle.

'G'day, Barney. Sorry to bother you at night but I thought it best with this one.'

Barney nudged Angus. 'What a shame. This snake fella interrupted your romantic night.'

Angus shook his head. 'No, I was next door when Amy yelled out.'

'Yeah sure,' Barney replied as he climbed onto the chair. The legs on it buckled a little and he put his arms out to steady himself. Amy had jumped up on the bench, where the sinks and mirrors were, her feet tucked up under her, well out of the way in case the snake decided to exit the shower. She watched Barney, hoping the chair wouldn't break and send him crashing to the ground. Thankfully, he regained his balance, his hands gripping the top of the wall as he looked down at the snake.

'It's a big one and you're right. It's a taipan, no mistaking it, and I'm guessing about two metres long. Bloody lucky it didn't bite you.' Barney said. 'Gawd, there's a lot of water getting wasted there. You could have turned...' He went to say more but Angus cut him off.

'What's your plan, Barney?' he asked as he gripped Barney's arm, steadying him as he climbed down from the chair.

'Okay. This is what we'll do. Angus, I want you to move that other chair to outside the shower where the snake is. I've got this.' He waved the thick stick in the air, the chain swirling around wildly. Amy wondered how precise his actions were, considering how slow and ungainly his body movements were. 'I'm going to be right here,' he pointed to just outside the shower door, 'and when I say open, Angus, you open the door and I'll whack it with this.'

Amy drew her feet up tighter and made sure her towel was tucked in around her body as Angus pulled a chair over near the door. He positioned it to the side so Barney had enough room to get past him.

The two men appeared calm and Angus almost seemed to be enjoying the moment.

'Ready? 'Barney said, his eyes focussed on the door. 'Okay. Go.'

Angus opened the door, his feet firm on the chair as he hung onto the top of the wall for balance.

The snake was curled up, its head still in the air when it turned to face the now open doorway. It moved slightly before Barney brought the thick chain down heavily on its body. He hit it again, his arm moving so quickly that the snake did not have time to escape. She held her hand over her mouth, amazed at the speed that Barney moved. It was obvious that he had done this before and she was relieved when the snake did a few final movements before lying still, its body broken into several pieces. She jumped a little as some of the pieces moved, the bit with the tail on it wriggling a little more before it also lay still.

'You got it.' Angus said, hopping down from the chair and moving nearer for a better look.

Barney reached over and turned the water off. 'Big bastard. Glad to get rid of him. We can't have him hanging around.' He grabbed a nearby bucket and using the shovel he had brought with him, placed the pieces of the snake into it. 'Mongrel taipan alright. They call them the fierce snakes. We have some of the deadliest snakes in the world. Kill you in a matter of minutes. I don't always kill them. Most of the time you can just get out of their way and they'll get out of yours. But in here, it's not worth it. Not everyone is young enough to climb over the wall. That could have been disastrous. You should buy a lotto ticket, Amy. Bloody lucky.'

She stared hard at the remains, for once lost for words. When she went to get down from the bench she remembered that she had nothing but a towel on. 'Angus could you please pass me my clothes? Those on the hook.' Angus leaned in and grabbed her clothes. Blood covered the tiles and bits of snake were splattered on the walls and floor. As she took her clothes from him she shuddered, the size of the snake still daunting even though it was now in several pieces. Angus continued picking up the pieces as they discussed different snakes and other experiences they'd had with them. Barny leaned back on the doorway jam, and lit up a cigarette, laughing and joking as if this was a usual occurrence and just part of his regular day.

* * *

Neither of the men took any notice when she got down from the bench and went to a shower at the other end of room. It was a relief to get into her clean clothes and she turned the shower on and washed her feet. This time she carefully observed the drainpipe opening and stood between it and the door. No more being trapped and never again would she take having a safe shower for granted.

As she flung open the door she frowned at Angus who was laughing loudly at something Barny had told him. Both men turned to her. 'What a night,' Barney said, thumping Angus on the back. 'It's not every night you see a naked woman climbing over a wall and mate, what do you think that snake thought when he looked up from the drainpipe, he must have thought ….'

'Stop,' Amy said, 'Enough!' She held her hand in the air, the other hanging onto her towel and toiletry bag. She slipped her thongs on and glared at them. 'Angus, I'm going back to the van and I'm opening that bottle of wine my mother gave us for a special occasion. I don't want to hear another snake joke. It's just as well you don't drink because I'll be having the entire bottle.'

She pushed her shoulders back and placed her hair, which was still wet and messy, back behind her ears. 'Goodnight, Barney, and thank you for getting rid of it.'

With that she stormed off, stopping just outside the building before quickly turning and walking back in. 'Torch please,' she said to Angus who already had it held out in front of him.'

She could tell he was trying not to laugh. 'How will I see?' he said.

Turning she flicked the torch on. 'I don't care. Goodnight.'

CHAPTER 42

*A*ngus let Amy sleep in the next morning. He made his cup of tea quietly and walked away from the campsite. Even though it was early morning the heat was starting to build and he thought how similar the countryside here was to where he was from some hundreds of kilometres due north. It was the same hazy horizon with only a couple of strands of cloud stretched above it. Paddocks stretched in every direction, the land flat and only a few head of cattle standing under a small piece of shade a half-dead tree offered. It was a harsh environment, but he breathed deeply. It was what gave him peace. He could lose himself out here and trouble-some thoughts that sometimes plagued him, lessened, and what was important became more focussed.

The sight of Amy climbing over the shower wall yesterday flicked across his mind and he laughed to himself. She'd done well so far with the camping, but the snake had her rattled and it hadn't helped that he and Barney had seen the funny side of it. He had tried not to look at her as she clambered over the wall but it wasn't something you got to see every day. Pushing his hat down on his head he thought about how close they'd become in the short time they'd known each other. Was it something more than friendship that he felt for her? If it was, he wasn't going to let it in. He didn't want to be responsible for messing up a good travelling experience and anyway, she hadn't indicated that she felt anything more for him either.

As he walked back towards the van he saw her step out, in the same little denim shorts she always wore and a bright t-shirt, signalling that she was ready for the day. He tipped the last of his tea out on the ground, little spurts of dust puffing up where the liquid landed. He'd have to try a bit harder this morning to be social. Perhaps attempt to make up for laughing at her last night. She waved to him and a smile crossed his face. How did someone wake up so happy every morning and with so much energy? It was a good feeling to be with her and maybe he should take on some of her exuberance, especially in the morning. He waved back. He'd cook her breakfast to make up for last night. Food worked with her every time.

CHAPTER 43

'Thank you, Angus. Is this to try and win me over because you laughed at me last night,' she said as she picked up the crunchiest piece of bacon.

'Perhaps,' he replied, casting his best smile her way. 'Here, I made you a coffee. White, one sugar, and stirred just the way you like it.'

'You're doing well but I don't forgive that easily.'

'I wish you could have seen yourself ...'

He stopped as she scowled at him. 'Okay,' he added, 'not another word about it. I promise. It can be our little secret that you had to climb in a very ungainly manner over a high shower wall, um, naked.'

A corner of his mouth quirked with amusement and she didn't answer, instead holding out her hand to accept the coffee.

'Thank you, and yes, I would prefer if we kept that to ourselves.'

'Sure. I won't tell anyone.' He chuckled. 'I can't say the

same for Barney though. You know how they love a story in these little towns.'

'Well, I'm still trying to get the image of Barney in nothing but his jocks sitting with Betty watching tv last night out of my mind.'

Angus laughed. 'That would have been something to see.'

'It was.'

They sat and chatted for a while and he made a special effort to answer with proper replies, rather than sliding into his usual non-verbal manner. It must have worked because soon she seemed to forget about his jokes last night and they talked about where they might travel next.

'I wouldn't mind staying here for a while,' he said. 'It's a good-sized little town. I reckon there would be some work here for me with the mines so close.'

She shaded her eyes from the sun and looked out across the park. 'I don't mind. Apart from the snakes it's a nice campground and it looks like we have it nearly to ourselves.'

He stood up and stretched. 'Let's go and check out the town.' He pointed to some rocky outcrops in the distance. 'We can ask where's good to go. Those rocks look interesting and there's a river over further. I saw it on the map. Not that there would be much water in it but could be worth a look.'

'Sounds good. And you promised dinner in town tonight. We'll celebrate me being alive.'

RHONDA FORREST

As she sat sipping her coffee she went over the events of the night before. A shudder ran through her body, and she perused the campsite, making sure nothing was slithering nearby. The wildlife was part of the experience and she didn't want to be too much of a city girl. But that was what she was. She'd seen plenty of snakes growing up on the coast but usually they were pythons or green tree snakes. Those ones were harmless and you would never kill them, unlike last night. She'd need to harden up a bit to match Angus's demeanour towards the creatures around them. He'd tried very hard this morning to be more social and amicable. Just as well, because last night was no laughing matter. No doubt it wouldn't be the last episode with wildlife, hopefully not in a shower next time.

She jumped up and noticed Angus tidying up the back of the van. She was supposed to make her bed and put everything away. 'Sorry,' she said. 'I meant to go back in and neaten that, but you distracted me with breakfast.'

He threw a bra and t-shirt at her, which she caught with her spare hand. 'Thanks. I am messy. That's just me.'

'We're all different,' he replied, holding up her towel which had somehow ended up underneath the bed in the back of the van. 'Every time I see this towel...' He stopped and folded the towel neatly, placing it on her bed which he had also made. 'Never mind. Let's get going and see what the little town of Gowrie has to offer.'

CHAPTER 44

The shops on the main street were just opening as they parked the van. The road was empty of vehicles, only a bedraggled dog trotting up the middle of it. A swoosh of dirt flew out from a doorway, a robust woman holding a straw broom following it, her strong sweeping movements pausing in mid-air when she spotted them. She leaned on the broom and smiled. 'New-comers. Welcome. Looking for a job?' She looked at Amy when she spoke. 'As long as you can serve coffee and cake and can hold a conversation, I have just the job for you.'

Amy laughed. 'Oh, sorry. No, I don't think so. Well not at the moment but I'll keep it in mind.'

The lady twisted her mouth and looked Angus up and down. 'How about your husband? Can he cook? Make breakfast? Hold a conversation?'

Angus went to reply but Amy cut in. 'Nope. He'd be no good. Doesn't speak before lunchtime.'

The lady put her hands on her hips. 'Okay, but can he cook.'

'Are you short of workers around here?' Angus asked, jumping out of the way as the lady started sweeping the pavement near his feet.

'Workers. What are they? Half of these businesses will end up closing down. No one wants to work, well not here. They all go to the mines. Big money.' She waved her broom in the air. 'Good day to you both. Enjoy!'

They continued walking, the lady disappearing into the takeaway shop that sold hamburgers, and fish and chips. 'Sounds the same as at home,' Angus said. 'Maybe we should stick around and work here for a while.'

'We'll see. I'm not that great at cooking and I don't really want to be serving coffee. I'm terrible at that too. Bookwork would be good.'

* * *

It hadn't taken long to walk along the main street. The town had all the usual amenities, much like Matfield, a hairdresser, newsagency and hardware. And, of course, the essential corner pub, which was always the central meeting place of any small town. On the corner of the street, three elderly men sat on a low brick wall. They were smoking and talking, watching Angus and Amy walk past.

Angus nodded and said hello, stopping for a chat as Amy continued. There was a clothes shop further on and she took the opportunity to look in its window while Angus chatted to the men. He was still there when she came back and when he saw her he said his goodbyes and walked toward her. The men all gave her a friendly wave and she smiled and waved back.

Angus looked as relaxed as any country local as he strolled towards her. His tan had darkened further and she tried not to stare as he sauntered casually up the street. 'I got the local knowledge,' he said as he caught up with her. 'There're some good spots along the river and a lookout and a scenic walk further out of town. They gave me directions to what they call a magical waterhole. Are you keen to have a look?' He didn't add the story that the men had told him about it being where young Indigenous people had once gone to secretly meet each other. He'd left out the magic of the story, the part about the waterhole being where love for another was created or that the local Indigenous people referred to it as the place where hearts join.

'Sounds good.' She laughed. 'They're all waving to us again.'

Angus shook his head. 'Everyone assumes we're either married or together.'

'And what did you tell them?'

A warm sensation ran through her body as he wrapped his arm around her shoulders, squeezing her in tightly to him. 'I told them we're just mates. C'mon, let's get going.'

She pushed her shoulder into him as he took his arm away. 'By the way, they're laughing right now. I don't think they believed you.'

He threw her the van keys, steering the conversation in another direction. 'Here, you drive. My turn to sightsee.'

CHAPTER 45

That afternoon as Amy drove back to the caravan park, Angus thought about what a great day it had been. They'd walked for miles along the riverbanks, following the well-worn paths of cattle, the trail eventually leading up through a rocky outcrop; the only raised part of the ground on the otherwise flat plains. Following the directions the men had given him, they wound their way through boulders and crevasses, climbing upwards until they found the caves and Aboriginal artwork that they'd been looking for.

It was the same as many sites throughout the region and reminded him of the waterhole on his property where he had taken Amy. The men had told Angus where to go because he had said he was from Matfield. Not many knew of these smaller hidden sites and that's the way the locals liked it to stay. It kept the artwork safe from most travellers unless they went off the beaten track. There were plenty of other popular and larger sites for travellers to visit.

The art was ancient, from a time before the arrival of Europeans, when only the Indigenous people lived on the land where they now stood. As they perused the sketches and markings of a people who had been able to survive in some of the harshest landscapes on the planet, they talked about how special the place felt. When they'd walked a bit further they found the rockpool the men had directed them to. Amy waded in cautiously, her questions about snakes and other vermin that might be around, justifiable after the events of last night. She wore a pair of cotton green shorts and a tan t-shirt that he had quickly worked out was her favourite; the swirly Celtic design in the middle, faded, and sections no longer visible. Her brown hair hung down her back, sleek and shiny when she resurfaced from bobbing under the surface of the water.

She'd been hesitant to enter the pool at first, but the clear water and heat of the day had proven too enticing and once she was in she had made the most of it and swum around, lying on her back and floating, her eyes closed, her body relaxed in the tranquil water.

Angus took off his t-shirt and waded in. Usually at these remote places he'd take off his clothes and go in naked, but today he'd be civilised and leave his shorts on. Besides, in this weather their clothes would dry off in no time. He floated around for a while, enjoying the refreshing water. It was a good way to cool off and he let the water swirl around him, watching an eagle perched on a rock higher up, observing the two of them.

Amy got out first, spreading her towel out and lying on her back, sunning herself. He kept glancing at her while she wasn't looking his way. Her skin was tanned and tiny droplets of water glistened on her skin. He dragged his eyes away from her, eventually getting out of the pool to lie on the rocks next to her. A couple of tiny clouds scuttled across the otherwise clear sky and the eagle took one more look before spreading its wings and soaring higher up the rock face. It disappeared around the other side of the outcrop and Angus closed his eyes, the sun soaking into his skin, the water residual on his body keeping him cool. It was the most peaceful he had felt in many years and he let his body sink into the rocks, enjoying the warm hard surface beneath him. It wasn't just the location that was causing the sensation of serenity, it was also the company.

When he turned towards Amy, he caught her staring at him, and they looked at each other before both turning to look back at the sky. Their silent connection magnified and he tried to still the strong feelings that swirled in his mind.

* * *

From the top of the rocky outcrop, the van looked like a speck in the desert. It was a long walk back and they were both lost in their thoughts, neither speaking the entire way. There hadn't been any conversation as they drove back out along the dirt road, the only time Amy spoke was to ask if she was on the right track. Silence descended quickly after that and now as Amy turned the wheel and steered the van into the park, Angus felt unsettled.

A nagging worrying feeling punched in his gut. Something had shifted today. When they'd laid next to each other at the rockpool, with nothing but prehistoric artwork above them and ancient rock beneath them, the area home to the longest living people in the world, he had felt like the earth itself moved. Like his heart had grown and thrown away some of the shackles of the past. Now it was like it had room for another person. A girl. A woman. Amy.

He'd tried hard to shake it off. A cold shower and a shave in readiness for dinner at the pub hadn't helped at all and when he looked in the mirror he lightly slapped his hands on his cheeks. Maybe it was better not to be too relaxed. When he was busy and focussed, particularly when he immersed himself in work, thoughts about women had been easy to block or talk himself out of. This time that wasn't happening.

She'd come out of the shower at the same time as he had. 'No snakes?' he asked, the words coming out fast as he tried not to instead shout out how amazing she looked. Blue jeans and a white off the shoulder top showed off her figure and he looked closer, she had even put a bit of makeup on.

'You're staring.' Her green eyes were bright in the afternoon sun and he realised that he was holding his breath and blinking hard.

'Just, well, you look a bit different.'

'So do you,' she said, looking him up and down. 'You don't scrub up too badly.'

'Thank you.'

'To the pub we shall go,' she said, laughing at him as she strode ahead of him back to the van.

Her jeans were tight and his eyes were drawn to her backside, which he was sure she was moving seductively from side to side on purpose. Maybe the old men in town had been right when they'd jibbed him about just being mates with Amy. 'Geez, sonny. Don't waste time. If you let that one get away you'll be sorry. What are you waiting for?'

* * *

It was Friday night and the pub was crowded. They'd found a table for two next to the side wall and he'd impressed Amy by pulling out her chair for her. He was well used to outback pubs but her eyes were going everywhere. On the walls, old pieces of farming machinery hung from heavy rusty hooks, their age dating back to the days of bullock carts and horse-drawn carriages. There wasn't a spare bit of wall that didn't have some sort of memorabilia on it; black and white photos of pioneers, the horns of bulls that stretched wide, as well as signed football jerseys, trophies, a collection of old bottles, stubby holders and even an array of bras the plaque above them declaring how much money had been raised for a charity. It was colourful, eclectic and typical of outback pubs.

'Wow, this place is incredible. So much to look at.'

The tables around them were filling up and families and other locals talked and joked with each other. It was a familiar setting, much like the pub at Matfield, yet the people were different, and no doubt Angus would be pleased that nobody knew him and he could be inconspicuous in amongst the crowd. 'What would you like to drink?' he asked Amy.

'I think I'm going to have a glass of white wine. To celebrate the day.'

'I'll be back. You have to buy drinks from the public

bar.' She watched as he made his way to the long bar at the front of the room. The middle of the room had lines of long tables, filled with a variety of people of different ages. It was likely they were families, out for a special occasion or like her and Angus, out to celebrate Friday night and the end of another week. Their chatter and laughter were noisy and happy, a few of the children going back and forth to an old piano that was tucked away in the corner. They laughed as they pushed each other for a position on the piano seat, their fingers pushing down the keys and adding to the vibrant hum of the room.

Her gaze was drawn out through the window next to where she sat. Two boys went past on skateboards, their bodies tall and straight as they glided effortlessly down the footpath. The street outside was quiet, although a number of utes and trucks were parked on either side, no doubt the occupants either here at this pub or at the other one on the next corner up. A group of teenagers gathered on the other side of the street and she watched as a couple of them lit cigarettes. She shuddered. They looked like high school students and even from a distance she could see that some of them still had their school uniforms on. Two of them were wrapped around each other, kissing right under the streetlight that flickered on and off, as if the bulb needed fixing.

Thank goodness she didn't have to think about students or school. If Angus wanted to try and find some work in this little town she was sure there would be something for her to do. Maybe she could even offer to clean at the caravan park. She wasn't averse to hard work, just not anything to do with education.

Observing the people in the pub had occupied her for some time and she suddenly realised that Angus had been gone quite a while. She leaned out and peered down the hallway to the public bar, trying to see where he was. There was a large group gathered around the bar, and she spotted him with two drinks in his hands. He was talking to another man and she wondered if he knew him. Looking back out the window she watched the group of teenagers move off, a couple of younger kids following them on their pushbikes. Probably not much to do on a Friday night in these little places she thought. No wonder there were so many people at the pub.

Outside, the night sky darkened and only a faint touch of red glowed above the buildings on the other side of the road. The last of the sunset disappeared from her view and she turned around to find Angus standing beside her. He placed her drink in front of her as he sat down opposite. 'Sorry to take so long. I got talking.'

She reached out and picked up her glass. 'I could see that. No hurry. There's plenty to look at. I like people watching. Was it someone you know?'

'No. Never met him before, but he was standing next to me at the bar while we waited for our drinks. Asked where I was from.'

Angus took a long sip from his drink. 'Your usual?' she asked.

'It's ginger beer instead of ginger ale this time. They make it in Bundaberg. It's refreshing.'

'Do you ever feel like a real beer? I don't drink alcohol very often, but on nights like tonight I enjoy a glass of wine. It was such a lovely day.'

He raised his glass in the air and clinked it against

hers. 'It was a great day, but no, it doesn't worry me. I have on a rare occasion had a beer or wine with a meal but I'm happy to stick to soft drink.'

'So was the fella at the bar from around here?'

'Yes, his name is Daniel. Turns out as soon as I said where I was from he asked if I knew Marcello. Can you believe it? You come all this way and one of the first locals you talk to knows your boss.'

'How does he know him?'

'They worked together years ago. Something to do with mining machinery. Daniel, that's the fella I was talking to, he did some of his apprenticeship with Marcello. Speaks very highly of him.'

'Small world,' Amy said as she picked up the menu Angus had placed on the table.

'He's also chasing a mechanic. Said he'll come and talk to me before he leaves. I tell you what, I don't think we're going to have any trouble getting jobs, anywhere. Everyone is chasing workers. Now what's on the menu.'

'I'm ravenous,' Amy said, reading through the choices.

'Me too.'

They took some time deciding what they wanted, their choice made quickly when the waitress came up beside them.

'What'll it be?' she asked. 'I recommend the rump steak. It's local.'

Angus looked at Amy and she nodded. 'We'll have two, thanks. Amy will have hers well done and mine medium. I'll have veggies and she'll have chips and salad.' He looked to Amy for confirmation and she grinned and nodded again.

The waitress picked up the menus and jotted down

some notes on her notepad. 'And would Amy be looking for a job? We're after bar staff, kitchen staff, and cleaners.'

Amy looked up. 'Oh, I'll keep that in mind. I might be looking for something. It depends on how long we stay.'

The waitress looked Amy up and down. She was about the same age as Amy's mother, her tight black trousers and collared black shirt, neat and professional. 'My husband, Ted and I, I'm Marion, own the pub and we're in dire need of staff. Come to us first. Everyone will be trying to hire you if they think you're going to hang around.'

'We're staying at the van park. We might stay for a while and work,' Angus added.

Marion squinted suspiciously at them, moving her head from Angus to Amy and then back again. She chortled loudly, causing a few of the customers sitting near them to turn their way. 'Oh my gawd, you're the youngsters staying in the van. You,' she said, pointing at Amy. 'You poor thing. You must be the girl in the shower. A taipan came up through the drain underneath you and slid across your feet.'

Amy felt her face burn and she was lost for words. That incident had only happened yesterday and Angus swore he wouldn't repeat it to anyone. Besides that, he hadn't been anywhere to tell anyone. She looked from Angus to Marion.

Marion tucked the menus under her arm. 'It's okay Luv, Barney gave me and the bar the whole story earlier today. Thank your lucky stars you're only a slip of a lass. Imagine someone like me having to get over the top naked and try and manoeuvre over the other side. Barney was impressed that you were agile enough to get over it, said he wished he'd been there to see it, and as he said it's not every night that a beautiful girl with only a small towel wrapped around herself knocks on his office door.'

Thankfully Angus answered for her. 'Amy was lucky and thanks for the job offer. She'll keep it in mind.'

Marion grinned at them again before striding off to the next table. By the way she was pointing and talking, Amy could tell she was re-telling the story to anyone who would listen.

'This food better be good and this place worth coming to,' Amy said. 'It seems like everyone in this pub already knows the story.'

'Small towns,' Angus quipped. 'You can't beat them.'

The meals had been well worth the wait and Marion apologised for the delay when she placed the plates in front of them. 'Think about that job,' she reminded Amy. 'I'll look after you and there aren't any snakes allowed in here.'

'You're not going to live that down for a while. Barney must have had an interested audience when he told it. I wonder if he embellished it a bit.'

'I'm just going to pretend that it never happened.' By now the wine had found its mark and she felt mellow, relaxed. She hadn't drunk much alcohol lately so even a small amount had an effect. 'That glass of wine has gone down well,' she told Angus. 'Although I can feel the effects. I don't think I'll have another one. Maybe a soft drink when you go to buy the next round.'

'Will do,' he said. 'That Daniel fella is making his way over here. He's keen for a worker as well. I told him to come and see me once we finished our meals.'

Just as he said that Daniel appeared next to them. He carried a baby in his arms and behind him was a younger woman who Amy thought must be his wife. She also had a baby in her arms. Angus stood up and shook Daniel's hand before introducing him. Daniel replied as he greeted them. 'This is my wife, Jess, and these are our twins, Ava and Ella.'

Amy stood up and tweaked Ella's toes. 'They are adorable. I haven't had much to do with babies, but there is something about twins that I love.' Ella held her arms out towards Amy and she naturally put hers out in response. Before she knew it the little girl was snuggled in her arms, her head resting on Amy's shoulder.

'She likes you,' Jess said. 'The twins are used to Daniel's large family so they're not shy, which is good.' Jess was a slight build, with dark brown eyes and wavy brown hair that fell onto her shoulders, pinned back by a clip on one side. She looked good considering her twins were still babies and Amy thought how busy the young mum would be looking after two.

Daniel also looked relaxed and happy. 'I hope we're not interrupting you,' he said, 'but we'll be leaving soon and heading home. These bubs need to go to bed. Can we talk for a moment?'

'Yes, sure,' Angus replied, pulling out a chair for Jess to sit down. Daniel moved another chair from nearby so they were seated together.

As they started to talk, Marion leaned over and cleared the table; the plates with nothing left on them testament to the lovely meals. 'Now, Daniel. Don't you go snavelling any of my workers. Young Amy might come and work here for me,' Marion remarked.

Amy laughed. 'You may not want me. I haven't worked at a pub before.'

'I'll have you pouring beers in no time. Don't forget to talk to me before anyone else.'

Daniel waited until Marion had gone. 'I'm dead serious about the job I mentioned before up at the bar. My young worker busted his ribs and he'll be out for at least three months. It's peak time for the cattle and there's a mountain of mining trucks and other vehicles to fix. The money is good so I don't think you'll find anything to beat the pay rate.'

'Three months?' Amy asked. 'That's quite a stretch.' She directed her last comment to Angus.

Angus ran his hand through his hair. 'We hadn't planned to stay that long in one place. More like a week in each. We've only just started travelling and the aim was to see as much of Australia as possible.'

'If you work for me for three months and do a good job, you won't need to work for the rest of the year. I'm telling you, what the mines have said they'd pay for these next jobs is some of the best money I've seen. I subcontract to them and have been doing so for years. I know you'll be good if you've come from Marcello.'

'How about you, Amy?' Jess asked. 'What do you do?'

'I recently studied to be a teacher. A music teacher.' She found it hard to continue. It seemed so crazy to say that she'd given it up after six months.

Angus finished for her. 'Amy came to my home town of Matfield. That's how we met. We're just mates. Travelling partners.'

'The school was not what I expected and now I've realised that teaching isn't for me. I can do other things though. I've worked in offices and shops as well as in education. There seems to be plenty of jobs around.'

'There is. Everyone is after someone. You'll see some of the businesses have had to close because they can't get staff. The bakery only opens three days a week now and the hairdresser is the same. It's not for lack of patronage, it's because there is no one to serve,' Jess said.

Daniel added in, 'I'm okay usually for staff because we have good people working for us and Jess still manages to do most of my bookwork. But with my mechanic out, I'm really in a fix. I've advertised everywhere but unless it's directly with the mines and a permanent position, mechanics don't want to come out here for a short stint. I can't compete with what some of the mines are offering.' He grinned at Angus. 'Mechanics like you are as rare as hen's teeth.'

Jess nodded towards Amy. 'Amy is rarer. At the moment they've combined classes at the high school. They're down about five staff. Same story. No one wants to come out here.'

'You don't have to worry about me and school. I'm not ever going back to teaching. I like the sound of pouring beers though.'

They'd sat and talked for a bit longer, both babies now asleep. Amy carefully passed Ella back to Jess as they got ready to leave. Daniel gave Angus his card. 'I'd love you both to come out for a visit and we can talk some more. We'll just be hanging around the house tomorrow and the workshop is right next door. If you're even remotely interested, give me a ring and come out. I realise you need to talk about it between yourselves. It may not be what you had planned, but it might also be too good an opportunity to pass up.'

Once Daniel and Jess had left, Angus and Amy sat looking at each other. 'Three months?' she said again. 'That's a long time in a town like this. I'm not sure I'd like it. It's smaller than Matfield. I don't even think it has a pool. For me it would be just like living in Matfield and that did not work out well.'

'I understand what you're saying, but this opportunity to work with Daniel and learn from him on these larger pieces of machinery would mean gaining more skills. They seem like a nice couple.'

She could tell that Angus was excited at the prospect and she wasn't totally against it. 'I just need time to get my head around staying here that long. Why don't we sleep on it, talk about it in the morning and then maybe go for a visit to their place if you're interested. If it's really what you want, it sounds like I can get work here at the pub.' She looked around, the tables still full of families enjoying the relaxed atmosphere. 'It may not take much to convince me. This place and the people here tonight have a good vibe about them.'

'Let's just wait and see what tomorrow brings, Angus said. 'Like you said we'll sleep on it and talk about it a bit more in the morning.'

They'd waved to Marion on the way out and she called out for them to wait. Pressing a piece of paper into Amy's hand she whispered. 'This is my number. Remember, I asked you first.'

CHAPTER 47

*A*my watched as a mob of kangaroos easily cleared the barbed wire fence that separated the van park from the paddocks. They moved in a group, the larger ones in front and the smaller ones trailing behind. 'They clear that as though it isn't even there,' she said to Angus, who also was watching them.

'Pests out here, especially in the dry.'

They sat in silence and when she finished her breakfast she hopped up and tidied the van. He had his back to her and was still staring at where the kangaroos had disappeared to. Quiet as usual, she thought and this morning even more pensive than usual. He hadn't mentioned the job or what they were doing today so she'd left it. He'd talk once he was ready. Once she'd neatened everything she cleaned up her breakfast dishes in the small tub they washed up in and dried them, making sure everything went back in its place. She was getting better at keeping things tidy.

By the time she came back, Angus had also packed up and was dressed, waiting for her.

'Coffee?' he asked.

'Sure, I'd love one.'

* * *

She waited for him to start the conversation.

'So did you think about what I was offered last night?' Angus asked.

'I have. I didn't think about the jobs we might be offered before we left. I guess I was just caught up in the adventure of it all and escaping school. It would be silly to think that everything was going to line up job wise for us at every place we stop. This wouldn't be a worry for you if you were travelling without me.'

'I really don't want to hear that again. This trip is not about me. We decided that from the start. We're a team, and a pretty good one so far. No, I'll go with whatever we work out. I'm enjoying travelling with you.'

She breathed a sigh of relief. She had wondered, not for the first time, if he was sorry he hadn't just gone with his original plans and travelled by himself.

'Thank you. That means a lot.' Deep down a wave of emotion overcame her. She would have been devastated if he had even hinted that it might be better if they parted ways or that this was not going to work out.

'I'd be happy to work at the pub. I'd have to learn how to serve and pour beers but it would be okay. The only thing I don't like about it would be that it would probably be mostly night work and on weekends. And that would be when you're not working.'

'Yeah, I thought about that also last night. There's a lot to see around here and plenty of places to camp not too far away. If we don't have the weekends, that might cut down on what we get to see.'

'There would also be the problem of you sleeping in the swag. Three months in the same place is a long while.'

'I thought about that too. I could buy an annexe or a large tent. That would give us more cover for cooking and throw some shade. Or there could be the option of renting one of those caravans.' He looked over towards the vans, the middle one still with a large sagging reindeer on its roof.

'Why don't we go and talk to Daniel and see what he comes up with? Maybe he has some ideas. He knows we're living in a van. From what Marion said, that's another reason they can't get workers. There's nowhere for them to live.'

* * *

Amy changed into something a bit more respectable than her usual shorts and t-shirt. She had brought a couple of dresses with her and she ran her hands over the fabric, enjoying the feeling of wearing something different. Angus came around the other side of the van and smiled, his eyes appraising her different attire. 'That looks great on you. Very summery.'

'There is only one season out here, isn't there.'

'Pretty much, although the winter nights will get cooler.'

She spun around, the floral fitted dress cool against her skin, the length of it to just above her knees. She still had her riding boots on. They were an essential in this dust. 'Hang on. Turn around again,' Angus said as he reached over. She felt his hands against the skin on her back and a shiver ran through her body. 'Just tucking your tag in. You look great.'

'Bit different from how I had to get dressed up for work every day.'

'You're really traumatised by those months at Matfield, aren't you?'

'I wouldn't say traumatised, that's a bit strong. But jaded, cynical, and annoyed. Yes!'

The drive out to Daniel's place wasn't far and the van moved along nicely on a road that looked like it had not long been graded. The countryside was mostly flat but when they neared the river the road dipped down and they crossed a new bridge, its surface quite a way above where the old one had been. They stopped in the middle of it and looked down at the dry riverbed, Angus pointing out the old timber stumps where the original bridge must have been.

'I'd say that one has washed away at some stage and maybe not too long ago.'

She peered through the open window, a large lizard basking in the river sand staring back at her with its large yellow eyes. 'I can't imagine this ditch having water in it. There's not a drop in it now.'

Angus pointed up into the trees. 'Look up there, you can see where it's been in past floods.'

She looked high into the trees, amazed to see clumps

of grass and debris caught between the branches of the gums that lined the creek. Even a tyre was stuck up there, its rubber peeling away, faded by the incessant heat that was often over forty degrees in these parts.

'It's very remote out here,' she said. 'I wonder how Daniel's wife, Jess, likes it. She looks so elegant and calm for a mother of twins and I don't think she'd be much older than me. No doubt she was born and bred out here. God, imagine me with twins. I'd probably leave one behind or forget to feed them.'

He laughed. 'You are a bit forgetful sometimes, but everyone is different.'

'Have you ever thought about having kids, Angus, you know when you meet someone one day and settle down.'

'I used to think about it. I love all those nieces and nephews of mine. How about you? You're so good with little ones?'

'It's not something I think about. At the moment I'm enjoying being selfish and free to do what I want.'

'I'm a bit the same.' He started the van up and crossed to the other side of the river. 'My problem is I'm always scared I'm going to stuff things up.'

She turned to him, frowning. 'What? I haven't heard you say that before. Why would you think that?'

He lowered his head to look through the windscreen of the van, a wide gate in front of them blocking them from going any further. 'I guess that's why I run from relationships. Worried about stuffing up someone else's life. Not my own, just someone else's. Now enough deep and meaningful, especially this early in the day for me. Get out and open that gate. I'm not going to remind you to close it. You're a country girl now.'

* * *

As she pushed the gate open she pondered over his words. She would have to continue that conversation at another time. It did explain why he often pushed people away or didn't get too involved with others. Would that be what would happen to them? A friendship that only went so far and maybe if it ever started to become too close he'd push her away. As the van drove through and she pulled the gate closed, she reminded herself to have a chat with him about what he'd said. He wasn't getting away with that comment so easily.

* * *

Angus had phoned ahead and Jess and Daniel were waiting on the verandah for them, two cattle dogs, one blue and the other red, barking and running out to meet them as they drove in. The homestead was impressive, with wide verandahs wrapping around the front and sides, fancy fretwork decorating each verandah post and a bull-nosed red tin roof shining as the sun bounced off it. It was typical of a country homestead, with a concrete path lined with a few small bushes leading up to three wide stairs. 'Oh, my goodness,' Amy said. 'Look at that house. That's the sort of home I've always dreamt of. A classic Queenslander, on wooden stumps and with wide stairs and a verandah. It's stunning.'

'Reminds me of Nana's house a bit,' Angus said. 'Those verandahs are great places to play when you're a kid.'

Daniel opened a gate at the top of the stairs and came down towards the van. He whistled for the dogs to come to him. They were quick to do as they were told and both sat in the dust at his feet. He extended his hand to Angus first and then to Amy. 'G'day. Glad you could come out. Don't mind these two, they're all bark and no bite.'

The blue dog wagged its tail and Amy put her hand out for it to smell. 'She's lovely. What's her name?'

'This red one is, wait for it, called Red. She's my dog and the blue one is Jess's. Her name is Rosie. There's quite a story behind these two dogs. I'll let Jess fill you in. Welcome to our home. This is where we live and over yonder,' he shielded his eyes against the sun, 'are the work sheds. Where all the action is. Come on up. Jess has some morning tea ready for you.'

Jess couldn't have been more welcoming and once again Amy admired how calm she was. 'You seem so relaxed for a young mum with twins,' Amy said to her as they sat down in the white wicker chairs that were spread around the verandah.

Jess let out a loud laugh. 'Are you kidding me? I'm only relaxed at the moment because both girls are asleep. It's chaos around here usually and if I get more than three hours of sleep without an interruption I feel lucky.'

'You don't seem much older than me.'

'I'm twenty-eight. Daniel's a bit older. The twins were, might we say, an unexpected, unplanned blessing. But we couldn't be happier. How about you? Daniel reckons you and Angus are just travelling companions.'

'Yes. We are. Just friends. Angus had been planning this trip with his van for quite a while and then we became friends. I was in an unpleasant situation with work and it was perfect timing when he asked me if I wanted to come with him. I was ready for an adventure and change, so the timing was perfect. We'd prefer to keep travelling together, so that's why we need to work out the job situation. I've always let him know that if he wants to travel without me and go his own way then I'd be fine with that. So far it's worked out well though.'

'It's funny how things work out sometimes, or rather sneak up on you. Daniel was my boss and I couldn't stand him. Then we became friends and then well, as they say, the rest is history.'

'Did you know each other at school out here?'

'Oh no. I'm from Brisbane; a city girl and with a very different upbringing from the one Daniel had. He's the fifth generation to live here. All his family lives in town. There's a mob of them and I love them all. They're my family now.'

'So are your family nearby?'

'I only have a brother and his wife, who also have twins. They live inland from the Gold Coast, at Tamborine Mountain. They come and visit a couple of times a year and we do the same with them. The mountain is often a cool retreat after here. It's a completely different landscape. I lived there for a year so I have a special attachment to the area.'

The men had stopped talking and came to sit with Amy and Jess. 'Jess isn't from the country either Angus. She's not keen on the snakes, same as me.'

Jess shuddered. 'I hate them.'

Angus took a biscuit from the plate Jess offered. 'I bet you have some stories to tell about coming to live out here when you're from the city.'

Daniel smiled and Amy thought what a good-looking man he was. He was tall and well-built, with dark curly hair and blue eyes. The close connection between him and Jess was obvious, his eyes following her movements as she talked.

'Oh, she has plenty of stories. She could write a book about her experiences from the moment she arrived here.'

'And before,' Jess added. 'I lived a very different life from most, as a youngster growing up. Some things are better left in the past. My brother is the same. We grew up pretty much on the streets. So, you can imagine what that was like. Luckily the job out here saved me.'

Daniel leaned over and kissed her on the cheek. 'And I saved you too.' Jess smiled and they all laughed. Amy watched Angus as he talked. She could tell he was relaxed in the couple's company and she was also intrigued about Daniel's business and what the job entailed if Angus decided to take it. A mechanic with the skills that Angus had was needed as soon as possible.

Daniel directed his next question to Amy. 'How about, you Amy? You mentioned last night you were looking for an admin job. You're not interested in any office work, are you? We could do with someone else to help. Jess has less and less time and with not much sleep she could do with a break.'

Jess added, 'I'd love someone to help with the books, but I understand that you're a teacher. I guess you'll go back to that.'

'No. No way. I had a terrible experience, and that job is definitely not for me. Maybe down the track I'll teach music privately, you know, one on one. I'm a piano teacher and that's the only way I'll work with kids again.'

'What a shame,' Daniel said. 'One of my sisters works in the office at the high school. In fact, if she gets wind of you in town you'll need to duck for cover. There will be no getting away from her. She's also in charge of the Parents' Committee and I know they've been offering all sorts of deals to entice teachers out here.'

Daniel was just about to take Angus over to look at the workshops when a four-wheel drive pulled up in a cloud of dust outside the gate. A young boy got out and opened it, waiting until the vehicle passed through before shutting it again.

Jess, who had just gone to check on the twins, reappeared. 'Oh, my goodness. Now you're in trouble, Amy. This is Daniel's sister, Belle, the one he was just talking about. Strange for her to call in on a Saturday. And looks like she has all the kids with her. Hers and Liz's. You'll get to meet all Daniel's nieces and nephews.'

The car had come to a halt right in front of where they sat, the dogs barking once again and leaping around the kids as they got out.

'Thank goodness the twin's room is on the other side of the house,' Jess said. 'They're a rowdy lot, this crew.'

Introductions were made all around and Amy surveyed the kids who appeared to be a range of ages. They were dressed up. The boys in smart shorts and collared shirts, the girls in pretty dresses. The youngest one swirled around to show Jess how pretty she looked. Jess picked her up and hugged her. 'This is Lea. She loves me don't you, Lea.'

The little girl put her hands on either side of Jess's face and squeezed her cheeks together before kissing her on her nose. 'Love you lots, Aunty Jess. You're my favourite.'

Belle made a beeline for Amy, shaking her hand firmly before looking her square in the eye. 'I won't beat around the bush and we can't stay long because the kids are going to a birthday party back in town. You're the teacher? The teacher who ran into the snake in the shower?'

Amy smiled back, 'Word gets out fast in these parts. I was a teacher, but not anymore.' She noticed Daniel roll his eyes and shake his head in Belle's direction. He had warned her about his sister's direct nature. Belle continued. 'Here's the deal. The high school is in a terrible situation. See these beautiful kids. Two at high school and the rest will be in the near future. Look at them. They're you're typical country kids. Polite, well-behaved and eager to learn.' She glared at them and they all stood up straight and smiled at Amy, almost as if they'd rehearsed the move. 'There are no teachers for them. At the moment the PE teacher is a lovely guy but …. well anyway, the PE teacher is teaching them English and history. He's trying his best but it's not great and it also means they miss out on sport. It's only a small school, about three hundred kids. We're down English, history and did someone say you were a music teacher? The kids wouldn't even know what a music class was.'

Amy took a deep breath and went to speak but she'd left it too late. Belle continued. 'Jackson come over here. Tell Miss Amy how long since you've had a music teacher. Better still, sing for her.'

'Aunty Belle,' the young boy protested. He looked at Amy. 'Mrs Chitty left when I was in year three. I'm in year seven now at the high school. I'm trying to learn how to read music on the internet but I don't get it. All my mates want to play guitar and the drums. The equipment is still there, locked away but there's no one to teach us.'

One of the girls pushed him to the side. 'That's nothing. My friends and I want to have a choir. We like singing. Some of our friends who moved to bigger towns are in choirs and they go to concerts and competitions and all sorts of cool things.' She took a step closer to Amy. 'Can you teach choirs how to sing that well?'

Amy felt trapped. All the little faces turned to her. It was a ploy, she knew it. Daniel's sister had obviously got word of her qualifications and had somehow known that she was going to be here today.

She looked towards Daniel, who held both his hands in the air. 'Don't look at me. I didn't say anything about you teaching. I mentioned that you were both coming out to talk about my offer of work.'

Angus leaned back in his chair, stretched his legs out and crossed his feet. 'Looks like I'm not the only one with decisions to make.'

Amy sat up straight, mindful that everyone including the two dogs was staring at her. 'I'm really sorry, but I don't teach in schools anymore. It's not for everyone. When you teach you have to put in more than one hundred percent, and I can't do that.'

Belle smiled at her. 'Our kids at the school here are mostly well-behaved. It's better than a lot of schools and the teachers who work there love it. It would be a great opportunity and a fantastic country experience for you.'

'That's exactly what they said about the last place. I'm really sorry. My mind is made up.'

Everyone's shoulders seemed to slump and Jackson scuffed his boots on the floorboards. 'We always miss out. I reckon the school should just close down.'

Belle put her arms around his shoulders. 'Don't say that. They'll get staff. It's just a bit hard at the moment.

Well, we tried. Come on you lot, say goodbye and let's head off to this party.' She turned to Amy. 'Don't forget if you change your mind, you can always come and chat with the principal. Harold Best is getting on, but he does a great job. I don't know who will replace him when he decides to retire.

'Maybe the school really will shut down,' Jackson said.

CHAPTER 48

*A*ngus and Amy stayed for a bit longer after Daniel's sister and the kids. Angus had walked with Daniel over to the workshop and had a good look around. To say he was impressed was an understatement. This workshop was ten times bigger than the one at Matfield and had state of the art equipment and tools. Daniel owned the business himself but contracted back to a mining company. He had written down some of the conditions and pay amounts on a piece of paper.

'I know it might not be exactly what you had planned when you left Matfield,' Daniel said as he shook both their hands, 'but have a good think about it. You could hone some extra skills with these new trucks coming in. Technology develops so quickly and it's essential to keep up with it. If you don't, you'll be left behind.'

They talked a bit more as they walked back to the house, Amy listening but not saying too much. The language of mechanics and trucks was foreign to her but if Angus took the job she might need to think seriously about the office work. It would be a steep learning curve but she was a quick learner and always up for a challenge.

Daniel reiterated to Amy that her best option would be teaching at the school. 'These kids are missing out on chunks of their education. I can't understand why teachers won't come out here and teach. The system is disadvantaging our country kids. It doesn't affect us yet, the twins are way off going to school but it will come around quickly. You've done all that study and it would mean so much to the town, but …. it's up to you.'

* * *

Amy was quiet on the drive home and Angus wondered if she was mulling over what Daniel had said. No doubt the kids had pulled at her conscience. Her face was set in a stern look and he gave her time to think until they reached the van park. For a moment he had the urge to lean over and pull her towards him, to draw her in and tell her it was okay to feel pulled from each side. She looked upset and he looked away when she wiped her hand across her eyes.

'Cup of tea?' he asked. 'I'll boil the billy and make us both a good strong cup.'

'Thanks,' she replied, her voice small, her movements slow and without her usual energy.

She'd cheered up a bit when he talked about the workshop and what Daniel had planned for him over the next three months. In his mind, he already knew what he wanted to do, but he'd wait and see what she said.

He looked at her expectantly and she must have realised the questions on the tip of his tongue. 'Oh sorry,

Angus. I'm so tied up in my own thoughts I'd forgotten that you're probably wanting to know what I want to do.'

'We're a travelling team, Amy. No pressure.'

'No, no, that's fine. I don't feel pressured at all. I'm more than happy to stay in the town for however long you want. We'll work out where to camp and I have plenty of choices with jobs. I think if you want the job with Daniel you should take it. The problem for me is I have too many choices.'

'Are you thinking about the bookwork with Jess?'

'I think so. As long as you don't mind, because she said I'd work from the office, there at the workshop. It's only two days a week though, so I'd have to find something else for the other days. I could always talk to Marion about the work at the pub.'

He stood up and came over, giving her a hug. 'Thanks, Amy. That's great. I have a good feeling about this place. We'll need to work out where to live though.' They both looked around the caravan park, the dust flying through the air from where a hawk had plunged down and picked up a small rat. She looked closer, or maybe it was a mouse. 'Survival of the fittest out here,' she said. 'Yes, I think we do need to look for somewhere else.'

*T*he next morning, she slept in. The interior of the van was hot and the small fan that ran off a battery had died during the night, the blades stationary, the air, hot and sticky. She threw the door open, immediately thankful that she had pyjama shorts and a matching singlet on because there was company outside. Lots of company.

A group of children, including the ones she had met yesterday, were gathered in neat rows, right outside the van. Behind them were six adults, an older man in the middle counting to three and then saying, 'Begin.'

She rubbed her eyes. Was she dreaming? Was she imagining that Angus was sitting in his camp chair to the side of the van, grinning from ear to ear? Shaking her head she blinked several times, staring from the group to Angus and then back again.

The children all started singing at once. The tune was a familiar one but at first she couldn't pick what it was. She put her head on the side trying to work it out. The adults, three women and three men, in the back row, who were a variety of ages, also started singing and she listened to an offbeat rendition of something that sounded vaguely like Waltzing Matilda.

A woman stood behind Angus, and Amy was surprised when she recognised who it was. It was Belle and she gave Amy a little wave and shrugged her shoulders. The singers continued until the song was finished, their bodies straight, their hands held in front looking like the most angelic children you would ever see.

The older man who had made a terrible attempt at conducting them, stepped forward and offered his hand for her to shake. 'I'm Mr Best. Harold Best. Principal of Gowrie State High School. We heard you were in town and thought we'd come and sing for you. We're in dire need of a teacher, especially for music at the primary school and well, we need teachers for most subjects at the high school but especially music. I'd like to offer you a position for however long you want. We could start with three months and go from there. I understand you're travelling so if you left after three months we'd understand. This contract, he waved it high in the air, is subsidised, like most of our other younger teachers' contracts are, by the Parents' Committee. It includes a much higher rate of pay than a beginning teacher, free rental of a house in town designated for teacher accommodation, petrol vouchers from the local petrol station and vouchers from the pub, hairdressers and just about every other business in town. Anyone with a kid at that school is willing to put up the extra to snavel a teacher like yourself.'

She stood up. 'I am overwhelmed. I've never had anyone make such an effort to try and get me to take a job.' She looked at the eager faces all staring at her. 'I'm only in town for three months.'

Harold looked at her, his eyes pleading. 'We will support you in any way possible. Our staff is small, but we all get along and nothing is too much trouble. You can ask the others here. I'm flexible and I totally understand if it's only for three months. We have a storeroom full of musical equipment that hasn't been touched in years. Our kids want music in their lives again.'

She closed her eyes and looked to Angus and then back to the kids, who stood still, their eyes fixed on her. Taking a deep breath, she replied. 'I'm overwhelmed. You don't even know me.'

'I may have made a quick call to a parent I know in Matfield. You taught his daughter piano at the primary school last term and their older boy was in your music class at the high school. They couldn't speak more highly of you. I didn't contact staff or the principal. I'd already heard along the grapevine about the management at that school.'

'Most of the staff were lovely.'

'Would you like to become part of our school? Even if it's only for a short while.'

She looked at the kids who were all standing still and waiting for her reply. Angus looked at her, also waiting.

'It would be very hard to say no, when you've gone to so much trouble and you all sang beautifully.' A loud cheer broke out amongst the kids and she waited until they were quiet again. 'You were very good, but I can see there is work to be done.' She looked at Angus, an expectant look on his face as he waited for her to give everyone her decision. 'I guess, well I guess, I will say... Yes.'

There was lots more noisy cheering and the students jumped up and down as they hugged each other. Angus came and stood beside her and she whispered to him.

'I notice they brought all the cute angelic kids. They didn't bring any of the bigger ones from the high school. I don't see any of the teenagers that were smoking outside the pub on Friday night.'

'No backing out now, Amy. We're both committed.'

'I can't believe I've just agreed to go back to teaching.'

Belle came up beside them. 'Coerced, bribed and nagged until you broke. You won't regret it. I promise. It will work out well because my other sister didn't realise Jess was looking for someone to help with the office over there. She's going to work for Jess and that frees you up for the school. We worked it out last night. Conspirators. We just needed you to agree.'

'Or weaken,' Amy added.

Harold handed her the contract. 'I did it up last night, just in case. You still have one week before school starts. How about I meet you at the house this afternoon and I can go through everything with you and Angus.'

'Oh, I forgot. A house. Wow.' She turned to Angus, 'That's not something we counted on.'

'Um, we're not a couple,' Angus said. 'We're not married. Just travelling mates. Is that still okay for us both to live there?'

Harold patted him on the back. 'Of course, it is. We're just happy to have you both here. Maybe if everything works out you'll stay until the end of the year.'

The other teachers gathered around, all wanting to introduce themselves and talk to Amy. Errol was the science teacher and he shook hands with Angus. 'Pleased to meet you both, and don't worry, we'll look after her. I'm at the high school and I'll make sure those kids toe the line for her. Harold runs a tight ship and the kids and staff all support each other. She won't regret it. Like many teachers here she might never want to leave.'

'Don't tell her that at the moment,' Angus said, 'One step at a time. You guys have done well to make her change her mind though. Well done.'

The house was all that Harold promised it would be. The furniture was basic but it had everything that was needed. It would also be more comfortable than the van. Her new boss arrived with his wife, her arms full of linen and towels, plus a large basket decorated with a bright yellow ribbon.

'Morning. I'm Ruby. This is from Marion and some of the others. She was disappointed you won't be working at the pub. But she has five grandchildren at the school so she was delighted when we told her what was happening.'

Amy took the basket from Ruby. 'You work so quickly. I can't believe this has all happened so quickly.'

Harold chuckled as he placed a bottle of champagne on the table. 'Belle called an emergency meeting last night. A large number of parents showed up. Marion is also very good at gathering the forces,' he said. 'We worked quickly because we didn't want to lose you.'

Harold and Amy sat at the table, while Angus busied himself by bringing in bags and other items from the van.

He kept glancing at Amy and giving her the thumbs up as Ruby bustled around, dusting and making sure everything was in order.

As usual there was a fair bit of paperwork to read, but Harold was steady and methodical and explained everything, stopping all the time to ask if she had any questions or concerns. Contracts, timetables and lists of other essential information were spread out on the table in front of her. This time though she understood what was being presented and so far everything seemed to be favourable.

The timetable was similar to what she'd had at Matfield. Two days at the primary school teaching music, then the other three days at the high school. She stared at the timetable for the high school, checking it over thoroughly. 'These are all music classes, plus there are quite a few spares in there. Will they be filled later?' she asked.

'No, no way. You are entitled to the usual spares and then I've given you some extra time away from classes because you're new and you'll find you will need that spare time if you decide to have a band or choir. It might be a bit messy to start with as no one has touched anything for a while. I'm leaving it up to you. We're here to help or come to for advice if you want, but I'm happy for you to run your own ship. These kids haven't had music for so long and I know there are many of them who so badly want to learn. They've really missed it.'

Everything so far appeared to be vastly different from her introductions at Matfield. She was still wary though. It all seemed too good to be true. As they waved goodbye to Harold and Ruby, Angus turned to her and playfully punched her on the arm. 'Well, well, well. Miss Coops.

Here you go again, although I'd say this time you're going to love it.'

She pushed him back. 'Let's just wait and see. It could all be smoke and mirrors. I'm still dubious about the high school students. From what I saw around town they look the same as kids that age anywhere do. Usually, the last place they want to be is at school or in my music class.'

CHAPTER 51

By that night Angus and Amy had moved everything into the house. It was a modest wooden cottage with a good-sized yard and within walking distance of the centre of town. Two bedrooms, a small lounge and a kitchen gave them plenty of space, along with a bathroom and a laundry taking up part of the back landing. A verandah ran across the front of the house, its wooden rails and posts and uneven wide timber floorboards, typical of a traditional country cottage.

Amy stood in the front yard with her hands on her hips. 'What happened Angus? One minute we're on the road, just a van and swag and off into the wild for an adventure and the next minute we're set up like a regular suburban couple in a house with furniture and both ready to start new full-time jobs on Monday?'

'You told me to turn left.' He smiled at her and put two cups of tea down on the wooden table that just fitted, along with two chairs on the front verandah. In the western sky the sun was dipping below the horizon and the air was still and silent. In the distance the sound of a truck rumbling further out on the main road could be heard, but other than that the town was still.

'Everyone must be inside having their dinner,' he said. 'It's so quiet.'

Amy looked up at him as she walked up the cracked concrete path to the two front steps. 'You know this is the sort of house I've always dreamt about. An old wooden cottage. Harold said this was the original school-master's house back in the early 1900s. They've reno-vated a bit and restumped, but apart from that it's much how it was.'

'Would have been a small school back then and no air conditioning.'

'He said the students used to sit under a big tree out the back to do their lessons. It was cooler in the shade than in the rooms. All the kids either rode horses or walked to school. He's going to show me the old photos of what it was like; the school library has a display on their wall.'

'What a difference between him and Elliot. You might really enjoy this job.'

'We'll see. I'm not jumping ahead too much.'

They sat together and Angus stretched his legs out in front and leaned back in his chair. The front yard was mostly dry grass with a concrete pathway and a couple of gardens along the sides. A low picket fence and wooden gate bordered the front, beyond that a dirt footpath and then a bitumen road. The edges of the road were broken and in some parts grass grew up through the cracks, a few potholes and bumpy bits a tell-tale sign the road needed repairs. At least it was bitumen though, which would mean less dust in the house.

He ran his hand over the weathered tabletop, noting some indents and carvings of those who might have sat and similarly drank their tea. His body relaxed and a feeling of contentment settled. There was something about Gowrie and the people they'd met that was reassuring and settling. Who knew, if Amy's job worked out maybe they'd stay longer.

He looked over to her, her face still turned to the yard as she perused every nook and cranny. 'Look there's an old water tank cut off and filled with dirt. That would make a great vegetable patch. I'd love to grow some herbs and veggies.'

'We could do that. We've got big water tanks and Ruby said there's a bore out the back that brings up good water.'

'At least we've got one good tree in the yard. Some shade.'

They looked up, the lanky gum tree somehow managing to throw some green into the landscape. Its leaves pointed towards the ground, the white bark of its trunk and limbs stark against the golden light of the late afternoon. He pointed upwards.

'Look. See that knob up there, to the left. There's a galah in there. I just saw it pop its head out.'

'Oh look,' Amy said. 'There's the other one further up the branch. They're a pair. Maybe they've got eggs or chicks in there.'

'Nana says that a pair of galahs is a sign of good luck.' Angus wanted to say more but stopped. Amy's face was flushed, the hazy afternoon light sending a beautiful glow over everything in its path. Her eyes were bright as she looked at him over her cup of tea. 'Suddenly I feel content,' she said.

He nodded, lost for words, a range of emotions flooding through him. He'd warned himself not to let this happen, but as he looked into her eyes he knew it was too late.

CHAPTER 52

ngus dropped her at the school gate at seven-thirty on her first day. She could have walked but he said it was more appropriate that she be driven, plus she had a couple of bags filled with books and other resources that she wanted to take with her. Harold had taken her off classes for the first day so she could set up her room and have a good look around. He'd been adamant he didn't want her coming in over the holidays. 'Plenty of time for that in the first week back. Enjoy what you have left of your holidays and I'll give you that extra first day to set up and meet everyone.'

Her parents had of course been over the moon when she rang and let them know what was happening. She could feel their satisfaction oozing over the phone and she listened patiently to their words of advice about taking it slowly and giving everything time. 'It won't be easy straight away, Amy,' her mother lectured. 'You have to give these places time. It's a shame it's only for a term but I suppose it's better than nothing.'

She hadn't let on that the possibility of longer work was there if she wanted. Her parents' gleeful reaction to the short stint of work had been enough. Her mum had organised a bag of clothes and shoes for her and posted them. Thankfully the parcel had arrived in time for the start of the term.

Angus came around her side of the van to open her door and she stepped out, his hand reaching out to take her bags from her. When she stood in front of him, he handed her bags back and looked her up and down. She'd worn her lucky dress. The one she had worn to the funeral, way back at the start of the year when she'd first met Angus. It was floral and a respectable length to just on her knees. Drawn in at the waist by a thin belt, the colourful designs made her feel fresh and motivated. Her hair was loose on her shoulders and she pushed her sunglasses back on her head, the glare of the sun already bright.

He stared at her for quite a while before reaching out and touching her on the arm. 'You look great and you also look happy.'

His touch sent tingles along her skin and when she looked up into his face she was struck at how close they had become over the last few weeks. He was like her kindred spirit, a best friend and no longer just a travelling mate but now a housemate as well.

'Thank you, Angus. I'm a bit nervous, but that's usual. I just hope the kids are okay. These first three days at the high school will let me know. So far it's all just been hearsay and paperwork.'

He leaned over and kissed her lightly on the cheek. 'I'm proud of you. Good luck.'

With that he turned and got back in the van, waving to her through the window as she took a deep breath, and walked up the pathway to the school office.

* * *

The office was the same as every other school office. Walls lined with hexagonal plaques filled with gold medals and engravings, a large honour board, as well as the usual photos of different school events and prizes that had been awarded to students. Artwork done by students and shelves lined with trophies as well as other school paraphernalia filled one wall and she cast her eyes around, noting how tidy and organised everything was. Two office ladies were busy talking to parents and she waited in line, trying not to listen to the conversation of two older students who were standing behind her. The office ladies picked up on it though and one of them with flaming red hair and bright red lipstick held up her hand gesturing to the parent to wait a moment.

"Excuse me,' she said to the parent before turning to the students. 'You two. Get up here now. Yes, you both.' She waved her hand at the students behind Amy who quickly stopped talking and walked towards the counter.

Amy listened intently. This woman was not someone to be messed with. 'Both of you, turn around and apologise to everyone in this office for your disgusting language. This is a workplace and your behaviour is completely inappropriate.' She waited for a moment. 'Hurry up.'

The boy and girl turned to Amy and a group of parents

who were in front of the counter. 'Sorry, sorry about the language. Forgot we were at school.'

The students had actually looked her in the eye when they spoke, and she nodded back to them to let them know she accepted the apology.

The red-haired lady waved them out. 'Get outside now. I'm not serving you until later. You can come back when I'm ready.'

They obediently shuffled out with their heads down, only looking up to say hello to a couple of parents who had been standing just inside the door listening.

The door shut behind them and the office ladies both looked up at her.

'Are you Amy Coops?' the younger one said.

She was embarrassed when her voice came out as a squeak. 'Yes.'

The lady with the red hair put down what she was doing and came from behind the counter. 'Sorry, every-one, you'll have to just wait a moment.' She stood next to Amy and took one of her bags from her. 'Pleased to meet you. I'm Doris.' She turned to the parents. 'This is Amy Coops, our new music teacher.'

There were lots of 'oohs and ahs' and, 'pleased to meet you', and a very loud 'welcome'. Amy nodded, keeping her eye on Doris as she led her through a hallway up to the end section of the admin building. She waited outside an open door, the sign on it stating, 'Principal'. Harold looked up from where he was sitting behind his desk and gave her a wave. He was talking to a man and his son, all of them standing up as their meeting finished.

Harold looked a little different dressed up in his formal shorts and collared shirt, but the same friendly smile instantly put her at ease and she sat down in the chair that he pointed to.

The first day of the term was always busy and she was surprised at how much time Harold spent welcoming her. He did want to know more about the experiences at her last school and she'd been careful to be professional in her responses. Who knew who out here? There always seemed to be some sort of connection and she didn't want to start on the wrong foot on her first day. She had however been honest and was surprised at the wobble in her voice when she explained she had been treated and the lack of support with behaviour problems in the classrooms.

Harold leaned over his desk, his hands wrapped together. 'Look I'll be honest. Our kids aren't angels and we've certainly got our fair share of problem kids. But we stick together tightly as a team and I will back you no matter what the situation. I will give you this advice though. Go in hard. Don't be too friendly to begin with, there's plenty of time for that once you get a rapport with them. Lay down the school rules and your expectations. The caring, warm and fuzzy stuff will come later. Just let them know what you expect in these first few weeks. They've had a run of different teachers so they are a bit out of sorts. I am going to speak to them today though and if there's any nonsense it will be me they deal with. On the other hand, you do need to develop your own behaviour management skills. We'll have plenty of time to catch up and there are a range of experienced teachers who will help you.' He stood up and reached over, and she shook his hand.

'Good luck,' he said, as he looked down at his watch.

'Nearly time to start. Come with me to assembly and I'll introduce you.'

* * *

The rest of the day consisted of sorting out her room and getting to know her way around. The room was large with her desk at the front, some shelves for books and two pianos on either side wall. A cluster of desks and chairs were set up in the middle and she loved the long row of windows that let plenty of light into the room. A storeroom at the back was full of musical equipment, most of it stacked on top of other desks and stands. She ran her finger over the cymbals. Like everything else in the storage area, they were covered in dust. Some of the instruments had large drop sheets over them so hopefully they were in working condition.

She closed the door to the storeroom. It was tempting to get in and see what she had to work with, but first, there were her books and resources to set up, paperwork to sort out and a laptop to pick up from the office. Several teachers dropped in to welcome her and before she knew it the three o'clock bell had rung and the teaching day was over. She listened to the noisy students in the hallway outside her room. They had been let out from other class-rooms opposite hers and the din rose above everything else, setting her nerves on edge. Yes, of course today had been good. She hadn't had to deal with any of the clientele.

* * *

That night Angus told her about his day at work. It was his dream job and Daniel was going to be great to work for. The workshop was large and organised and the equipment the latest the industry had to offer. 'It just feels so right,' he told Amy. 'I haven't felt so excited about a job before and the opportunities to learn new skills.' She'd listened and asked a million questions before they discussed everything about her day.

A weight lifted from his shoulders as she talked. Although she hadn't met the students yet, everything else seemed to be positive. The students hadn't been the major problem at Matfield anyway. She seemed calm and excited about beginning her music lessons tomorrow. They talked more over the meal he'd prepared and they both agreed their first days had been a success.

For Angus though, today had been more than just a new job. There was so much to look forward to. He liked the town, the people they'd met and most of all the time he and Amy were going to spend together in a place where there was a bit more space and comfort than the van. For a longer stint like three months, everything seemed perfect. He watched her as she cleared the dishes. Her face was glowing and her attitude, optimistic and happy.

By the time he was ready to go to bed, he felt like he'd turned a major corner. Something in his mind had shifted and the dreaded churning in his gut that often occurred had disappeared. A new start in a new town. Regret no longer lingered. It was time to move on.

*a*my waited outside her classroom door for her first class of students. Harold had checked on her earlier and made sure she had everything she wanted. 'Sorry about the state of that storeroom. I had plans to clean it out, but sometimes holidays are more important. Get the kids to help you if you want. They'll love that. Anything but real schoolwork.'

Now as she prepared to greet her first class she stood up straight, her shoulders back and a stern look on her face. She wanted to start on the right foot. A group of students lingered at the port racks, some with books in hand, others too busy talking to get organised or notice she was there waiting. Using her best teacher voice, she called out. 'Students, year ten. Lining up, now.'

Most of them turned their heads towards her and she called out again. 'Line up now. We have a lot to do.'

A few of them sauntered over and before long the rest of them followed. 'Straight line thanks.'

She waited and then waited a bit longer. Keeping the

same stern face, she stood silently until they had all stopped moving. It was hard not to smile but she kept her face straight and tried not to show how surprised she was. They were silent. Not a sound. All of them stood still, their eyes focussed on her as they waited to enter the room. 'Good morning, let's go in.'

Right from the start she made clear her expectations. No one was to speak when she was or when any of the other students were. Hands up for questions and respect at all times to everyone. She rattled off some other rules, waiting for the usual responses or complaints, but every eye was on her and no one spoke. The silence unnerved her and she stumbled over her next words, however quickly righted herself and carried on with her introductions. Once she was on track there was no stopping her. When she talked about where she had studied and the music she liked she noticed their interest piqued even further. Usually, she didn't reveal much of her private life but some of them asked questions about who she had seen in concert, or who her favourite musician was.

She'd been to more music concerts than she could remember and in a variety of different locations both in Australia and overseas. When she rattled off some of the big-name artists she had seen and mentioned Glastonbury, Blues Festival and some other concerts she had been to over the years, she could see they were interested.

By the time she finished speaking and started giving directions about cleaning out the storeroom, she felt confident and in control. Sure, there was some noise and chatter when they started moving the gear out of the room, but they interacted pleasantly and asked her where she wanted items placed. When she gathered the class back together, just before the bell went and regrouped them to finalise the lesson, she felt like she was off to a good start. A few of them even stayed behind to talk to her after the bell went. They wanted to ask about instrument lessons and what they were going to be learning for the rest of the term.

Overall, the first class had gone well and the lessons that followed were much the same. The year sevens had been the unruliest and she had kept three in at lunchtime and made them dust the instruments and sweep out the storeroom. She'd turned some music on and helped them clean. They had stayed even after she said they could go and one of them even apologised for being rude. At three o'clock she breathed a sigh of relief and cast her eyes around her now organised and neat classroom. This was a different experience altogether than her previous one. As she closed the door behind her a sense of satisfaction filled her and excitement about what she had planned for the lessons in the coming weeks. Wait until she told Angus about the day. Hopefully, he'd be home not long after her.

When she called via the office to pick up a key, Doris jumped up and asked how she had enjoyed her first day of teaching. 'And don't forget, you just come here and ask us all your questions. We've both been here for years. What you need, we can get and what we can't get the community will help with.'

Amy popped her head into Harold's office. 'Come in. Come in,' he waved his arm in the air and gestured for her to sit down. 'How did you go?'

For a moment she felt like she was going to burst into tears but she held it together. 'I enjoyed it so much I feel quite emotional about it. Maybe it was just first day luck, but the kids were good, the lessons went well and so many teachers and staff have asked how I'm going and offered help. Mr Senior sent some of the older boys over with music posters and they put them up on the wall for me. Another teacher brought a new sound system and player in for me and even the canteen lady popped in with morning tea and a hot coffee for me. I am, to say the least, overwhelmed.'

'Good. That's how it should be,' Harold said. 'Now grab the key you need and go home. Make sure you don't stay here late in the afternoons and go easy on yourself for some of your lessons. In other words, be kind to yourself. We like to look after our staff and that way we won't burn out. Any of us.'

'Are there any meetings I need to know about?'

'We have one each month, usually the second Wednesday afternoon. But I'll send an email out and let you know. We try to keep the meetings to a minimum, usually they're not required and teachers have enough to do without sitting through useless instructions and the latest fad that will be here this month and gone the next. We focus on the programs we have in place and what you can do in the classroom.'

He stood up. 'Welcome again, Amy Coops. I have a feeling you are going to make a very positive impact here.'

She'd nearly skipped out the door. What a difference.

CHAPTER 54

$\mathcal{I}$t wasn't until she got outside that she remembered that Angus had dropped her off this morning. Tucking her bag under her arm she walked out onto the street, turned left, and started walking home. The weather had been mild today and she was grateful for the lack of heat in the sun. Maybe she could get a push-bike. A couple of kids on skateboards sped past her, one of them had been in her class today. 'G'day Miss. See you tomorrow,' he called out, before bending low and doing some fancy jumps on his board before flying down the street. A flock of galahs that had been sitting in a gum tree on the side of the road, squawked and flapped their wings as his skateboard clattered past them, their pink and white bodies stark against the backdrop of the sky. She swung her bag and strolled casually, checking out the other houses and buildings on the way. When she got to their house, she stood on the pavement and stared at it, still in disbelief that she was going to live in such a gorgeous little cottage.

* * *

By the time Angus arrived an hour or so after her, she had showered and changed into shorts and a T-shirt. The lasagne she had prepared was cooking in the oven and she had re-organised the lounge room, adding a rug and some framed pictures that her mother had added to a delivery that had recently arrived. As she looked around she thought how already it felt like a home. When Angus came in through the front door her heartbeat quickened and she pushed her hair back from her face, taking a glance in the mirror to check she looked okay.

Daniel had given Angus work uniforms and boots and as he slipped his boots off before coming inside she thought how good he looked. His dark hair was tousled, his shirt was dirty and untucked and there was a smear of dirt on his cheek. He bent down and placed a box on the ground that had more work boots in it. 'More gear from Daniel. He's certainly looking after me.' When he stood up he pulled his other hand from behind his back. 'These are for you,' he said, reaching out and passing her a bunch of flowers. 'Congratulations on your first day of teaching.'

'Oh Angus,' she said. 'Thank you.'

They stared at each other and she felt her face flush. When he looked at her like that a warm sensation ran through her body and she wanted so badly to wrap her arms around him. As if he read her mind he took a step towards her, his eyes locking with hers. They stared at each other without speaking. Without warning he leaned forward, his lips pressing gently against hers. She responded by kissing him back and when his arm came up and wrapped around her back, pulling her in closer, she pressed against him, the warmth spreading through her body.

When they finally stopped kissing, she tilted her head back and looked up at him, smiling as he ran his hand gently over her cheek. 'I didn't mean for that to happen.'

'Me neither,' she whispered.

She reached up and ran her hand over the dirt on his face. 'It's good to see you. Kiss me again.'

He took the flowers from her hand and put them on the nearby couch, before wrapping both arms around her and pulling her in tight against his body. Her body felt like it was on fire and when his lips closed on hers she put her arms around his neck, his hands strong as they held her.

Eventually they pulled apart and Angus took a step back. 'Geez, what just happened?' he said.

'I'm not sure,' she replied, 'but I think it's meant to be.'

Angus stared hard at Amy. He wanted to wrap his arms around her and taste her lips again, but he looked down at his clothes. Dirt and grease stains marked his new work shirt and his shorts were dusty, his hair also messy and dusty.

'I'm going to have a shower and freshen up. I'm covered in dirt from work, otherwise, that may not have stopped where it did.' He'd kissed her quickly again before dragging himself away. She hadn't replied, instead a faint smile on her face, almost as if she was in shock. It had all happened so quickly and wasn't what he planned. The bunch of flowers was just to show how proud he was that she had taken a step toward renewing her teaching career. It wasn't supposed to pan out like this. But when he'd seen her as he came in through the door he wanted to bundle her up and hold her close. Hold her close forever.

Turning the shower on he scrubbed himself. Where to now? Had he just complicated their plans, or was this supposed to be? He was just about to turn the shower off when a voice sounded nearby. He turned, the water from the shower splashing across his body, his mind reeling as he looked to see Amy coming through the bathroom door. She came to stand near him, just outside the reach of the water.

They looked at each other for a long time. 'Are you coming in?' he finally asked, rewarded with a wide smile on her face.

'I thought you'd never ask,' she replied.

'Come here,' he said, his body tensing as he reached over and gently pulled her t-shirt over her head. She turned around and he undid her bra clip, caressing her back as he pulled it from her body and tossed it on a basket in the corner. When she stepped out of her shorts and underwear he had trouble standing still, but he waited until she stepped towards him before taking her hands and pulling her under the water with him.

* * *

That night they'd slept in Amy's double bed. Even after he'd fallen asleep, exhausted from their lovemaking she'd pressed her naked body against his and wrapped her arms around him. She was never going to let him go and only the thought that tomorrow was her second day of teaching and she needed to be at her best, made her close her eyes and go to sleep.

They'd woken at the same time during the night and their bodies had responded to each other. When he kissed her and looked deep into her eyes, she'd taken deep breaths and clung to him as he made love to her again. He'd told her over and over how beautiful she was and that her body was driving him crazy. She whispered back, 'I'm never going to let you go. What an afternoon and all because of a bunch of flowers.'

He leaned on one elbow and looked down at her, stroking her face and gently pushing strands of hair back from her face. 'The best day of my life was when I turned left with you,' he told her. 'I love you. I love you so much I don't ever want to be apart.'

'I love you too, Angus. I think I have from the minute we met. We just needed to be friends first.'

When he rested his head on her shoulder, she ran her hand through his hair, his words mumbled as he tried to stay awake. 'I don't know where we'll end up or go from here,' he said.

'It doesn't matter,' she replied. 'As long as we're together.'

* * *

Back in Matfield, Nana sat on her back verandah watching the moon rise over the small outhouse and dry shrubs that lined the backyard. A few rusty pieces of old farm equipment lay disused further down the yard, their shapes now lit by the moon as it threw its light across the scene. Two galahs nestled into each other on the branch of the gum tree and she drew her gaze from them to the owls that had just landed on her clothesline. A warm breeze blew across her cheeks and she ran her hand over her wrinkled skin. In her other hand, she held the post-card that had arrived that morning. It was from a small town called Gowrie that was south and to the west of where she sat. She knew where it was but had never been there. She held the card to the light, looking over the top of her glasses. So, friends had become boyfriend and girl-friend. Her lips curled up in a smile and she turned the card over, the front showing a town much like every other outback town in Queensland.

Angus and Amy, she thought. They met on a dusty road. They became friends. They turned left. And they fell in love.

~~~

ABOUT THE AUTHOR

Rhonda Forrest is an Australian author who juggles writing and publishing, alongside teaching high school students. She writes captivating contemporary fiction and historical romance about relationships, family life and social issues, set amidst beautiful and uniquely Australian landscapes.

After bringing up three daughters and traversing several careers, Rhonda went on to teach creative writing, English and history. Her passion for literacy, history and travelling around Australia fuels her novels. Along with her husband, she divides her time between Tamborine Mountain and a century-old cottage with a rambling garden overlooking the waters of the Whitsundays.

Recent novels bring to life the remarkable characters and settings that make up the unique Australian heritage and take the reader on a journey from bush to beach, with steamy romances, riveting history and eclectic characters.

Some books are available in audio and large print and you can also find some titles available in Portuguese, Publisher- Leabhar Books Brazil.

If you enjoyed this book or any of Rhonda's other books, you can make a big difference by writing a review, or leaving a star rating on Amazon, Goodreads or Book-bub. A personal recommendation to family, friends, libraries and book clubs is another great way to share the books with others. You can also follow Rhonda on Face-book, Instagram, Goodreads and Bookbub.

Website - https://www.rhondaforrest.com/

ALSO BY RHONDA FORREST

OUTBACK QUEENSLAND ROMANCE SERIES

With a cast of eclectic characters and set amidst the rugged outback of Australia, the **Outback Queensland Romance Series** will introduce you to stories of friendship, resilience, and loving relationships that come together to triumph over obstacles defined by the past.

Two Heartbeats (Book 1) is followed by the sequel, *Time Will Tell* (Book 2)

Turn Left (Book 3), *A New Start* (Book 4), *Outback Magic* (Book 5) and *Echoes of the Outback* (Book 6) are stand-alone books with some links to the other books in this series.

'A dingo howls, a star falls.
Don't worry for me, I'll be home soon.'

We'll Meet Again trilogy is an epic World War II saga that will take you from outback Queensland to the jungles of New Britain, then back to the peaceful hinterland regions of the Sunshine Coast and Tamborine Mountain. Based on actual events that include the invasion of Rabaul, and the tragic sinking of the Montevideo Maru, these are emotional stories of love, survival, and the resilience of the families who waited for their loved ones to return.

SALTWATER ROMANCE SERIES

SALTWATER ROMANCE SERIES

From the wild freedom of 1970s Australia to the tangled emotions of the present day, the Saltwater Romance Series delivers three powerful love stories.

Set against the rainforests of North Queensland, the Whitsundays, and the golden shores of Stradbroke Island, these novels explore first love, rebellion, second chances and the journeys that lead us back to ourselves, and to the ones we can't forget.

***Sample chapters from Nothing Without You are in the back of this book. Enjoy!

BINDARRA CREEK ROMANCE

Bindarra Creek Romance

BEYOND THE GATE - Mystery Romance at Bindarra Creek

CHRISTMAS AT FORREST GLEN - A Bindarra Creek Romance

A MAGICAL SUMMER - A Bindarra Creek Small Town Christmas Romance

A WINTER'S PROMISE - A Bindarra Creek Christmas in July Romance

ALSO AVAILABLE IN A BOX SET - CLICK HERE!

SILKWORM SECRETS SERIES (Book 1 and 2)

Growing up next door to each other in 1960s suburban Brisbane, Ruby and Bobby should have an idyllic childhood. However, Bobby's home life is vastly different than the loving security of Ruby's family, and not even the sanctuary of their shared treehouse set high in a mulberry tree can offer him the safety he needs.

Emotional and layered, *Silkworm Secrets* is a moving story about the secrets children keep, the power of friendship, and a love that overcomes the hardships of the past. *Forever More*, continues the story of Bobby and Ruby and reminds us of the good and bad in people and that a loving family can come in many different forms.

WHITSUNDAY ROMANCE - YOU MAY NEVER WANT TO LEAVE!

Love by the Jewel Sea - Book 1

Summer by the Jewel Sea - Book 2

The Lure of the Jewel Sea - Book 3

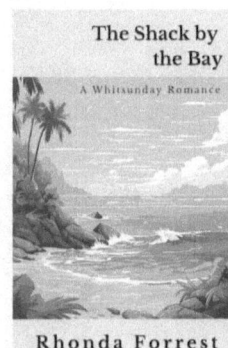
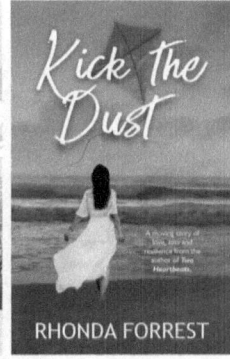

THE SHACK BY THE BAY - Whitsunday Historical Romance

Romantic and purely Australian, *The Shack by the Bay* captures the pristine beauty of the Whitsundays and the wartime memories of older Australians while introducing an eclectic blend of friends and family.

ALL MY HEART - A Tranquil Bay Romance

A small town and school - She only had to last six months.

KICK THE DUST - Contemporary Romance

'If I close my eyes, it's easier to hold onto a memory. When I open them, I think it might really be there in front of me.'